MW01591090

THE
TROUBLE
WITH
RABBITS

KELVIN V.A ALLISON

Copyright © Kelvin V.A Allison
2021 All rights reserved
This edition published in 2021 by
Paranoid*Pigeon Publications.
This novel is purely fictional and any resemblance
to people living or deceased is purely coincidental.
No part of this publication may be reproduced or
transmitted, in any form or by any means,
without permission of the author.

This book is dedicated to
Jess Kingsley

Chapter One

With a lurch, I rose into a sitting position, pain lancing through my brain with the sudden movement. Instantly my head began to spin, the dirty room about me seeming to swim before my blurred vision and I gagged, slapping a hand over my mouth as the warm flood of vomit surged up my throat. Eyes streaming with tears I twisted to the side, forcing myself to my hands and knees just in time before the hot rush of bile and lung butter poured from my open mouth to splatter down upon the old flagstones of the floor beneath me. For several minutes I stayed in that position, on all fours, the sour taste of bile in my mouth and throat and the bitter stink of it mingled with the snot which was now hanging out of my nose like one of Spiderman's webs. With a groan I wiped my nose and the escaping mucus with a thumb, scraping the offending filth upon the ground beside the pile of vomit then I was leaning back to sit on my heels, my other hand reaching up to wipe the tears from my eyes.

Which is when I saw it.

Well, when I say it, I mean me.

I saw me.

Well not me but what I was wearing.
For quite some time I sat there staring at the arm which I had raised to clear my tears, my eyes locked to the white sleeve before me, my mind struggling to come up with a reason that I would wear anything that had such a thing.
As if in slow motion I raised my other arm, shaking my head as I saw the same white material upon that limb, my eyes narrowing as I realised it appeared to be faux fur like on a costume. An eyebrow rising in question, I rose to my feet on shaky legs, staring down at my body in disbelief, taking in the one-piece white outfit that I was wearing, the legs disappearing into an old pair of worn and dirty black work boots. Cursing, shaking my head I staggered back, hands leaping to the front of the outfit, fingers seeking some buttons or a zip fastener.
I nearly cried out in relief when I found the latter, my fingers tracing to its top to try and grab the tiny metal handle only to discover that it was stuck fast, refusing to move even a fraction of an inch. Swearing aloud, I lowered my gaze, eyes widening as I studied the zip upon the front of my chest, the surface of it shiny and wet looking, the metal tag lying flat down.

Glue.

I was glued inside the damn outfit.

With a snarl and a series of garbled expletives I threw every bit of energy that I had into forcing the zip open, proceeding after several minutes to only have given myself a headache from the stress of doing so. With another groan, I raised my hands to my face and cursed again as I felt the circle of material about my features. Which meant only my hands and face were not in the suit. Struggling to comprehend what was going on I stood there, staring about the gloomy stone room that I was standing in, my stomach lurching even more as I realised that it was a cell with bars set into the small window of the worn wooden door that stood before me. Nausea took me once more and I staggered back against the wall behind me, my right-hand snaking round to my arse as I felt the soft cushiony bundle between myself and the stone. For a moment I stood there, my hand squeezing the item which seemed to be sewn to the back of the outfit that I was wearing, the overall shape making me think of an apple size pom-pom. Then I was raised both hands to the top of the hood that was fastened about my face, each one

taking hold of the long ears that were sticking up above my head, the material held in position with what felt like lengths of bendable wire.
I was still holding the ears when my eyes noticed the words which were written on the stone of the wall above the wooden doorway, each letter a different size, each of them daubed in what looked disturbingly like dried blood.
Run rabbit run.

Chapter Two

It was hard to put into words just how I felt seeing those words above the door of the cell. Of course, there was confusion, but it was mixed with a heady combination of fear and dread. Lots of dread.

After all, let us be honest, it's one thing to wake up in a cell yet quite another to wake up in a cell dressed as a rabbit with such ominous words written upon the wall above you in dried blood. What did the words mean?

They were obviously directed at me but why?

I had heard such a phrase before in the old song of the same name, and frowning I stood there, trying to recall the rest of the lyrics, my brow furrowing as they suddenly came to me, *"Run, rabbit, run, rabbit, run, run, run...Don't give the farmer his fun, fun, fun"*

I swallowed hard then, my stomach lurching.

Was someone intending to hunt me?

No, of course not.

That was just ridiculous.

There was obviously another more logical reason for me being locked in a cell and glued inside a rabbit costume, there simply had to be.

Yeah, right, of course there was.

Taking what I had hoped was a steadying breath, I took a step forward towards the door ahead of me, then another, a curse escaping me as I stepped in the pile of vomit upon the cell floor, the squelch as it flattened beneath my boot making me feel suddenly sick once again. Grimacing, trying not to think about the mess beneath my boot, breathing through my mouth so as not to breathe in the sour stench which seemed to have surged up around me once again, I took yet another step, on towards the wooden door set into the damp stone wall. With shaking hands, I reached out, my fingers brushing against the worn wood of the door, recoiling as they felt how damp and cold the surface was, then I stepped up to the bars, staring out at the gloom of the hallway beyond. With wide eyes, I stared as far as I could see to both the left and the right, frowning as I realised there was nothing in the hallway except the stone wall opposite me and the floor beneath it. Sighing, feeling sick with the myriad of emotions which were assailing me I lowered my forehead and bumped it forwards against the door before me, gasping as it swung back into the frame by maybe half an inch as my weight pressed on it, an ominous creak coming from the rusty hinges. "What the fuck?" I muttered, stepping back and staring at the door as it slowly began to swing back again, the movement barely noticeable but there all the same. Then I reached out with a hand, holding onto one of the metal bars in the window and pulled gently. With another loud creak that made the hairs rise on the back of my neck beneath the costume I was wearing, it swung inward and with a trembling hand I released the bar and grasped the door, pushing it open to reveal the shadowy hallway beyond. For a moment I was a child once again, standing in the open doorway staring along the upstairs hallway of what I knew was my parent's home, wanting to use the bathroom but my fear of what may lie beyond my door, hidden in the darkness, keeping me rooted to the spot.

Then with a curse and a deep breath, I stepped quickly forwards and out into the dark hallway. Heart hammering in my chest, I turned my face to the right, staring off into the gloom as far as the stone wall that sat some ten feet beyond the door I had emerged from, then I turned and looking down the hallways to the left. My eyes narrowed as I saw the six other cell doors which were built into the same wall as mine, before drifting on to the two doors set into the opposite wall, one either side of a large wooden table, an assortment of items upon its surface. Grimacing I turned my attention to the old Victorian looking lantern which hung from a hook built into the stone wall opposite the cell doors and I shook my head in confusion again. Where was I?

Frowning, I took another deep breath and stepped in the direction of the table, my steps loud in the stillness of the hallway and I froze, licking at my suddenly dry lips, regretting it instantly as the sour taste of the vomit returned. Screwing my face up I bent at the waist, coughing and spitting on the floor in a bid to be free of the vile taste, only to let out a strangled scream of pure and utter terror as there was movement before me in the gloomy hallway. Hands raised before me to ward of any impending attacks upon my person, my body still bent at the waist I tried to hurry back, my feet catching on each other and with a cry of fear I fell, landing hard upon the flagstones.

I was on my hands and knees in seconds, heart fluttering in my chest like a wild creature trying to escape the confines of a cage. Then I cursed once again, staring up in shock at the confused and scared looking faces of the six people that were standing outside the other cell doors, each of them dressed in white rabbit costumes.

Chapter Three

Time seemed to slow as the seven of us stared at each other, the six-standing people in the rabbit costumes turning and staring at each other in confusion and suspicion, and grimacing I forced myself to stand, fighting both my shaking legs and lurching stomach as I did. Then I leaned against the wall behind me, staring at the half dozen as they turned back around to look at me. For a second no-one spoke then I shook my head, pushing myself away from the wall. "I take it you guys just woke up in the cells too?"

"Yes," the closest of them to me announced, her voice breaking as she spoke and I turned my face to look at her, taking in her dark eyes and the make-up about them which had run down the pale slightly freckled skin of her cheeks, evidence that she had been crying. My own blue eyes drifted to her full lips, arched and full, and then I turned away from her, looking to see if anyone else fancied answering the question I had asked. Instead, they all stayed silent, eyeing me and each other with undisguised suspicion. I did not blame them.

After all, this situation that we had all found ourselves in was fifty shades of fucked-up crazy.

Standing there, faced with the near complete wall of silence, I leaned back against the cold stone wall behind me and studied my fellow rabbits; my eyes drifting over them slowly one at a time, focusing on the details that I could see from the circle of their faces, the only parts I could see other than their hands. Like I said the closest of them to me was a pale skinned young woman, her age hard to decipher but something was telling me she was in her mid-twenties. Turning from her, I studied the next rabbit in the line, frowning as I saw the flat brown eyes of the man staring back at me from behind the lens of his rectangular black framed glasses, his mouth a thin line between the gingery brown of his beard. For a moment, we held each other's gaze, neither of us blinking then I smiled slightly and shook my head, letting my eyes drift on to the tall black man that stood behind him, his skin dark against the white of his suit, silver stubble peppering his cheeks and his chin. As I studied him, he nodded at me, the movement barely perceptible and out of pure instinct I did the same. His deep brown eyes softened as I repeated the motion then he sighed heavily, perhaps relieved to find a friendly reaction. Or maybe he just had gas. Feeling suddenly awkward, I looked past him to the last three of them; two women and a man. The latter was standing with his hands clasped before him like a naughty schoolboy, his thin face and high cheek bones giving him a delicate feminine appearance as he stared back down the hallway at me past his fellow rabbits. Frowning, I turned my gaze to the two women, realising just how different they were at once, despite the fact I could see so little of their features. The closet of them, stood just behind the black man, was a woman of around thirty. As I studied the woman, her scared eyes stared back at me from behind her glasses and her bottom lip caught between her teeth, her right hand rising to brush the few strands of light brown hair that had slipped from the confines of her hood, away from her attractive features. For a moment I found myself unable to look away from her eyes, my breath catching in my throat at the raw sexuality that the vulnerability in them ignited inside me but then I forced myself to get my act together. Letting out that same breath, I forced myself to look past her to the other woman, the last of the group. Whereas the woman with the glasses and the light brown hair looked ready to run, her face etched with concern, the last woman was a creature of confidence, her crystal blue eyes meeting mine without fear, her chin held high and the muscles in her cheeks tight as she clenched her teeth tight. I was still staring at her, thinking to myself that she looked ready to kick arse when the soft voice of the first woman dragged my attention back to her. "Why are we here?"

I held her gaze in silence for a moment, not sure what to say then I decided that the truth was the best option and I shrugged. "I have no idea."

The woman nodded, emitting a shaky breath as she slumped back against the wall beside her and I reached out, gripping her nearest shoulder and giving it a gentle squeeze. "Hey, don't cry."

She nodded, dragging a white furred forearm across her eyes, smearing her black make-up even more then I turned from her as the deep voice of the black man addressed me, thick with an American accent. "Do you have a name?"

I nodded, smiling grimly. "Of course, I do...it's..."

For a moment, I stood there staring at his face, my mind racing as a deep, dark jolt of dread

coursed throughout my body me and he nodded. "You don't know your name either."
All I could do was shake my head.
He was one hundred per cent right.
I had no idea at all who I was.

Chapter Four

Wide-eyed, I stood there, meeting the gaze of the black man and then his choice of words dawned on me and I shook my head. "Wait…you don't know who you are either?"

He winced. "I don't have a clue. When I woke up in that cell a few moments ago I couldn't recall anything about who I am"

I grimaced, the fear in his brown eyes unnerving me and I turned to each of the others, meeting each of their gaze in turn. "Can't any of you remember who you are?"

There was a sobbed response from the young woman beside me and then the grim-faced man with the glasses and the ginger beard shrugged: his accent placing him as a Londoner. "I wish I could remember something…but there's nothing there except a few vague memories"

I nodded at him, frowning as my earlier memories of standing at my bedroom door and staring off into the darkness of the landing returned to me. I could recall that but other than that there was nothing. Nothing at all.

"What is this place? Where are we?" a voice with a midlands accent asked then and I raised my eyes at the question, turning to fix my gaze upon the woman with the glasses; ginger beard, smudged make-up and the black man doing the same. She seemed to cringe under the combined weight of our stares and took several steps back, treading on the foot of the woman behind her. "Watch what you're doing for fucks sake!" the older woman snapped, quickly moving away, forcing the thin faced man that was stood at the far end of the line of rabbits to do the same. "Hey, look I'm sorry," the woman with glasses turned quickly, the expression upon her features lost to me as she faced the woman she had bumped. "I didn't mean to tread on you." "Just stay away from me princess," the other sneered, her tone as cold as ice. "Understood?" "Come on now," the black man took a step towards the two women, raising his open palms before his body. "There's no need for us to argue amongst ourselves. We are all in this together!" "Are we?" the older woman raised an eyebrow, turning her wrath upon him. "Are we really? How do I know that one or more of you didn't bring me here and put me in this fucking outfit?" "Don't be ridiculous," the pretty boy shook his head, drawing her attention to him as the black man took the opportunity to step back away while she wasn't glaring at him anymore. "Why would any of us do that?"

"You tell me," the bitchy woman snapped, moving towards him until only inches separated them. As he flinched and stepped back, she cast the rest of us an amused look then turned back to him. "Do you know any of them?"

"No, no I don't" he admitted, and she laughed bitterly, stepping back away and gesturing at us. "Then tell me, how you know one of these freaks isn't responsible for putting me in this suit!"

"Fuck you," ginger beard snarled, the middle finger of his right hand extending towards her.

"Oh, very grown up," the woman held his gaze, clapping, the sound loud in the hallway. "How very mature of you. My statement stands, it could be any of you!"

"She's right."

Everyone turned towards the voice, the woman smirking, and I realised with shock that it had been me that had spoken. Shrugging, meeting the eyes studying me I nodded and sighed. "I don't know any of you people. It could be any of you that brought me here."

The silence that descended upon the seven of us was heavier than words can describe and cursing beneath my breath I shrugged, "I'm just stating facts. Don't shoot the messenger."

"If only," the bitchy woman sent me a cold smile. Resisting the urge to bite back I turned away, resting my forehead against the stone wall and closing my eyes as I tried to stay calm, my senses overwhelmed by the anger which had coursed through my body at her vile attitude.

"What the Hell is this?"

Frowning, I turned my head to the side, still leaning against the wall, watching as the effeminate man stood beside the table, staring down at it and the objects it was holding. With a sigh, I pushed myself away from the wall, moving over to stand beside him as the others joined us, seven faces all staring down at what lay there. For some time, I simply stood there, eyes drifting over the items upon the wooden surface and then I shook my head, muttering aloud. "What the fuck are all these for?"

"Quite an odd assortment," the voice of the black man drew my attention and I turned to find him on my right side, ginger beard and smudged make-up standing beside him. Turning, I stared back down at the items; a large brass ring with a several keys upon it, a small torch, a screwdriver, a hammer, a tin whistle, some string, an envelope and a small glass bottle with a label on the side. As if in slow motion, I reached out, retrieving the bottle, and raising it before my face. On the other side of me the woman with the glasses and the midlands accent gasped and swore. "What does it say?" The laugh that escaped me was confused as I turned to nod at her. "It says drink me." "Don't be so fucking stupid," the older woman snapped, her hand reaching past Midlands to snatch the bottle from my grasp, and I turned and watched as her eyes widened as she read it, then passed it back to me. "What is going on?" I shrugged, placing the bottle back on the table and on my right Ginger Beard spoke up. "Check the envelope, there might be something in it." Nodding, I reached out and picked it up, casting a look at those about me before tearing it open and withdrawing the stiff rectangle of card from within. Casting the now empty envelope back to the table, I raised the white card up before my face, hearing the mutters and curses as those around me began to read over my shoulder –

Hello, my dears, you are awake then. The game is now in play. All you need to do to win is stay alive. You cannot win of course but it's worth a try, don't you think? You may each take one item from the table before you, no more, no less! I will be watching so no cheating you sneaks! Best wishes,
Oliver Queenheart

Chapter Five

"Who the fuck is Oliver Queenheart?" Midland's accent muttered and I turned to look at her, seeing her brow furrowed in utter confusion.

"I have no idea."

"Let me take a look at that," the black man muttered, taking the card from my hands, his lips moving as he reread it silently, and I turned back to the table before me, reaching down to pick up the hammer upon it, testing the weight.

"Whoa! What are you doing?" Smudged Make-up gasped: her voice thick with fear as she stared at me. "What are you going to do with that?"

"Nothing," I told her, hefting the tool in my hand, feeling the balance. Glancing down, I studied it intently, noting how the handle and head were cast from the same piece of metal. It was a heavy-duty piece of work, something that could pack a punch if needed. I frowned at that sudden thought, wondering how I knew that. Was I a builder?

"Don't touch any of that stuff!" the older woman snapped, moving to the end of the table to stare at me past the effeminate man's shoulder. "Are you crazy?"

With a pinpoint of anger growing between my eyes, my fingers tightening about the handle of the hammer, I turned and met her gaze. "Listen to me luv, I don't know about you, but I want to be armed. I don't know who Oliver Queenheart is, but he is talking about killing us, we need to make use of anything that we can!"

By the time I had finished I was nearly shouting and at the end of the table the woman blinked hard, her expression telling me that she wasn't used to being spoken to in such a manner.

Fuck her.

She was going to have to get used to it.

"She is right," Ginger Beard stepped alongside me, reaching down to pick up the screwdriver before stepping back, Smudged Make-up taking his place as she picked up the torch and flicked the button on. Instantly a thin beam of light, the diameter of a pound coin shone from the end of the torch, illuminating the dust motes which were hanging in the air about us in the hallway.

"Easy with that honey," the black man warned her suddenly, concern upon his features. "We don't know how long the battery in that thing is going to last. We might need it to get out!"

With a nod and a weak smile, Smudged Make-up turned the torch she was holding back off and stepped over to join Ginger Beard and the screwdriver he was holding. As if realising that there were only four items left upon the table, the remaining people about me all surged forward, hands grasping for what lay before them and I stepped back over to join Ginger Beard and Smudged Make-up, the three of us watching as the four human rabbits pushed at each other in desperation. As if on some unspoken cue they broke apart and turned towards us, staring at the objects they held in their hands and out of instinct I did the same. On the left of the small cluster, the bitch was stood holding onto the brass ring with the keys upon it, smirking as she spun them about her fingers while beside her the black man stood staring down at the small bottle that he was holding in his right hand. At his side, the effeminate man was holding the small tin whistle up before his face, studying it intently, eyes narrowed while beside him the attractive woman with the Midlands accent was looking down at the string in her hands as if she had drawn the short straw. To be perfectly honest I was not sure that she had not. I was about to turn my face back towards the grinning bitch with the jangling keys when I frowned and crouched slightly, my eyes fixed to the object which had suddenly caught my eye in the shadows beneath the wooden table.

"What is it? What's wrong?" smudged make-up asked beside me, and I shook my head, dropping to my knees and scooting over the floor towards the object, the four people before the table quickly stepping out of the way, casting me looks as if I had gone totally insane. For a moment I knelt there, my right arm extended, fingers brushing through the cobwebs and then I rose to my feet again, staring at the brown paper package I had retrieved from the floor. "What have you got now?" the bitch snapped, throwing me a sneer but I ignored her, placing the package down and tearing the paper from it to reveal the book within. There was a collection of gasps and curses from about me and a throaty chuckle from the black man, and then I shook my head, reading the title of the old novel aloud, grim amusement in my voice. "Alice's adventures in Wonderland, why am I not surprised."

"Do you think this is some kind of joke?" the bitchy woman snapped, shaking her head at me. "No, no not at all," I stated, picking the old book up and turning it over, unable to avoid admiring the book and the artwork etched upon its cover. It looked old. And expensive.

"Is that a bookmark?" the effeminate man asked suddenly, stepping alongside me and pointing to the thin corner of paper which was protruding from the pages at the top of the book. "Maybe it's another letter from this Oscar Queenheart."

"Oliver" Ginger Beard corrected, and the bitch sent him a grim look, an eyebrow arching up. "What are you...his best friend?"

Ginger Beard met her gaze with an equally cold one followed by a grim smile. "Why don't you just fuck off, you miserable old cunt."

As the woman swore back at him the black man turned, hands raised as he stepped between them, his deep voice calming. "Hey now, come one people, don't do this. Whoever this nut is that has kidnapped us, this will be what he wants to happen, us fighting each other!"

I stood stock still beside the effeminate man, watching as Ginger Beard nodded, stepping back near the young woman with the smudged make-up only for the bitch to turn her attention on the man that had stopped the argument. "You keep your nose out of my business, do you understand me?"

The black man gave a chuckle, shaking his head in the rabbit hood, "You need to calm, lady."

"Fuck you."

He sighed heavily at the insult, turning to look back at me and I gave him a shrug. Placing the book back down upon the table. I flicked through the pages, pausing as I came to the piece of paper the effeminate guy had noticed. "What does it say?" the woman with the Midlands accent asked, suddenly close on my right side and I felt heat course through me as I felt the swell of a full breast push against my arm though her costume. Cursing under my breath, determined not to get turned on in my current situation, I shrugged and retrieved the paper, holding it before me as I read through it. "Well, are you going to read it aloud or do we have to guess what it says?" the bitch snapped from where she stood and I turned my head, staring angrily at her, my irritation returning.

Then the woman beside me placed a hand on my arm, squeezing gently, her voice soft. "Ignore her, don't bite, she is so not worth it."

There was a snort from the older woman, and I nodded, clearing my throat as I began to read aloud. "Read this quickly. You do not have much time before Oliver sends the Dumbdee twins after you. I can help you get home but first you will have to find me. I do not however know where I will be as I am myself am hiding from Oliver on pain of death, but I will help you locate me if I can. Look for my light, it will guide you to me. I wish you luck, but I do not expect to meet you all, the twins are too good at their work. Yours, Mackenzie Hatter."

As a chorus of murmurs rose about me, I could not help but smile. "Curiouser and curiouser."

Chapter Six

The seven of us stood in silence, passing curious and scared looks back and forth, each of my new companions no doubt thinking the same as me.

We were dressed as rabbits.

A bottle on the table had said, 'drink me'.

And now we had received letters from a pair of men with the surnames Queenheart and Hatter. Plus, I had found an old copy, possibly a first edition, of Alice's Adventures in Wonderland under the table. It stood to reason that whoever had abducted us all was a fan of the novel.

What other explanation could there possibly be? For some reason that only their fucked-up fruitcake of a mind knew, they had taken us all against our will, dressed us in this manner and then dumped us here in this abandoned set of cells with these clues to tease and confuse us.

But who?

It had to be someone that we all knew, someone that we all shared a link too. But with our memories currently absent there was no chance just yet of any of us figuring out who it might be.

"Fuck this! I'm not waiting around here playing silly fucking games, I'm going now!"

I turned my face towards the older woman that had been nothing but a pain our arses since we had met, as she stormed past me and the woman with the Midlands accent, stopping before the first of the two doors built into that wall, testing the handle with her fingers. As one, the other half-dozen of us watched as she cursed, stepping back and glaring at the door as she realised that it was locked, then she bent slightly, separating one of the keys upon the brass ring and sticking it into the keyhole that was set in the door face. There was a click as it sprung the lock then the woman staggered back, gasping and swearing in shock, her free hand clasped to the left side of her chest, the brass ring of keys she had held falling to the ground. "Are you OK?" the effeminate man was at her side in an instant, obviously a much more forgiving person than any of the rest of us considering her attitude thus far. Much to my surprise instead of berating him, she shook her head and stepped back once again, pressing her back up against the wall between the cell that I had awoken in and the one from which the young woman with the smudged make-up had appeared, her face pale. Confused, I stared at her for a moment, stunned to see no trace of the former arrogance on her features, her face instead wearing a mask of complete and utter fear. Then I was moved over to the door and crouching to retrieve the brass ring. Rising to my feet I turned and held my arm out, offering it to the terrified looking woman only for her to shake her head, her blue eyes widening. "I don't want them, you keep them!"

"I can't," I stated, shrugging. "The letter said we can only have one item each."

"Then give me the hammer," she muttered, her eyes flickering from my face down to the weapon I was holding and then back again, a measure of her former confidence returning. "I will swap the keys for it!"

My head was shaking even before the bitch had finished talking. "No way, the hammer is mine."

"What is wrong with the keys?" Smudged Make-up asked, her voice barely audible, "Why did you scream?"

For a moment, the bitchy woman stayed silent, her lips clenched tight together, the muscles of her face flickering beneath her tanned skin then she was shaking her head. "The key...the key which I stuck into the lock…it turned to dust…as soon as the lock opened… it just turned to dust!"

"Don't talk shit," Ginger Beard muttered, shaking his head and she shot him a scathing look, but stayed silent. Frowning, I bent by the door again, placing the brass ring down, brushing at the floor beneath the lock with my now free fingers. I grunted, surprised as my fingers brushed what felt like ash and then I retrieved the brass ring and rose once again, meeting the gaze of my new companions.

"There *is* some kind of dust on the ground."

"This is an old building by the look of it," Ginger Beard shrugged. "There is dust everywhere."

"He's right," the black man agreed, nodding at first Ginger Beard then me. "Keys don't just turn to dust."

"I know what I saw!" the bitch shrieked, the sudden sound loud enough to make me flinch.

"Hey, it's fine," Midland's accent suddenly announced, drawing everyone's attention to her as she addressed the angry woman. "If you want me too, I will take the keys…you can have the string that I took from the table."

The laugh that escaped the bitch was bitter. "I don't want your string you stupid woman!"

Midland's accent smiled and shrugged. "Then keep the keys, it doesn't bother me, I was trying to help you out."

For a moment there was silence as the two women held each other's gaze and I raised an eyebrow as I saw the power shift from the bitch to the woman with the glasses as the former sighed and nodded. "OK, I'll swap."

Smiling pleasantly, Midland's accent stepped towards her, handing over the length of string that she had been holding then moved back to me as I passed her the brass ring, the keys upon it jangling together as she did. Trying not to chuckle, I reached down with my now free hand and grasped the handle of the door that the bitch had unlocked with her apparently dissolving keys then turned my head back to smile grimly at my companions. "I have no idea what is on the other side of this door, but we may need to run. I am not stopping, just so you know. No disrespect but I am the most important person to me. I am running and not looking back. I suggest you all do the same."

There was a murmur of agreement and then I turned the handle and pushed the door open.

Chapter Seven

As much as I had intended to charge into the room and dash for safety if I could, I froze on the spot before the door was even halfway open, my nose wrinkling at the stench that washed out and over us like a wave. Despite my best efforts I was forced to raise a hand to my mouth, my eyes narrowing as I turned and stared at those who were gathered behind, seeing the disgust on their faces as they too covered their noses.

"What the Hell is that smell?" Smudged Make-up asked, her voice nervous and I turned to meet her scared eyes, my voice tense as I replied.

"It's the smell of death."

"It is?" she asked, raising an eyebrow, her eyes growing even wider. "How do you know that?"

"Yeah, how do you know that?" the bitchy older woman asked, her voice making my skin prickle with irritation. But it was a good question.

Try as I might I had no idea what my name was or how I had come to be in this place, but I also knew without question that the smell that was coming out of the room before us was the smell of something dead, something decomposed.

Who the fuck was I? What was I?

A funeral director? A mortician?

How was I so certain that the smell was death? Shaking my head, pushing the questions aside in my head aside for now, ignoring those of my companions, I stepped closer to the door and peered into the room that stood open before us, my eyes straining against the total darkness. Movement at my side made me turn my head and I smiled grimly as the woman with the smudged make-up moved alongside me, surprised to see her standing this close to the room and the foul stench. Then she raised her right arm, the torch that she held in her hand cutting a swathe of light through the darkness. "What can you see?" the black man was on my other side, voice low as if he feared speaking loudly might disturb something lurking within. Shrugging, I shook my head, taking a tentative step into the room, "I can't really see anything." As I edged forwards Smudged Make-up kept level with me, shining the torch ahead of us as we slowly moved into the room, step at a time until we were stood several metres from the door, our bodies close together out of pure instinct as she turned her hand, shining the light about the room, illuminating little due to the small diameter of the torch beam. I was about to begin moaning about it when suddenly the beam went off and we were thrust into near darkness, the only light coming from the rectangle through which we had entered.

I spun towards it then, seeing the concerned faces of Ginger Beard, the bitch, Midland's accent and the effeminate guy as they stared in at us, their own eyes widening, and I realised they could no longer see any of us in the room.

I jerked, gasping as hands grasped at me, raising the hammer to strike at the hideous monstrosity which had crawled out of the darkness to suck my soul from my body, my stomach knotting in dread and I suddenly needed to urinate. But then Smudged Make-up cried out, her breath on my face and I realised with relief that the hands on my person had been hers not some beast.

"Turn the damn torch back on!" I snapped at her, some ancient primal fear of the darkness and what might lie within its shadowy folds, surging up from within my core but beside me the woman was sobbing, her voice a whine.

"It won't work, the batteries must be dead!"

I swore, grasping at one of her hands, gripping it tight in my own as I began to edge back across the dark room, using the concerned faces of our new companions ahead of us in the doorway as a guide. We were halfway towards them when they parted, moving aside to allow the black man into the room, one of his hands holding the lantern that had been hanging outside in the hallway before him, his lean features grim.

In that moment, as he moved to stand alongside me and Smudged Make-up, my fear of the darkness receded back whence it had come. For a second, I stood there watching the strange shadows that the dancing flame within the lantern was casting upon the walls and then I frowned, staring about me at our surroundings. The room was large, maybe thirty feet wide, stretching back the same distance, wood cupboards lining the walls at both knee and head height except for the far wall where a marble worktop sat gathering dust. My eyes drifted over to a large sheet covered object that was positioned several feet from the marble worktop, the covering upon it stained with what looked like blood and various other dark fluids. I stood there grim faced beside the black man and Smudged Make-up, the three of us eyeing the mysterious object dubiously, as the other four in our small party suddenly discovered the courage to join us. As one we advanced upon it, fanning out about the shape in a horseshoe, each wrinkling our noses at the awful stench. "What do you think is under it?" Midland's accent asked, throwing me a questioning look from where she stood between Smudged Make-up and Ginger Beard and I shrugged. I had my suspicions, but I did not want to be proved right. Let someone else be the hero.

As if reading my thoughts, the effeminate man took a step forwards from where he had been stood between the bitch and the black man with the lantern, one shaking hand reaching forward. "Don't do it, son!" the black man warned, his voice barely audible and I glanced at him beside me and saw him cringe as if he had intended to merely think the words, not speak them aloud. The effeminate man grasped at a corner of the sheet and drew his arm back, frowning as it moved but then seemed to snag on something. "Don't," I warned, my voice sounding strangled, and along from me, Ginger Beard grimaced. "Just leave it mate, don't worry about it." Then the thin man gripped the material with both hands, yanked his arms back even harder and with a liquid sound the sheet came free.

Chapter Eight

Like a magician revealing the rabbit in the hat, the effeminate man whipped the dirty sheet away from what lay beneath, displaying what had been hidden. Closest to the object, the effeminate man suddenly dropped the sheet and fell to his knees, a torrent of vomit flooding from his mouth to splash down upon the ground before him and I gagged as the stench of it reached me, reminding me that I had done the same not so very long ago. On the far left of our small group the bitch had gone pale, her hands clasped to her face and on my right side, Ginger Beard was staring at the scene before us with undisguised shock, one arm draped about the shoulders of the woman with the smudged make-up as she sobbed and shook her head. Only myself, the black man on my left, and the woman with the Midlands accent seemed unaffected by what had been revealed to us all. Not that I was not disgusted by what had been under the sheet. Far from it, but I knew that I was not as disturbed by it as I should have been. Which had me not only questioning again just who I was but also throwing glances at the man and woman either side of me, wondering just who they really were at the same time.

Then I turned my gaze forwards and stared with fascination at the fat rabbit in the dentist chair. Taking a deep breath, I took a step forwards and to the side, shaking my head as I studied the gore and blood encrusted rabbit suit that the fat man had been wearing when he had died.

Although died kind of sounds too gentle for what had obviously happened to the poor unfortunate that sat before us in the blood covered reclining chair, his face frozen in terror. Mutilated, tortured, violated.

Those are perhaps more fitting words to describe what had been done to him but even they did not convey the misery that he must have gone through before he finally breathed his last and gave up the fight to stay alive.

Letting out a shaky breath that I did not realise I had been holding, I edged ever closer, my eyes drifting to the leather straps that held his wrists and ankles in place on the chair, and then moving on to settle upon his fat face. His features were waxy and grey, mottled bruises showing on his skin, but it was his eyes and mouth that unnerved me the most, the latter frozen in a silent scream and the former staring straight ahead, the colour all but gone from his wide eyes leaving them like clear frosted marbles.

"Why would someone do this to a human?"

I turned at the black man's question, shrugging as an answer evaded me and then we were both staring back at the terrible injuries upon the body, my mind listing them as I found them, trying to form them into some order making me wonder if I had OCD normally. His throat was cut, the wound stretching from ear to ear, the width of the cut showing me that it had not been a normal blade that had inflicted the wound. Again I felt my stomach knot, wondering where this knowledge came from and I forced myself to look on, noting the twenty eight stab wounds to his chest and torso, each done with a thinner needle-like blade, then I was staring with morbid interest at the pile of intestines which had slipped through the deep cut in the meat of his belly, the blade responsible having sliced with ease through both the white costume and the numerous layers of the obese man's bulging stomach. I turned my head as another retching groan from the effeminate man dragged my attention and I watched as he heaved again, chundering more vomit onto the ground where he was kneeling, tears streaming down his face. "Is that a piece of card?" the voice of the woman with the Midlands accent drew my gaze back towards her as she gestured towards the chair where the man was strapped. "There beneath his right arm, can you see it?"

Grim faced, I watched as Ginger Beard removed his right arm from the shoulders of Smudged Make-up and stepped forward, taking a deep breath as he reached out, fingers probing by the dead man's right elbow. Then he withdrew a small piece of card, slightly bigger than one that a businessman might give you, his eyes narrowing behind his rectangle glasses as he studied it. A high-pitched chuckle made me turn, my eyes widening as I saw the bitchy woman standing there giggling, her attractive but cold features etched with mirth as she stood there in her white rabbit suit and howled with laughter. "Are you OK Miss?" the black man asked, the shadows on the walls swaying as he stepped towards her, the lantern swaying in his grasp as he studied her. "Is there something funny?"

Instead of replying she gave another howl of laughter, holding on to her sides and wiping an arm across his mouth the effeminate man rose to his feet and sent her a look of disbelief. "What are you laughing at?"

She fell silent then, thumbing the tears from her eyes as she stared at each of us in turn, a strange smile upon her face. "You sad little fools. Don't you see what is going on here? Haven't you figured out what's going on?"

There was a brief silence then I shook my head at her. "No, why don't you explain it to us."

"This is a game," she chuckled, spreading her arms wide and grinning broadly. "I don't know how or why but this is obviously some kind of grand set up for television, we have probably all be hypnotised by somebody or set up by our family and friends."

I shook my head and sent her a grim smile. "I don't think that's likely is it. You having friends."

"Fuck you," she snapped angrily, flicking me her middle finger. "This is all to test our reactions!"

"Are you fucking crazy?" the woman with the smudged make-up suddenly shrieked at her, moving to stand alongside me. "Is that your problem? Are you a mental?"

"How dare you?" the bitch snapped, her smile fading from her face to be replaced by a snarl. "Just shut up!" Smudged Make-up screamed at her, interrupting the woman mid-sentence, one arm pointing at the grisly display in the reclining leather chair. "Do you really think they would kill someone just for TV?"

With a mocking chuckle, the bitch strode over to the man in the chair, one hand reaching out to scoop up a greasy length of grey intestine in her hands. "None of this is real, you stupid girl, it is all special effect make-up!"

"I wouldn't be too sure of that," Ginger Beard announced, stepping alongside me, Smudged Make-up, the black man and Midlands Accent, the small white card still clasped in his hand. With a grim glance at me and he cleared his throat, "Listen to what is written on this card...this naughty rabbit wouldn't run...the rotter tried to steal our fun...so we strapped him down upon this bed...and hurt him lots till he was dead."

Beside the dead man in the reclining chair, the bitch gave a high-pitched giggle and shook her head. "I don't understand."

"What our friend is trying to say is that this is a real dead body we have here," the black man announced, his deep voice grim. "This is all real, now why don't you be a sweetheart and put his intestines down."

Chapter Nine

"Do you think she is going to be OK?"

I turned my face towards the effeminate man as he waited for a reply to his question, seeing the concern upon his features and then I followed his gaze as he stared at the limp form of the snotty nose bitch as she lay beside the chair where the dead man was strapped, the woman having not moved since she had passed out.

"Does it really matter?" Midland's Accent answered before I could even speak, her tone amused as she too stared at the unconscious woman. "At least she is quiet now. She was beginning to wear on me."

"Me too," Smudged Make-up muttered, stepping forwards to glare at the unconscious object of our conversation. "Why is she so fucking horrible? There's no need for it."

"She is scared," Ginger Beard stated, his face as impassive as ever, his eyes still emotionless behind his rectangle glasses. "She is scared and so she is trying to show she isn't by being overly confrontational. I've seen it a lot."

As he finished talking, I raised an eyebrow, picking up on something he had said and beside me the black man tilted his head to the side, watching the ginger man intently, "Seen it a lot? Does that mean that you are getting your memories back?"

Ginger Beard frowned, starting to shake his head in confusion before his eyes widened as he realised what it was that he had said and, in that moment, I knew the words had left his mouth instinctively with no real thought behind them.

He knew but he could not remember how.

The same way that we all knew what the book Alice's Adventures in Wonderland was about and the way we all knew what the bitch had been referring to when she had mentioned reality TV shows. We had not lost all our memories, we still functioned to some degree.

We all knew what cheese tasted like.

We all knew what the colour purple looked like.

We just did not know who we were.

With a heavy sigh, I shrugged and turned away from the woman, moving over to stand beside Ginger Beard as he once again began studying the small card that he had read out to us all.

"So, we are definitely being hunted then?" I stated and he grimaced and gave a nod.

"It looks that way to me."

"But I haven't done anything," the effeminate man took a step over to join us, the colour gone from the circle of his face that I could see. "I am an innocent man!"

"Are you?" the black man asked him suddenly, making the younger man turn towards him. "Yes!"

"Are you sure?" the black man continued, the lantern still held before him as he spoke, the flickering flamer within it casting strange patterns of light upon his features as he continued. "Because I have no idea whatsoever who I am. I'd like to believe that I am an innocent man too but for all I know I could be a serial rapist or a child killer!"

Smudged Make-up let out a small moan at his words and took a step away, casting concerned glances at me and Ginger Beard as she moved behind us and the black man laughed and shook his head, genuinely amused. "Honey, I wouldn't worry, for all we know you could be the most dangerous person in the room."

"But I'm not," she shook her head, eyes wide in disbelief as she looked at us. "Honestly, I'm not!"

"That's his point," I stated, meeting her frightened gaze. "You might be."

"Exactly right," the black man nodded, smiling grimly. "Maybe whoever is hunting us has good cause to want us dead."

"Fuck them if they do," Ginger Beard's voice was cold. "I'm not going to lie down and give up."

"Me neither," I agreed, the same sentiment being spoken about the room by Smudged Make-up, the effeminate man, Midland's accent and finally the black man as he smiled, nodding at us all. "So, we need a plan to stay alive."

"We get out of this building," Ginger Beard nodded, face grim. "We find our way out and then get clear of this place, put as much distance between us and those who are hunting us as possible. It's the only way I reckon."

There was a murmured chorus of agreement and then the effeminate man gestured towards the door we had entered by. "There is another door out in the hallway, past the table where we got our items from, that must be the way out."

I bit my bottom lip, resisting the urge to add that he was stating the obvious and instead I nodded, avoiding his gaze as he hurried past me to the doorway of the room. With a smile at me, Midlands Accent moved to follow him, Smudged Make-up following suit and then me, Ginger

Beard and the black man were staring down at the unconscious figure of the bitch, each of us frowning and casting each other grim looks.

Chapter Ten

By the time we were back out in the hallway several minutes later, the black man still holding the lantern and the bitch slumped over the right shoulder of Ginger Beard; Midland's Accent, Effeminate Man and Smudged Make-up were standing several feet up the hallway near the table, all three waiting for us to join them. "Nice of you to wait for us," Ginger Beard muttered, one hand clamped to the back of the bitch's legs as they hung down the front of his broad body, the rabbit tail of her costume looking odd as it hovered beside his face. The effeminate man looked uncomfortable, shifting his feet as he gestured towards the black man, "He had the lantern, it's too dark for us to go on without it, otherwise I might have done." Despite my best efforts I laughed aloud at his honesty and beside me the black man smiled and shook his head, his teeth bright. "It's nice to be appreciated."

As he moved past the group, leading the way off up the hallway, the light from the lantern shifted upon the walls as it swayed within his hands and I watched, shaking my head as the bizarre procession of human sized rabbits followed him, ears swaying above their heads as they walked. I turned, meeting the eyes of Ginger Beard as he stood with the bitch over his shoulder. "You surprise me, I didn't think you would offer to carry her."

He gave a bitter chuckle. "Hey if I had my memory, I probably would leave her behind but until I know who I am, who we all are, I am not leaving anyone behind."

"No?" I raised an eyebrow. "You a hero, eh?"

He laughed again. "I don't know, maybe I am. But no, the real reason I won't leave her behind is because how do I know she isn't my wife?"

I frowned, eyes drifting to his left hand. "Are you married? You are not wearing a wedding ring."

He nodded, face grim. "I know that, but I am also pretty certain that when I was abducted and brought here, I wasn't already glued into a rabbit suit. Whoever put us in these outfits also took our old clothes, maybe they took our jewellery too. Lots of people wear rings, don't they? But have you noticed that none of us are? Maybe they took them all, maybe the woman with the Brummie accent is my wife, maybe the black guy is my gay partner. The bottom line is we don't know."

Then he was walking past me towards the others, and I grimaced, nodding slowly as I considered all that he had just said to me.

He was right of course.

And there I had been earlier, preparing to charge into the room and make a bid for freedom, ready to leave the others behind me. Feeling sick I turned and studied the small group that I had nearly deserted as they stood before the far door in the hallway, wondering if Ginger Beard was right, if one or more of them meant more to me than I realised. I cursed as it dawned upon me that I was stood alone in the near darkness at the opposite end of the hallway to the others and I shuddered as the shadows seemed to form around me as if they were living creatures that had grown brave now that the lantern had moved away from them.

As I reached them, I slowed, watching as Midland's Accent crouched down before the doorway, raising the brass ring of keys that she had swapped with the bitch before her only to pause. "Hey, these keys all look the same."

"Just try one in the lock," the effeminate man urged, sounding impatient. "Come on, let's get out of here before whoever killed that guy in the other room comes back and does the same fucking thing to one of us."

"Yeah, come on, hurry" Smudged Make-up nodded, bending down slightly to watch as the attractive woman with the glasses and the Midland's Accent selected a key and inserted it into the lock, turning it to the side. My vision was blocked for a moment as Smudged Makeup stepped to the side but then both her and Midland's Accent were gasping and cursing, stepping away from the door while the effeminate man was crossing himself and staring at the lock in complete disbelief.

"What's wrong?" me and Ginger Beard both asked at the same time and with a grim expression, Midland's Accent shook her head and turned to meet our questioning stares.

"She was right, the key turned to dust as it undid the lock. I swear I nearly had a heart attack."

"Miss, keys don't just turn to dust," the black man smiled kindly, shaking his head. "Like I told sleeping beauty earlier, they just don't."

"This key did," the effeminate man nodded, face nearly white. "I don't know how or why but it turned to dust and crumpled away to nothing. I swear it's true."

The black man frowned, shaking his head again but staying silent and I exchanged a bewildered look with Ginger Beard before joining the conversation. "Could something scientific have happened to the metal to turn it to dust, like some kind of fast erosion?"

There was a series of shrugs and blank expressions and then Smudged Make-up was shaking her head, her voice grim. "It wasn't anything scientific, it was magic."

The laugh was halfway up my throat when beside me the black man seemed to jerk as if he was a sleeper awoken by an alarm clock and with wide eyes, he repeated her last word, the syllables rolling of his tongue as he tested the sound. "Magic."

"Are you OK?" I asked him, trying to force a smile but the look in his eye stopped the expression from reaching my face. "Have you remembered something?"

For a moment he stared back at me in silence, his eyes travelling over my face as if he were seeing me for the first time but then he heaved a controlling breath and seemed to suddenly get himself together as he faced me. "No, I'm sorry but I haven't."

I nodded and he frowned. "Are you OK?"

The smile that lit my face then was genuine as I nodded, feeling no shame about lying to him. After all, he was lying to me.

Chapter Eleven

For a moment no-one in the hallway moved, each of them standing and staring at me and black man as we smiled at each other, perhaps sensing something had changed in him as well, perhaps not. But it was there, I was sure of it. There was a look in his eyes that had not been there before, a look not only of knowledge but also of fear. And if his memory had returned what could he recall? I held his gaze for a moment longer and then nodded, stepping past him and gesturing to the door as I looked at the others. "Well regardless of what the matter with the key was, the door is open, who is coming with me?"

There was a pause from them all and then Ginger Beard nodded, moving to stand beside me, still carrying that oh-so irritating load over his shoulder. "Yeah, I am."

"Me too," effeminate man nodded. "We all are."

"Good," I smiled, meeting the gaze of the black man as he stood at the back of the group. "Then let's go."

Turning away from them I reached down and grasped the door handle, starting to turn it only to freeze as the deep voice of the black man stopped me. "Karl."

"What did you just say?" Ginger Beard asked, staring back at him curiously through narrowed eyes. "What are you talking about?"

There was a momentary silence as the black man chewed the inside of his cheek, his eyes drifting over us all then he shrugged, the light from the lantern jerking and shifting with the motion. "My name is Karl."

For a moment no-one moved and then they all backed towards me and Ginger Beard as we stood by the door, suspicion and fear in their eyes as they stared at the black man as he stood holding the lantern. It was understandable I guess, human nature for us all too suddenly suspect him of something nefarious simply because he knew who he was, and we did not. Suspicion fuelled by fear and jealousy.

But in truth for the level of reaction that his words received by those about me, he might have just as well have announced that was carrying a bomb or that he was sick with a highly infectious case of Ebola or Covid 19.

We had been a group of seven but now there were two groups standing in the corridor. One of them numbering six and the other one. "How long have you known?" I asked him, already certain that I knew the answer and he shrugged and sighed, looking down at the floor for a moment before raising his eyes to meet mine again, features set with a sad expression. "A couple of minutes. It was when the word magic was used. It prompted something. I do not know why but my name returned to me. I am Karl Mackal, but that's all I can remember."

"That's it?" Ginger Beard asked, his tone angry.

"That's all I can remember," the black man, Karl Mackal, nodded at him. "I know without question that is what my name is, but I cannot remember anything else about my life, what it is I do or why I came to be here."

There was another drawn out silence as he stared at us and we stared back at him, then I nodded. "Fair enough."

I turned back to the door then, wrenching it open to reveal nothing but darkness beyond and half turning my head I called back. "Hey Karl, how about you bring the lantern over here so we can see what we are doing."

The light grew stronger behind me as the black man slowly approached, stepping past me and out through the doorway ahead into what lay beyond and I joined him, my eyes widening. Whatever it was I had expected to find this was not it. We were stood together at the top of a set of rickety wooden stairs which led away and down to our left, running about the round walls of the old brick tower in which we appeared to have found ourselves, only a thin wooden banister preventing anyone from falling into the void in the centre of the tower. For a second, I stood studying the steps as they descended to the limit of the lanterns reach before appearing to be swallowed up by the darkness below. I grimaced as the image of a huge mouth waiting to swallow us came to me and then I frowned, my eyes fixing to the rope which hung down from above our heads, descending into the centre void to vanish like the steps had.

"What do you think that is?" I muttered, raising my eyes to stare at where it was tied off on a wooden beam above our heads and beside me Karl Mackal shrugged, his brow furrowed.

"I honestly have no idea."

The wooden landing beneath our feet creaked in complaint suddenly, the floor seeming to shift slightly as the rest of our small party edged out onto it to join us and I cursed, taking several steps down the stairs, fear gripping my stomach in a vice hold as I called out. "Spread yourselves out, I don't think these old stairs can take the weight of us all in one place."

There was a moments panic as everyone did as I asked; Ginger Beard moving behind me on the stairs with the bitch still slung over his shoulder, followed by Karl and the lantern, then Midlands Accent, then the effeminate man and finally Smudged Make-up at the rear of the procession, the young woman having somehow managed to get the small torch working again. We stood together on the stairs in silence for a moment, each of us throwing each other grim looks then we began to descend the stairs, down into the darkness, into the mouth of madness.

Chapter Twelve

Have you ever been in an old building and felt the floor creak beneath your feet, filling your heart with dread at the prospect of it giving way beneath your weight, sending you crashing through to the floor below? Well, that is exactly how I felt as I made my way cautiously down the old wooden staircase, the only difference being that if I fell through them, I had no idea how far I would fall before I hit the ground.

I shuddered as I suddenly considered the fact that maybe there was no floor beneath us, the insane thought making me feel as if I had spiders crawling through my hair beneath the costume I was wearing and I giggled insanely.

Of course, there was a floor down there.

To think otherwise was just unrealistic.

Because waking up glued into a rabbit costume with amnesia in a creepy building was normal.

Yet try as I might, I could not shake the thought that every time I put my full weight upon one of the steps it was going to break beneath me, and I would begin my fall. And so, with my heart in my mouth I continued down as quickly but as carefully as I could, mentally aging a year each time a step creaked beneath the boots I wore.

Then finally, thankfully we reached a landing, a section of wood stretching out on the same side of the tower that we had entered on, a door standing halfway along its length while the rickety wooden stairs continued downwards at its far end. Groaning, my body streaked with so much sweat beneath the costume that I was wearing that it felt like I had been dipped in melted butter, I forced myself to walk over to the door and test the handle, nearly crying out with relief as it opened without any trouble. Stepping inside I sighed in relief to feel stone tiles beneath my feet once again and as Ginger Beard, Karl and the others joined me I turned and studied our surroundings, illuminated by the lantern. It appeared we were in a waiting area: a wooden bench resembling a church pew was pushed back against the longest wall and beside that sat a small wooden table, the plant in the pot upon it long since dead and withered away. Turning back from the plant I watched as Ginger Beard knelt on one knee, laying the still unconscious bitch that he had been carrying down upon the wooden bench with the help of the effeminate young man and Smudged Make-up, the latter helping the bearded man to rise, a coy smile upon her make-up-streaked face.

Was she attracted to him? Surely not?

There had to be a better place to meet people than in a strange building when you were on the run from a threat you did not understand, surely?

Turning away from them I stood watching as Karl, how odd was it using his name now, set about lighting the lantern that was fixed upon the wall opposite the bench with the lantern that he was holding, stepping back as it finally took, the combined glow of both lanterns filling the waiting room with a warm, healthy light.

"Hey, look at this," Midland's Accent called out to us and I turned in her direction, finding her standing in front of the rooms only other door than the one through which we had only just entered, her eyes studying it with interest.

"What have you found?" I asked, moving to join her and she gave a humourless chuckle and pointed at the door, her gaze meeting mine.

"What do you make of this?"

My eyes narrowed as I studied the bronze plaque nailed to the door then I shook my head, unable to believe the name engraved upon it.

"Dr Mouse?"

Midland's Accent nodded, turning her head to meet my gaze, her eyes sparkling. "I know right? Dr Mouse, Dormouse, coincidence?"

"Not in this place," I grimaced as I reached out to try the handle, nodding as it opened. Turning, I addressed the black man. "Karl, any chance we can borrow your light for a few minutes?"

With a smile and a nod, he made his way over to us and passed me the lantern. "Sure, it's not my light after all, let's call in a communal light." Feeling awkward in the face of his friendly manner, I nodded in thanks and took the lantern from him. Then stepping through the doorway, I found myself in what was obviously someone's personal study or office, although it was clear that it had not been used for quite some time. Wrinkling my nose as the musty smell of stale air filled my nostrils, I let out a breath and instantly regretted it, knowing that I would be breathing the foul air back in. Grimacing I turned my head, my eyes passing over the expensive looking burgundy leather chair behind the thick oak desk lined with green felt, and then I was studying the series of bookcases which sat back against two walls, a third taken up by several wooden cabinets with drawers. "This place hasn't been used in years," Midlands Accent muttered, close by my right side but I stayed silent, my eyes still travelling over the room carefully, studiously. On a whim, I placed the lantern down upon the desk and made my way to the cabinets, my eyes drifting over them as I reached where they sat, my brow furrowed as I realised that I was searching for something but not knowing what it was I was trying to find. "What are you looking for?" Karl had entered the room, his deep American accent startling me for a second as he strode over to join me and I shook my head, my head shaking in confusion. "I don't know but when I see it, I'll tell you." For a moment he studied me in silence but then he smiled that white toothed smile, his brown eyes amused. "I guess that's fair enough. You are quite perceptive after all. You knew that I had got some of my memory back upstairs even before I had admitted it didn't you?" "Yeah," I nodded, turning away to look back at the cabinets before me. "I knew that you had." He chuckled at my admission, seeming intrigued by the fact. "How did you know?"

"Honestly?" I asked him, waiting for him to nod before I continued. "It was your eyes. They seemed to change from how they were."

"You are a good judge of people," he nodded, his eyes narrowing as he gave a smile. "What is it you do back in the real world do you think?"

He had me there.

I had no idea and so I shrugged. "I don't know."

"Not even an inkling?" he asked me, frowning.

"No," I stated. "Not even an inkling, it's as if all of my memories have just turned to dust."

Karl was already nodding when I snapped my face back away from him, eyebrows rising as I stared down at each of the drawer handles in turn, my mind racing as I realised what I was looking for, prompted by my own words. "Dust!"

"What's that?" Midland's Accent moved over from where she had been studying the books on the bookcase to join myself and Karl, her features curious as she sent me a puzzled look.

"There!" I pointed to the top drawer on the left set off cabinets, the index finger of my right hand pointing to the thick wooden handle of the drawer, the area free of the thick dust which seemed to cover every other handle there.

"I don't understand," Midland's Accent shook her head, but Karl looked suitably impressed. "You think there is no dust because someone has recently used this drawer? How on Earth did you manage to think of that?"

Again, I shrugged, my hands dragging the drawer concerned open to its fullest reach, the three of us staring in at the horde of paperwork which had been placed in a series of binders and separate drawer files. Without even waiting, Midland's Accent stepped before me, her fingers flipping through the files within the drawer, humming a tune to herself as she searched for something. Nearly a minute had passed by before she was turning and holding up a sheet of A4 paper in her hands, a smile on her face.

"What the Hell is that?" I asked her, my eyes locked to the item and she gave a grimace.

"The drawer is full of sheets like this, each has got seven names upon it, this was the last page in the drawer, and it has the name Karl Mackal on it. This must be us!"

With shaking hands, I took the paper from her, holding it before me as I studied the names upon it, my brain seeming to ignite with excitement as I recognised my own, the memory of my true name returning in a rush of emotion. I was Morgan, Morgan Carew.

Chapter Thirteen

Five minutes later we were back inside the other room with Ginger Beard, Smudged Make-up, effeminate man and a now conscious bitch. Except they no longer needed to be called that. Well, the bitch did but that is another matter. Suffice to say that with the presentation of the list of names to them they had each recognised themselves as I had and then announced what their real names were. Sat glaring up at me from where was half-slumped on the long wooden bench was Tori Rice, her face pale as she breathed in quick shallow breaths, looking like she was about to throw up all over herself and the floor. To her right stood the young woman that I had been referring to as Smudged Make-up, her features still set with the smile that she had been wearing since she had remembered that her name was Amber Dale. Alongside her, his feminine features set with an even larger grin than the one that Amber wore was Ian Towel, his eyes bright as he beamed back at each of us in turn. As I stood watching, the broad-shouldered man know known to us as Craig Musdye, reached up and scratched at his ginger beard, his features as grim as ever and his eyes narrowed behind his rectangle glassed as if deep in thought, his other hand clenched tight about the handle of the screwdriver that he had selected from the table. He caught me looking at him and I nodded, smiling only for him to give a weak effort back before he moved to sit at the far end of the bench from Tori Rice. There was a moment of tension as she glared at him, perhaps unaware he had carried her down the stairs instead of leaving her behind.

Or perhaps she was aware and did not care at all.

She seemed the type.

Either way there was something about the man's demeanour that bothered me a great deal. Had he remembered more than just his name? When my own name had returned to me it had not come with a series of memories and images, instead I had simply seen the name and known that it was mine. Had Craig seen more than that? I jerked slightly as a hand touched me lightly upon the shoulder and I turned my head, staring into the face of the woman with the glasses and the Midland's Accent, the woman that I now knew as Andrea River. "Are you OK?"

She nodded, then stepped back, gesturing for me to follow her as she turned and headed back into the room where we had discovered the piece of paper with our names written upon it. I paused for a moment as I saw Karl Mackal sat behind the desk in the leather chair, a horde of paperwork spread on the surface before him, and he looked up, smiling at me. "Morgan." Nodding, I made my way to stand opposite him, our eyes meeting over the desk. "What are you looking for? What are you doing with these?"

"Searching for answers," he explained, nodding once. "I am trying to find a link between us and the people whose names are on these other sheets of paper."

"Any luck?" I asked and he shook his head.

"Not yet I am afraid. The only thing that any of them have in common is that every name on these sheets has a line through them except for ours, as if someone has ticked them off."

"Maybe these other people have been brought here and hunted too?" Andrea suggested, her voice low and behind the desk Karl grimaced and nodded at her, his voice thick with dread.

"Yes, that was the impression I got. When they have killed someone like the poor fellow in the room upstairs, they tick his name off on the list."

"Which is why ours are not crossed out yet," I added, glancing between him and Andrea.

Behind the desk Karl winced. "I wish you hadn't used the word yet. It implies that some of us are going to die."

"We will if we don't get out of here," I nodded at him. "I am sure of it. Whoever put us in the cells obviously knows where we are, the first place they will come looking for us is here right? That is how they caught the guy upstairs, remember the card that Craig found?"

Karl raised an eyebrow, then nodded. "Ah the ginger bearded man, yes, the card said that the man had been killed because he wouldn't run."

"Which means whoever these sick fucks are, they will come here first to check for others who also try to hide or not run from them," I pointed out. He nodded, pushing himself to his feet although there was a brief flicker of something hostile behind his eyes. For a second I stood there staring back at him, wondering if I had really seen the look of anger that he had shot me but by then his brown eyes were meeting mine once again with no malice in them whatsoever. "Are you OK Morgan?" he frowned in concern. "Yeah, I'm fine, come on, we need to go."

As he moved out from behind the desk and we both turned towards the door, Andrea stopped us with a cough and together we both looked to find her standing by one of the bookcases, her expression hard to read. "Morgan, I wanted to show you these books."

Casting Karl a confused look, I nodded and turned back to Andrea, moving over to stand beside her, the black man following suit. "Sure, what's the matter with them?"

She shook her head. "There is nothing the matter with them, but I noticed them while you two were looking at the cabinet earlier. It says on the door that this was the office of a doctor, right? Well, these books are about psychology and the mentally insane."

Both Karl and I nodded, him speaking. "Go on." There was a brief pause then she shook her head and shrugged. "I don't know, I just thought that what if this isn't real? What if one of us is insane and they are imagining everything that they see about them, including the rest of us?"

Once again me and Karl exchanged looks and I raised an eyebrow. "Are you being serious?" She nodded. "Deadly, I mean really? Keys that turn to dust, rabbit costumes, clues, the fact that we have been told we are being hunted by someone called Queenheart, then we find a letter from someone with the name Hatter and now we are in the office of Dr Mouse which sounds like dormouse. And what were the twins called? The ones which are supposed to be hunting for us?"

"The Dumbdee twins," Karl answered, nodding at her. "You think that is meant to refer to Tweedle Dum and Tweedle Dee, right?"

"Isn't it meant to mean them?" she gave a scared laugh, her head shaking. "What if I am right?"

"What if you are wrong?" I countered as I held her gaze. "Do you want to wait here and find out when the people come looking for us?"

"No," she shook her head. "No, I don't."

"Then we better get the fuck out of here now," I snapped, harsher than I had intended but unable to stop myself. In truth her words had frightened me more than I could put into words. What if she was right?

If one of us was insane and the rest of us were nothing but their other personalities or part of their mania it meant that there was a chance that I was not real and that terrified me.

After all I felt real, but then do multiple personalities know that they are not what they think they are?

"Morgan? Are you coming?"

I jerked my face to the left at Karl's question, blinking hard as I did so, trying to focus on what was going on then I nodded. "Yeah, let's get the others and get out of this place."

We were at the door when the black man suddenly cursed and turned back, meeting my questioning look with a smile. "We had better bring the lantern with us, the other one can't be removed from the wall."

Nodding I stood beside Andrea, watching as he picked the lantern up from the desk, accidently knocking several sheets of paper from its surface to the floor in the process. Shaking his head, he turned back towards us, raising one foot to step over them when he froze and stood staring down at the spilled papers, his expression one of complete surprise. As he bent to retrieve it from the floor, me and Andrea moved back to his side, a frown upon the woman's face. "What is it?"

He stayed silent for a moment, eyes scanning and then re-scanning the paper that he was holding and then he passed it to me. "I have found another name that isn't crossed out, it looks like somebody else has escaped them."

Nodding, I took the paper from him, my eyes drifting down the six crossed out names that were written on it then fixing on the last name at the bottom, my brow furrowing. "Charles Lutwidge Dodgson? Where have I heard that name before?"

When Karl spoke, his voice was grim. "That my friend is the real name of the author known as Lewis Caroll, the man who wrote Alice's Adventures in Wonderland."

Chapter Fourteen

"I don't understand what you are saying?" Tori Rice stood chuckling at us a few minutes later, obviously having recovered from her bout of unconsciousness with no ill effects. "Are you trying to say that the author Lewis Caroll was brought here and hunted like us?"

"If we are right about the names on the other sheets of paper, yes," Karl nodded, his deep voice strained as if he was trying not to lose his temper with the arrogant woman. "That is exactly what we are trying to say."

She laughed then, waving a dismissive hand at him. "It's a ridiculous theory, that book was written in the twenties, are you seriously expecting us to believe that people have been brought here and hunted since then?"

"Actually, it was written around 1863 but it was first published in 1865," the effeminate Ian spoke up, drawing everyone's attention and beside him the young woman Amber gave a murmur of surprise and threw him a smile. "How do you know that?"

Ian opened his mouth to reply, frowning as he stopped and shook his head. "I...I don't know, but I know I'm right just as much as I know that my name is Ian."

For a moment, the rest of us eyed him in silence and then Tori was sneering at him. "Well, that makes even less sense. If he was alive in the 1800's there was no way that he was brought here and hunted."

"She has a point," Craig muttered, the man's voice grim and turning I saw him standing back against the far wall, his mouth a downturned gash within his ginger beard, his eyes emotionless. "That would mean that there is some kind of organisation behind this to have kept it going for such a long time."

Beside me Karl grimaced, biting the inside of his cheek as he stared back at the others and then he shrugged and smiled. "Fair enough, we were just trying to let you know what we had found, you don't have to believe it."

"I don't," Tori sent him a sneer and he laughed. "Why doesn't that surprise me?"

"Meaning?"

He shrugged again. "Meaning that from the moment we all awoke and found ourselves in this damn place you have done nothing but rock the boat and upset people."

"And what are you supposed to be?" she laughed bitterly, "Our morale officer."

Anger flashed through the brown eyes of the black man then and in that instant, I knew that I had not been mistaken earlier when I had seen his sudden rage. With a curse, he shook his head and took a step back towards the door that led to the stairwell. "Morgan thinks we should be gone from here and I agree, we should go now."

Standing with her arms crossed over the chest of her rabbit costume, Tori sent him an angry look. "Don't tell me what to do!"

"Fine with me," he smiled pleasantly. "Stay."

Then he was striding out through the doorway and cursing I hurried after him, Andrea River at my side. By the time we were on the wooden landing, Karl was already eight steps down the rickety staircase, bringing him almost opposite us and I grimaced, calling out to him. "Hey, hold on, we should wait for the others!"

He stopped walking at the sound of my voice, turning his head to look back at me and the woman at my side. "Why? So, we can be ridiculed by that woman?"

"Karl please," Andrea shook her head. "You have the lantern, don't go and leave us in the dark!"

Instead of replying, he simply stood there in silence and in that instant, I knew that he was going to walk off and leave us behind on the rickety staircase in the darkness. But then he sighed heavily and nodded. "OK, I'll wait."

As if on cue, the door opened behind us and a concerned looking Amber appeared, Ian and Craig behind her and a miserable faced Tori at the rear and fearing that the landing would not support our weight I quickly hurried to the descend the stairs after the black man with the lantern, Andrea following quickly behind me.

For several minutes we made our way down the stairs without speaking, the only sounds being the creak of the steps beneath our weight and the occasional gasp or curse from one of us when we thought we were to fall. Then after a seemingly endless descent there was a call from ahead of me on the staircase from Karl. "I think we are nearly at the bottom!"

He had barely finished his words when he cursed aloud and as I watched him, he leaned back against the wall of the tower staring in horror at the centre void of the stairwell. Concerned, I did the same, frowning as I saw nothing but the rope hanging down to my right and I stepped closer to the railing and looked down into the void. For a moment I stayed still my eyes locked to the large white form that was hanging on the end of the rope and then I took a steadying breath and began descending the stairs again, moving to stand beside Karl now that he had continued and reached the ground floor. Neither of us spoke as we stood there, waiting as the rest of our party joined us one at a time, each new arrival heralded by a curse or a gasp of shock as they saw the figure in the dirty white rabbit costume hanging from the noose. Shaking my head, stomach threatening to betray me I stared in grim fascination at the figure on the end of the rope, my eyes drifting over the dead man's bloated face, his eyes sunken and popped and his tongue black and swollen.

"Oh my God, he stinks," the voice of Tori Rice broke the silence and I almost smiled as I heard her gag in disgust. "Look, he's shit himself!" Lowering my eyes, I saw the filth upon the floor beneath his body, the faecal matter no doubt having fallen out of one of the legs of the rabbit costume that he was wearing then I frowned and dropped down to stare at it more intently.

I heard the curious mutters from those about me and then the voice of the bitch was whining again, her tone disgusted as I reached out and retrieved the small white card which had been stood amongst the pile of shit like the flag of a proud explorer. Rising once again and grimacing as I studied the object in my hand, I read the words written upon it aloud so my companions could hear me. "This angry rabbit tried to fight, till round his neck the noose went tight, he begged and begged for us to stop, then in the stairwell he went...plop."

There was an ominous silence as I cast the card to the ground then the deep voice of Karl was chuckling grimly at my side. "I don't know what's worse, the bodies or the damn poetry."

Chapter Fifteen

Shaking my head, I chuckled grimly at his comment and then I turned my head to the side to regard the young woman with the smudged make-up, Amber Dale, curiously as she made a soft grunting sound and raised both of her hands to her cheeks, her eyes widening.

"What is it? Ian asked her, his feminine features concerned as he turned his face towards her, the ears of his hood wobbling. "What's wrong?"

"Other than the dead man hanging on the end of the rope in front of us?" the bitch, Tori sneered.

"Shut up you, nasty cunt," I suddenly snapped, surprising both myself and those about me, the stunned expressions on the faces of all but her and the confused looking Amber slowly turning into smiles as they stood looking at me. For a second or two silence reigned, me and the bitch glaring at each other and the others watching, then I addressed Amber. "What's up?"

She held my gaze in silence for a moment and then she narrowed her eyes as if trying to remember something, her voice barely audible as she spoke. "I...I saw something."

Instantly we were all spinning about, our eyes fixed to the single door which was set into the wall of the tower behind the dead man hanging from the rope, no doubt each of us expecting to find somebody standing there watching us all. "No, I mean I saw something in my head, I think it was a memory or something," the young woman explained quickly and as one we all turned back to stare at her, Craig raising an eyebrow as he stepped closer to the woman. "What did you see? Did you see how you came to be here? Did you see the people responsible?" She shook her head, meeting his gaze and wincing slightly. "No, no sorry, it was nothing like that at all."

"So, what did you see exactly my dear?" the velvety tones of Karl asked as he stood beside me, his expression kindly. "Do you think you can tell us...are you able?"

Amber Dale nodded, smiling slightly as she raised her face and met his eyes. "In the memory I am in a well-furnished room sitting upon the lap of an attractive lady. I don't know why but I think she's my mum."

"How lovely," Tori chuckled without humour, shaking her head. "What a lovely story...can we go now?"

She fell silent as everyone, but Amber turned towards her and with another shake of her head, she raised her hands, palms facing us and stepped back away. "Fine I'll shut up."

"I wish you fucking would," Craig stated angrily.

"Hey now," Karl was stepping between the two of them, sounding for all the world like an angry teacher with two unruly students. "The pair of you please. Amber is trying to talk us through something here, let us listen!"

"Sorry," the broad man nodded at him, then turned his face to look at the young woman. Tori however just made a face and moved to stand over by the door, folding her arms across her chest and glaring back at the rest of us as Karl prompted Amber. "Please, continue."

She nodded, taking a deep breath then. "Like I said, I am sitting on the lap of the woman, mum, and she is reading to me from my favourite book. She is reading to me from Alice's Adventures in Wonderland."

"Shit," the curse from Ian had us all turning to regard the effeminate young man for a moment and then Amber was continuing, her voice thick with fear, her eyes wide as she looked among us.

"Then mum stops reading, and she looks at me and tells me that it is not just a book, she tells me that I must be ready because one day the Queen of Hearts and the others will come and try to take me. Just like they took Great Grandfather."

A heavy silence settled over us as she finished talking, her eyes moving over each of us in turn as she winced. "I am just telling you what I saw."

"I don't know what to say," Karl stated, turning to look at me and I shook my head at the man. "Don't look at me, none of this makes sense."

"Oh, you aren't going to tell me that you believe her," the bitch Tori was laughing bitterly, taking a step back towards us. "Don't you think it's convenient that first the American here comes up with some hare-brained suggestion that we have been abducted by a centuries old group of kidnappers who have also abducted Lewis Collins and then by pure coincidence Amy Winehouse here experiences a memory involving the book that the man is famous for writing."

"Lewis Carrol, you dumb twat," Craig grimaced at her. "Lewis Collins is an actor."

"Whatever," she snapped angrily, regarding him with a sneer for a moment before turning her angry gaze upon each of us in turn. "Look, I just want to get out of here. I do not have any time for fairy stories. I want to go home!"

Despite my wanting to shout at her to shut her mouth I held my tongue, realising that as irritating as she was, Tori was talking sensibly. With a heavy sigh I nodded. "I hate to admit it, but Tori is right. We need to get out."

Without another word, I skirted around the dead man hanging on the rope and made my way over to the door which the bitch was standing beside. Not even bothering to make eye contact with the hateful woman, I tested the handle, relaxing inside as I felt it turn and then I opened it wide, stepping through into the dark wide corridor beyond. I paused only long enough for the others to walk in behind me, the light from Karl's lantern illuminating the gloom as I studied the wooden floorboards and the walls of the hallway with their flaking white paint. Then I hurried towards the first of the three doors that lined the wall opposite me. Cursing as I found it locked, I hurried onto the next one, casting a look back as Andrea bent down before it with the brass ring of keys in her hands and I froze, calling back to her. "Wait."

"What?" she turned towards me, both eyebrows raising, a confused smile upon her attractive features. "What's wrong Morgan? Don't you want to get in there?"

"I don't know," I stated honestly, my eyes drifting to the ring. "How many keys are left?"

"Six."

"What's wrong Morgan?" Craig asked, curiously.

"It looks like all the keys are the same shape doesn't it, and each time a key has been put in a lock so far it has turned to dust when the lock has clicked open," I pointed out. "If there are only six keys left then we need to make sure that we don't waste them, right?"

"Why worry?" Ian stated, moving into view beyond Andrea, a smile on his features. "There are six keys but only three doors, where's the problem, Morgan?"

I was about to open my mouth to reply when Karl beat me to it. "There are only three doors here but what if there are another five doors somewhere beyond these?"

There was a unified groan from the others and then Craig moved past me to stand on the door

to my left, his fingers on the handle. "Let's try each door and see if they are locked before we panic, some of the doors have already been unlocked, maybe some of these are too."
I nodded at him, turning the handle of the door before me, opening it wide only to curse as I found what looked like a small cupboard before me, the back of it less than a foot from the door, an old broom sat inside. Feeling stupid, I stepped back into the hallway to find that the door where Craig had been stood was open and he was nowhere in sight, Karl standing where I had last seen the broad man with the glasses and ginger beard. Casting a look back at the rest of the party, seeing the four of them watching curiously, I moved alongside the black man and stared into the room which Craig had entered, frowning as I saw him hurrying back out, his face grim. He reached us a second later, brushing us aside and shutting the door quickly behind him, before bending at the waist and spitting down on the floor, raising an arm to wipe across his mouth as he cursed once more. "Are you OK?" I asked in concern. "What was in there? Another body?"

He shook his head, forcing a grim laugh. "No, just rotting meat, there were flies everywhere, damn, I swear there was a dog in there on a hook. Who the fuck are these people?" Grimacing, I rose, patting him upon the back as he continued to spit and curse and then I moved back to stand beside the rest of our companions. "Do you want me to try a key?" Andrea asked, looking up at me from where she was still crouched beside the door, the brass ring of keys clasped in her hand. I paused before answering, turning to watch as Craig approached us then I looked back at the woman and nodded at her. "Yeah, why not."

Throwing me a grim smile, she turned back to the door and inserted one of the keys into the lock, her hand turning to the right and I watched in disbelief as I saw for the first time how the key seemed to fold in upon itself and come apart into black flakes which fell to the floorboards before the door. Rising, Andrea tested the door handle, throwing me a weak smile as she opened it wide before her. She winced and raised a hand before her eyes, half turning her head away as cold grey sunshine flooded through the opening, filling the hallway with grim light. Cursing, I turned my head away, avoiding looking at the light for several moments until my eyes had adjusted to the change in brightness and then I turned back towards it, stepping past the still stunned woman, aware that my companions were still struggling with the glare. My left hand raised at an angle before my eyes, my right gripping tight to the handle of the hammer that I had taken from the table, I edged my way through the narrow hallway which ran adjacent to the door, travelling the ten feet of its length with careful steps, ready for whatever tried to stop me.

I moved carefully over the weathered and broken door which lay at its end and then I stepped out into the open space beyond, finally free of the building in which I had awoken.

For a moment I stood there, vaguely aware of my small group of companions as they gathered about me, but I was far too busy staring up in confusion at the two suns in the grey sky, one red and one blue, to pay them any attention. Where the Hell were we?

Chapter Sixteen

"Er...why does it look like there are two suns?" the nervous voice of Amber asked as she moved to stand alongside me, and I turned to look at her curiously. She met my gaze with wide scared eyes, the look of disbelief and fear on the woman's face, matching the feeling of dread that was gripping my stomach in a vice hold.

"I don't know," I stated, trying to smile back at her but failing miserably. "But it can't be good." She nodded, looking back up at the pair of suns and I turned to look at the others, finding them stood in a cluster several feet away staring back at the building from which we had only just managed to escape. My eyes drifted over it and the area in which we were now stood for a moment and then I heard the voice of Ian. "Oh my God, look at the plaque above the entrance!" Instinctively I did as he had said, grimacing as I saw the plaque, just as Andrea read aloud. "St Alice's Asylum? Oh my God that's creepy."

There was a disdainful snort from Tori, and I grimaced and took several steps away from both them and Amber, my eyes slowly taking in my surroundings. I raised an eyebrow as I took in the black metal fence that enclosed the area where we were now stood, waist high and bent in places, then my eyes drifted back to the building itself. My brow furrowed as I studied it, shaking my head as I took in the absence of windows and the old bricks that made up its walls. Then I was looking higher, tilting my head back as I stared at the old-fashioned gable roof set with various turrets, getting the general feeling that the building would not have looked one bit out of place in a Charles Dickens novel. But it was not just the architecture of the building that had the hairs rising on the back of my neck beneath the hood of the costume I was wearing.

It was the buildings overall shape.

As I stood looking up, I estimated the building was two stories high and maybe forty feet wide.

But that made no sense.

No sense whatsoever.

After all, hadn't we just spent what felt like a lifetime walking down through the building via the rickety wooden stairwell that had wound around the inside of the tower, a journey which must have taken us down at least ten stories.

So how was the building so low?

Licking at my suddenly dry lips, I stepped to the left, walking parallel to the front of the building until I was level with the corner and then I was staring at the side of it, shaking my head as I did so, my expression grim, my stomach lurching.

"What's wrong?" Karl called out to me from where he stood beside the others and I threw a nod in the direction of the side of the house, my hand with the hammer in it gesturing for him to come and join me. He reached me moments later, his face concerned, Craig and Andrea coming along with him and I turned to glance back at Tori and Ian, finding them both still looking at the plaque high above the front door. Turning to my three companions, I found them staring at the side of the building and I stayed silent, waiting for them to see the problem.

"Fuck me," it was Andrea who noticed first, a hand leaping to her mouth and the brass ring of keys jangling in her other hand as she took a quick step back, shaking her head as she sent me a look of complete and utter shock.

"What am I missing?" Karl frowned, turning to stare back at us and then Craig was swearing.

"Fucking hell...where's the tower that we walked down?"

The black man snapped his head back towards the side of the building so quickly that I half expected him to suffer whiplash, but then he was stepping forwards, shaking his head, his voice low. "This isn't possible."

"Tell me about it," I nodded, gesturing with an arm back towards where Amber Dale was still staring up at the grey sky. "And did the rest of you notice the two suns?"

They turned with me, the trio muttering and cursing as they finally noticed what me and the young woman had seen upon first leaving the bizarre building behind us and once again a chorus of curses and exclamations of disbelief rose from them as they stared up at the sky.

"Where do you think we are?" Andrea muttered and I met her gaze with a shrug and a grimace. "Honestly? I have got no fucking idea."

Turning away from them all, I strode forwards, making my way down towards the rusty old gate that sat at the far end of the metal fence away from the building that it surrounded. I paused, my eyes drifting over the shapes that had been placed within the metal of the gate, frowning at what looked like octopi and squids, and then I opened it and made my way out to

stand in the dead grass beyond the metal fence
staring out at the view. It seemed that the
building in which we had awoken was atop a
small rise and from my elevated height, the
surrounding land was laid out before me.
It was hard to tell which way was which what
with the two suns in the sky, but my senses told
me that east lay to the left of where I was
standing. Frowning at how I might know such a
thing, wondering again who I was when I was
not dressed as a rabbit and suffering amnesia, I
turned my face in that direction. In the far
distance there seemed to be a large area of
broken-down wooden buildings, like a hastily
built shanty town. For several moments I
studied it intently, trying my hardest to discern
if there was anybody moving there but then I
cursed, realising that such details would be lost
to the distance. Just to the south of that strange
town, sat an area of greenery looking for all the
world like a private London park, the trees and
bushes that made it up loomed over by a high
white tower, its upper reaches lost amid fog. For
some time, I stared at that pale monolith, my
eyes narrowing and then I turned my face to the
south to the trio of buildings that lay beyond the

sea of dead withered grass between them and me. Chewing on my bottom lip I studied the buildings intently, trying to figure out what the huge building and the two much smaller ones were and then I moved my gaze onwards, raising an eyebrow as I took in the sight of the large church or Cathedral which sat atop a large hill to the very south of where I stood. Then I was turned about slowly, frowning as I realised that the entire landscape was surrounded by what looked like a dense forest on every side except the south east where an almost black sea stretched to the horizon. I turned as my six companions began to gather around me once again and then the bitch Tori was speaking, her tone as irritating as ever. "So...where do we go?" Despite my intense dislike for the woman, I had to admit that it was a damn good question. Where indeed?

Chapter Seventeen

"Do you think that they will be OK on their own?" Andrea asked me nearly ten minutes later as me, her, Karl and the bitch Tori were making our way over the sea of dead grass in the general direction of the Cathedral on the distant hill. I frowned at her question and stopped walking, turning my head back to stare at the three figures that were walking away from us towards the shanty town that lay in the east, their white rabbit costumes making them easy to spot as they travelled across the grass. "Yeah, they'll be fine," I nodded, hoping that I was right. In truth, I had grown to like the solemn looking Craig and the young woman Amber in the brief time that I had known them, and I genuinely wished that they were with me, Karl and Andrea and not Tori, who had done nothing but moan and whine since we had begun walking away from St Alice's Asylum. Turning back towards the distant Cathedral I began walking again, casting my thoughts back to before we had set off on separate journeys. I had finished studying the land laid out before me and then turned to throw the others a grim look, telling them that I intended to head for the

Cathedral and try and get help. Instantly there had been turmoil as people both agreed and disagreed with my plan, Craig stating that he wanted to head off to the shanty town and seek help there if he could. Faced with the onset of another huge row I had shaken my head and raised my hands for silence, waiting until everyone was listening before I continued, stating that I was going to the Cathedral and that Craig was heading off his own way. Anyone who desired to join us was welcome. Which was how I had ended up with Tori. Sighing heavily, wishing once again that she had chosen to go with the other group, I focused on the landscape before me as I walked, constantly on the lookout for any sign of danger headed in our direction. We had been awake for what felt like nearly two hours now and there had still been no sign of the Dumbdee twins that we had been threatened with in the letter from the mysterious Oliver Queenheart and as much as I hoped that meant that they were not coming after us I knew better. People had already been killed by them. It was only a matter of time before they got on our trail and came hunting us down, eager for blood. I shook my head and grimaced as I considered that thought, my stomach knotting at the fact that there were people somewhere out there who had the intention of killing me and my new companions. Perhaps it was better that our party had split into two separate groups. That way if these people were after us it gave them more than one lot to focus on. Hopefully, that meant that at least some of us could get to some form of help. Standing on the hill staring out over the landscape it had been obvious that wherever we were it was not a normal place. And that was not because of the two suns or the structurally impossible building we had just escaped from. No, the land had a weird almost surreal feel to it, an almost fantastical dreamlike quality that unnerved me. The words of Andrea back at the Asylum came to me then and I frowned as I considered what she had said. '*What if one of us is insane and they are imagining everything that they see about them, including the rest of us?*' Could she have been right?

Was all this just the creation of a tortured mind? Letting out a breath, I shook my head and moved my eyes to study my three companions as they walked with me, Andrea on my right and

Karl and Tori up ahead. If Andrea *was* right then it stood to reason that the real person, the insane person that had created the rest of the personalities, the fractured identity's if you will, was one of us four. Surely if it were one of the other three then we would now not exist as they weren't with us.

Was that how it worked?

Sighing again I turned my gaze from my companions to stare at the Cathedral ahead of us, closer than it had been but still extremely far in the distance and I realised with knowledge no doubt gained in my real mysterious life that we would need to walk for another two hours before we reached our destination. A smile touched my lips as the thought occurred to me, for if I was still getting these unexplained fragments of information coming into my head then surely it meant I was real.

Didn't it?

"What do you think that place is?"

I looked around as Andrea spoke, frowning as I studied the trio of buildings that she was pointing at some distance to the left of where we were walking, the largest appearing as if it were at least several storeys high and the other two looking like simpler one storey buildings.

"I don't know," Karl shook his head, staring over at the buildings as he walked, the interest in his voice evident. "Maybe we should head over and take a look."

"Screw that," Tori cursed, shaking her head as she strode ever onwards, not bothering to even turn her head and look over at the trio of buildings. "Who cares?"

"We might find help there," Andrea offered, her tone hopeful and I stopped walking, she and Karl doing the same as we exchanged glances, thinking the same. Up ahead of us Tori suddenly seemed to realise that she had been walking on alone and with a curse she stopped and spun about, hands moving to rest upon her hips. "What now?"

"I think we should check them out," Andrea stated, looking at me and Karl, and I nodded.

"Yeah, I think you might be right...Karl?"

The black man shrugged and smiled. "Why not, it's not as if it is that far off our course is it."

Andrea nodded, smiling and then the expression slipped from her features as the bitter, acidic voice of Tori sounded. "Oh, you have to be fucking kidding me."

Grimacing, I turned towards the woman, finding her still standing some distance away. "What's the problem?"

"I don't want to go to those buildings."

"Why ever not?" Karl raised an eyebrow as he faced the obnoxious woman. "Don't you want to find help?"

She stayed silent for a moment, her lips moving as if she was not sure what to say and then she was shaking her head. "I don't want to go there. I thought we were going to the Cathedral on the hill to try and get help."

"We were and now we are going to head to those buildings and see if we can find help there," I explained, trying to stay calm. "If there's no-one there we can continue on to our original destination…it's not a biggie."

"How about someone asking me what I want to do," she snapped angrily. "This is a democracy not a police state."

Beside me Karl nodded, smiling at her. "OK, everyone who wants to head to the buildings first raise a hand."

Not bothering to hide my smile as me, Andrea and Karl all stuck an arm up in the air, I met Tori's gaze. "OK?"

The look of sudden anger upon her face was priceless. "No!"

"Why not?" I asked pleasantly. "We put it to a vote like you wanted...this isn't a police state after all."

Karl and Andrea laughed, then Tori flicked me her middle finger. "I suppose you think you are funny?"

"I have my moments."

For a moment, a silence hung over the four of us and then Karl shrugged and smiled at the woman that was standing by herself facing the three of us. "The bottom line is that we are going to head over to the three buildings to try and find help, if you want to come with us then that's fine with me, if not, well, that's fine with me too."

Tori stayed silent, her bottom lip caught between her teeth as she glared back at us and I gave a weary smile, worm out with her attitude. "So, are you coming with us?"

Her smile when it came was broad and bright, but the light never reached her blue eyes. "Fuck you, fuck all three of you, I don't need you!"

Then she turned back away and continuing off across the sea of dead grass. Frowning, I watched her until she had been walking away for nearly a minute and then I sighed and shook my head, turning to face my two remaining companions. "And then there were three."

Chapter Eighteen

"It's a hospital" Karl muttered in surprise as the three of us stood before the largest of the three buildings some twenty minutes later, what remained of our small group having made our way towards it across the dead grass. I nodded at his words, my eyes studying the rusty sign which hung above the buildings large entrance, proclaiming that it was St Alice Hospital, the letters written in a strange almost calligraphy style font. This was the second time that we had found a building named after this mysterious St Alice. Who the fucking Hell was she?

Alice in Wonderland?

I gave a grim chuckle at the thought, cringing as the number of times that novel seemed to be tied in with what we had experienced so far returning to me. What was going on?

An image of young Amber entered my head then, her face pale beneath her smudged make-up as she had told us the memory that had returned to her, claiming that her mother had warned her about the dangers of the Queen of Hearts when she had been just a little girl. There was every chance that her mother had been just some fruit loop, trying to trick the young Amber into believing the story was real for who knows what reason. But there were the other coincidences and links to the damn book, the same book I had found under the table back in the dirty hallway bordering our cells.

"Hey, did you notice the windows?" the voice of Andrea dragged my thoughts to the here and now and turning my head I watched as she gestured up at a bank of windows above the front entrance sign, my eyes widening as I saw the prison like bars across their openings.

What hospital kept their patients locked up? Agreed some mental hospitals did but we had awoken in the asylum which meant that this building was obviously nothing of the sort.

So, what then? Why the bars?

Throwing my two companions a grim smile, I stepped forwards, pushing open the large wooden doors of the entrance and stepping through into the gloomy small room beyond, devoid of everything except a door several feet ahead of where I was standing. I frowned and cursed then, wishing suddenly that we had chosen to bring the lantern from the asylum.

"Damn, it's gloomy," Karl muttered as he and Andrea joined me, the man voicing my thoughts.

"Maybe the windows will let light in," Andrea offered, and I nodded, watching as Karl moved forwards and pushed open the door that sat ahead, vanishing from our view as it swung shut behind him with an ear-splitting loud creak.

"Morgan, I'm scared," Andrea stated suddenly, her voice breaking, and I threw her what I hoped was a reassuring smile and stepped forwards towards the door that Karl had just departed through, gesturing for her to join me.

"Come on, everything will be fine. We will find help then get the Police here to rescue us. Trust me."

I turned away from her then so that she would not see the doubt that was probably evident upon my features and pushing open the door I stepped through into the large, wide corridor that lay beyond. The first thing I saw was Karl, the black man standing several feet in front of me, head tilted back as he stared up at the ceiling overhead and I did the same, my eyes widening in surprise as I saw how high it was. The next thing that caught my eye was the seemingly endless rows of beds that lined each wall of the corridor, all devoid of mattresses and sheets, appearing as metal and spring wire skeletons, cold and unwelcoming. Shaking my head at the sight of them I returned my gaze to the ceiling and frowned. Whereas from the outside the building had appeared to be several stories high indicating that there was more than one level within, the building consisted of just one level on which we were now standing, the ceiling vanishing high above us amid the gloom and shadows. Once again, I lamented the absence of the lantern and then I stepped forwards to join Karl, my footsteps echoing off the stone floor, the only audible sounds except for the dripping of water off in the distance.

"Oh my God it's cold in here," Andrea moved to join us having followed me through the door.

"It's because of the thick stone walls and the windows," Karl nodded, gesturing to the numerous broken panes of glass that ran around the large room, the weak grey sunlight that was shining through them being just enough to allow us to see our surroundings. Frowning as I saw my breath misting in the air before my face, I shivered and turned my head to look around us, realising that it did not look much like a hospital at all. On the left side of the wide corridor not far from where we stood was an open door and then another three beyond that, each about fifteen feet apart. Turning my head to the left, I studied the door that lay there and then moved my eyes to look at the other two doors that sat some forty feet beyond it, these closed and some distance apart from each other. Turning back to Karl and Andrea I shook my head. "The place looks like it is deserted." Karl frowned at my words, nodding. "I was thinking the same thing...there's no-one here." Nodding I stepped back towards the door. "Shall we head on to the Cathedral then?"

"Oh God," Andrea groaned, rolling her eyes behind her glasses. "That Tori woman will be unbearable now."

"You mean she wasn't already?" I sent her a smile and she nodded and grinned, the warmth of that broad smile making my heart skip a beat and I swallowed hard and quickly turned to look at Karl, surprised to find he was now standing over near the open doorway on my left.

"What are you doing?" Andrea asked him, concerned. He shrugged, throwing us a grin. "Well, we might as well check this place out while we are here don't you think? We might be able to find stuff to protect ourselves."

Without waiting for us to reply he was gone again, striding into the open doorway beside him and sighing, I moved to join him, Andrea sticking close behind me. Striding into the room I stopped, surprised to find that it was little more than a walk-in cupboard, Karl standing several feet within it, his eyes travelling over a dusty set of wooden shelving covered in seemingly dozens of old-fashioned glass bottles, each bearing a tiny white label. As I stood there staring at Karl and the shelving, Andrea made a strange soft grunting noise behind me and then she stepped alongside the black man, her free hand reaching out to collect a bottle and raise it to her face to read, her brow furrowing slightly. "Anything interesting?" I asked hopefully and Karl shook his head, raising the bottle he had taken from the table and showing it to me. "No...I was hoping there would be a similar bottle here so I could figure out what this is but alas there isn't any that seem to match." Shaking her head slightly, Andrea made a strange face and placed the bottle that she had been reading back on the shelf, retrieving another and studying the label before putting that back too, her features thick with confusion.

"Are you OK?" Karl asked her, moving back to stand beside me in the doorway, "What's the matter my dear?"

"I'm not sure," she shook her head, throwing the pair of us that same strange look she had just worn. "I have no knowledge of my past whatsoever, but I know what these liquids in the bottles are and I know what they do."

"Go on, we are all ears," I urged her, and she nodded, turning once again to the small glass vessels that filled the shelving system.

"The labels on these bottles say that the liquids in them are *Resperine* and *Paraldehyde*. The first of them, *Resperine* is known as the very first anti-psychotic drug. As far as I am aware it was mainly used in the early 1920's and is derived from the shrub *Rauwolfia* which is native to India, Africa and South America. *Paraldehyde* is a hypnotic drug and was introduced sometime around the late nineteenth century. It was used as an effective treatment for alcohol withdrawal, anxiety and insomnia."

For a moment me and Karl stayed silent as we stared back at her then I raised an eyebrow. "So how do you think you know all this stuff?"

She shook her head, shrugging. "I don't know, like I said I have no other memories returning but I know that what I just told you two is one hundred per cent right."

"Maybe you are a chemist or some kind of nurse or doctor?" I suggested and she shrugged again.

"I guess I could be...I wish I knew."

"Smell this," Karl extended the bottle that he had taken from the table towards her, and she took it, holding our gaze while she placed the brass ring of keys down upon the shelf beside her and then unscrewed the cap of the bottle and sniffed at the contents. Instantly she was gagging and moving it away from her nostrils, trying to get the lid back on to it as she coughed and wheezed. Stepping forwards, Karl took both the bottle and the lid from her, placing it back while he eyed her with intense curiosity, and I grimaced and shook my head, concerned for the woman well-being. "Are you OK? What is it?"

"It is some kind of acid," she stated, meeting my gaze and beside me Karl let out a long whistle.

"Damn, the label upon it says Drink me."

"You're lucky you never," I stated. "Really lucky."

"What do you think these drugs are doing here?"

We both turned to look at Andrea, me having no answer for her question but Karl coming up with one. "Could they have been used to drug us and bring us here?"

Andrea nodded. "Sure, I guess they could have used them on us but there are lots more modern and more powerful drugs that could be used. Besides where would someone get all this stuff? I doubt that these drugs have been available for probably over a hundred years!"

Karl nodded, biting at his bottom lip as he frowned, then he turned. "Thoughts Morgan?"

I shrugged. "I haven't got any. This is just too fucked up."

We all spun about as beyond the room we heard the creak of the door to the foyer opening then the faint tread of footsteps coming our way.

Chapter Nineteen

For a second the three of us stood there staring at each other with wide eyes and then I was spinning towards the open door and ducking behind the wall beside it, my companions following suite. Beyond the doorway, out in the wide corridor, the footsteps came closer, pausing at the doorway and I swallowed hard and gripped tighter to the handle of the hammer that I was holding, readying myself to leap from my hiding place and bring it down over the head of the person as they appeared. I tensed as a shadow fell across the doorway and raised the makeshift weapon I was holding high above my head. A body appeared in the gloom of the doorway then and with my heart lurching in my chest, I gritted my teeth and attacked. In that moment Andrea let out a shaky gasp of fear, unable to control herself and as I brought the hammer down, I heard the familiar, irritating voice of Tori Rice mutter. "Is someone there?" With a grimace, I pivoted at the waist and the head of the hammer slid past the side of the woman's face by a fraction of an inch. She screamed then, falling backwards out of the door and cursing I dropped the hammer and hurried after her, my companions joining me as I tried to calm her down. For several moments she stayed down upon her back, desperately trying to crawl away like a deformed crab but then she stopped, eyes widening as she stared back up at the three of us. Then the screaming and swearing began as she surged to her feet and threw herself at me, fingers reaching for my eyes. Cursing I got my arms up between us, grasping at her wrists to protect myself only to curse in pain as she kicked me hard in the right shin. "Calm down!"

"Fuck you!" she screamed, kicking me again, her face a mask of rage. "You tried to kill me!"

Then Karl and Andrea were between us, faces grim as they tried to force us apart only for the black man to stagger back as she freed an arm from my grasp and struck him upon the nose. Then in a blur of movement, Tori was grunting in shock and dropping back to her rump as Andrea stepped in close and hammered a hard and fast punch into her unprotected face.

"Stay down!" the attractive woman with the glasses warned as she jabbed a finger down at the sobbing Tori. "Just stay down!"

Shaking my head, I stepped up alongside Andrea, casting a surprised look at her. "That was quite a punch."

She nodded. "Maybe I work out in my real life."

"Maybe," I smiled grimly, turning to look over at Karl as he stood several feet away, the fingers of his right hand trying to stem the blood that was running from his nose, and I winced. "Are you OK Karl?"

Instead of answering immediately the black man shook his head, eyes glaring angrily at the woman on the ground and then he was meeting my gaze, his voice bubbling with anger. "I think she has broken my nose."

"Don't blame me!" she sneered, one hand-held to the side of her face where Andrea had struck her. "Morgan tried to smash my brain in with a fucking hammer!"

Sighing, shaking my head, I turned back to meet her gaze. "We thought you were one of the ones hunting us, what the Hell were you doing sneaking up on us like that Tori, are you mad?"

"Yeah, I thought you were heading on to the Cathedral," Andrea stated, staring at the woman.

"On my own?" Tori shook her head as if the woman from the Midland's had suggested the most insane thing ever. "No way was I walking around here by myself."

Shaking my head, I resisted the urge to point out that she had willingly chosen to leave us after we had invited her to come with us to the buildings. There was no point in arguing with the irritating woman. I had already learnt that in the brief time that I had known her. So instead, I nodded, turning from her and casting another look back at Karl. "Has the bleeding stopped?"

He nodded, throwing the woman another look of anger before looking back at me. "Yeah, for now. It still hurts like a mother fucker though!"

I frowned at him then, surprised by his foul language despite his pain and I was vaguely aware of Andrea also regarding him with surprise, an eyebrow raised as she stared over at him. Then I turned round to point a finger at Tori as she rose to her feet. "If you are going to cause trouble..."

"No!" she snapped, her hand still rubbing at her cheek as she stared at me. "I am not going to do anything daft!"

I smiled at her, nodding and then the expression slid from my face. "For your sake you better fucking not."

Chapter Twenty

For a moment I thought she was going to make a funny comment to my threat but then she nodded and forced a grim smile. "Hey look, if it means I am not on my own then whatever, can we start again with no arguments."

Shaking my head, I turned away from her not bothering to agree with her terms. After all there was no point. She was bound to piss me off again before too long. Striding away from her, Karl moving to join me, I made for the next door on the left wall, testing the handle and opening it when I realised that it was not locked.

"What is in there?" the voice of Tori asked as she and Andrea moved up to stand behind us and I grimaced in sudden irritation, hating having to now be nice to the confrontational woman.

"It's another storeroom, it looks like it is just filled with boxes of canned drinks and food."

"Could it be supplies for our captors?" Andrea asked and turning my head to look back at her.

"That'd be my guess."

Beside me, Karl gave a shake of his head and headed on towards the next door, muttering as he went. "We are wasting time looking for the wrong things."

"Wrong things?" I called after him, shaking my head. "I thought we were looking for help?"

"Of course," he nodded, turning towards me with a smile on his face. "That came out wrong."

"Did it?" the question left me before I had realised, and he shrugged and grinned at me.

"Of course, it did."

"OK," I nodded, suddenly feeling a strange sensation as the black man held my gaze, a feeling that I could not place washing over me. Then I forced a grim smile and moved over to stand beside him as he opened the next door in the row, revealing another storeroom filled with piles and piles of what appeared to be old grey woollen blankets and starched white linen sheets. At the discovery of yet another such room, I turned my head to the side and studied the face of the black man, frowning as I saw the muscles clenching tight and then unclenching within his silver stubble cheeks. "You OK?"

"Of course," he nodded, turning and nodding at me. "I was just hoping that there would be something lying around which could be of some use to us!"

I nodded and he shrugged again. "You know like I said earlier, weapons and stuff that we could use to defend ourselves from the people that took us, the people that are hunting us down" Holding his gaze, I fought to keep the frown from my face, trying to figure out what had changed in the man I had been coming to trust. "This door is locked," Andrea called out and I nodded, looking past Karl to see the woman with glasses as she knelt before the last of the doors on the left of the wide corridor, a grim-faced Tori standing behind her, arms folded across her chest as she stared at the door ahead. "Problem?" I asked as I moved to stand beside them, wishing that I had not asked as Tori turned towards me, fully expecting the woman to begin whining at me again. Instead, she shook her head as she lowered her hands, a finger pointing at the door which we were gathered in front of. "This one looks different."

"Different?" I shook my head. "In what way?" She sighed, rolling her eyes. "Can't you see?" Biting back at angry retort, I turned back to the door, narrowing my eyes as I stared at the deep dark walnut of its surface, shifting my gaze down to the brass handle and the lock. Then I nodded as what she was talking about dawned on me. Frowning, I turned my face to stare at the doors which we had already tried, noting the peeling paint and their weathered surfaces, then I looked back at Tori. "You're right!"

"But what does that mean?" Andrea asked, looking up at the pair of us from where she was knelt before the door, a key held in her fingers.

"It means that there is something important behind it my dear," the deep voice of Karl Mackal snatched our attention, his brown eyes fixed unblinking upon the door, a strange little smile upon his face. "It is probably the reason that it is locked, and the others weren't."

"Any idea what could be in there?" I asked him and he turned me, a confused look upon his face.

"No, but it has been locked up for a reason."

"Open it," Tori stated. "Let's see what's in there." Nodding, Andrea inserted the key in the lock and turned it to the right, the metal of the item once again turning into black flakes in her hand and falling to the floor. She rose then, reaching down to the door handle and turning it, pushing the door open wide before her. For a moment, the four of us stood staring in through the open door revealing what looked to be a well-lit, elaborately furnished office. Then Karl spoke, his voice barely audible. "Come into my parlour said the spider to the fly."

Chapter Twenty-One

Together we moved forward, Andrea entering the room first, then me, Tori close on my tail and then finally Karl at the rear, the four of us spreading out when we got inside the room, Karl closing the door behind us. Standing between the two women I turned my gaze slowly about the room, shaking my head at the opulence of it all when compared with the barren rest of the building that we had seen so far. A large desk dominated one wall of the square room, the surface of it highly polished and carved with great care and detail, a large green leather chair sitting behind it by the wall where a lit lantern hung upon a hook set in the bricks. To the left of the desk stood an enormous bookcase, hewn from what appeared to be the same type of wood and crammed to near overflowing with books of every size and colour, many of them appearing to be old.

"Who do you think these are?" the voice of Tori had me turning to find her and Andrea standing before a series of framed photographs upon the wall opposite the desk, many in black and white but a few in colour. Moving to stand with them I let my eyes drift over the photographs, noting the old-fashioned clothes in the majority of the black and whites, the quality of the pictures grainy and shadowy, making them appear aged. "I recognise that woman!" Andrea suddenly stated, a finger rising to point at one of the colour photographs. Frowning I studied the picture that she had indicated, my eyes settling upon a middle-aged woman with brown hair and a kindly face, a broad-shouldered man with silver hair standing at her side, arm about her shoulders. Turning to look at Andrea, I felt my stomach knot as I saw the look of fear and disbelief in her eyes as she swallowed hard. "I recognise the man as well."

"Where from?" I asked, my hands reaching out to hold her by the shoulders. "How?"

For a second she seemed to look right through me as if I weren't there, her eyes filling with the prospect of tears and then she blinked, meeting my gaze. "I don't know, I can just remember the woman lying upon a hospital bed, she is bleeding profusely from the mouth and nose, coughing and choking, her back arching in pain as she is sobbing and screaming...and the man...that man is standing there in a tweed suit shouting at me angrily, asking me what I have done."

Her words trailed off then and I let out a shaky breath, pulling the woman into a loose embrace, my right hand gently stroking the back of the white rabbit costume that she was wearing.

"So, what did you do?" the voice of Tori asked, breaking the silence and I released Andrea, allowing her to step back to shake her head.

"I have no idea at all, but the vision is so clear...it is definitely something that has happened."

"Do you know she is?" Tori asked her, surprising me with her soft tone. "Do you know who he is?"

"Oliver Queenheart." the deep voice of Karl announced and together me and the three women all turned to find him seated behind the desk, looking as at home there as he had back behind the desk in St Alice's Asylum. He held our gaze for a moment as he sat in the leather chair, his fingers drumming upon the seat's arms, the bottle of acid before him on the desk. Then he was talking once again, gesturing to the front of the desk with a finger. "This is the office of Oliver Queenheart and the pictures upon the wall are of him."

Frowning I stepped closer to the desk, my eyes lowering to study the bronze plate that was screwed to its surface - 'DR O. QUEENHEART'

I met the gaze of the black man again. "So how do you know the pictures on the wall are him?"

"Logic," he smiled. "Why would he have photographs of another man on his wall?"

"Maybe it is his brother," Andrea suggested as she moved beside me, and Karl laughed softly.

"Perhaps but that makes little sense. You just told us that the man in the photograph was shouting at you for some reason...perhaps whatever it was that you did to upset him is the reason that you were brought you here."

I was vaguely aware of Andrea turning her eyes upon me and sighing I met her gaze. "He could be right."

"Hey this is odd," the voice of Tori had me turning back to find her still standing staring up at the photographs upon the wall. "The guy from the photo that Andrea pointed out is in every one of these."

"Don't be daft," Andrea shook her head, moving over to stand by the other woman's side. "Some of these pictures look really old. How can he be in them all?"

Tori shrugged. "I don't know but he is...look." Standing before the desk I watched as the head of Andrea's rabbit costume moved first one way then another as she studied the photographs, the long ears swaying above her head and then she turned back to stare at me and Karl, her face pale, "She was right! How is it possible that he is in all of these?"

Chewing the inside of my cheek, I held the gaze of Andrea and Tori as they both stood staring over at me, suddenly angry that since we had awoken back at the asylum everybody had been looking to me for guidance and support, and then I sighed heavily. "I have no idea. I am afraid I don't have a book with all the answers in it!"

"I do," the voice of Karl made me turn, my eyes widening as I saw him removing a large leather-bound book from one of the drawers on his side of the desk. As he placed it down, me and the two women moved around the desk to stand behind him staring down at it in curiosity.

"What the Hell have you got there?" Tori asked and Karl Mackal chuckled, looking up at us.

"This is the private journal of Dr Oliver Queenheart. If we are lucky all the answers that we seek will be in here"

Then he opened the journal wide and together we began to read the words upon the pages.

Chapter Twenty-Two

12th October 1785

Finally, after years of fruitless searching I believe that I have finally found the correct three men to assist me in my research of the occult. The first is Dr Thomas Mouse, my colleague at the hospital, the second is a Mr Mackenzie Hatter; a gentleman who has made quite a name for himself as a landscape gardener to the rich and the last is Father Archibald Hare, a somewhat disillusioned Catholic priest. We have named ourselves the Order of the Shadows and tonight we held our first meeting at my home where many ideas, thoughts and plans were exchanged. For the first time in years, I am excited about the future. After the death of my wife Alice, I did not expect to ever feel joy again.

21st February 1786

Today, after months of naught but talking, our Order came into possession of a manuscript that allegedly contains a spell that grants transportation to another plane of existence. Thomas acquired it from one of the patients on the ward for the insane wretches where he works. It would appear to activate the spell one must simply utter the sentence of power that is written upon the manuscript and to return to this world you must simply say your true name whilst looking into a mirror. We are going to test the spell tomorrow night.

22nd February 1786
Tonight, is the night. The hours seem to pass too slowly by far and I can barely control the excitement coursing through my veins and yet I must control myself until the rest of the Order arrives at my home. We have sworn allegiance to each other after all.

14th November 1786
What madness is this?
The spell worked as promised. We were all transported one at a time to a strange land where the sky is grey, and two suns hang suspended above the blasted land. On nearly all sides the land is surrounded by an unnatural forest where spiders the size of horses' dwell, ready to feast upon any that might dare to venture into their domain, while in the south eastern corner there sits a sea so black as to

*make one's heart lose hope of ever feeling joy
again. There exists in this land a hospital, a
cathedral, an asylum and a garden of beauty,
almost as if they had been drawn from our very
minds, an area suited to each of us.*

*There also sits a tower in the east, hewn as if
from one single piece of marble, rising into the
grey sky above. We stayed in that strange land
for several hours, exploring as much as we
dared before we came home. When we arrived,
we discovered that while we had been away
eight months had passed in this world.*

1st January 1789

*I tire of this world with its petty laws and rules.
The others and I are spending more and more
time in the strange land that we have named
New London. On our fifth visit there we
discovered that it had its own lifeforms; hostile
and dangerous creatures which resemble some
bastard hybrid between shadow and tar. It
would appear after some investigation that they
are the servitors of the ancient rabbit-like deity
that the spell calls upon for its power; the dread
lord Tsugoth. Now each time we journey to New
London we ensure that we always take at least*

half a dozen homeless people or miscreants with us that will not be missed, as food for the shadowy creatures of death.

15th July 1794

What have we done? Stupidly we have taken too many of the down and outs of this world through into new London and now they number nearly a hundred, somehow having learned to escape the shadow creatures better than we had expected them too. Worse, with the absence of food they have resorted to cannibalism. The only saving grace is that they appear to fear the four of us and stay hidden away in the slum area that they have built in the north east. We in turn keep to our buildings and I have named them all after my dear beloved Alice.

To keep the shadow creatures satisfied we have taken to bringing people here to hunt and kill, having learned from our mistakes with the homeless wretches that merely turning them loose did not work. So, to ensure that they do not escape and become trouble like their predecessors have, we dress the newer abductees in white rabbit costumes in honour of Tsugoth and we join the hunt. I have even taken to employing a couple of large, twin thugs from the real London; Jim and John Dumbdee, to carry out the execution of the hunted upon their capture. To make matters a bit more palatable I have discovered that there are many people in the real world willing to pay a tidy sum to make others yet disappear. Add this new-found source of income to the fact that while in New London we do not age and we will soon become rich men.

29th April 1862
Damn him, damn him to Hell.
Our best laid plans have been potentially sabotaged and unravelled at the hands of an opium addled author! The man owed a close friend of mine a large sum of money for unpaid gambling debts and as he was unable to pay I arranged for him to take part in the next hunt in New London.
Somehow though he managed to escape from our clutches and take Mckenzie as a prisoner. For days Thomas, Archibald, the twins and I searched with no success. Then we found McKenzie sitting within the garden which he had claimed as his own, weeping like a child as

he told us how the author had made him see the light and that we were little more than murderers. In a fit of stupidity McKenzie had given the author his own mirror and told him to recite his name, thus enabling him to return to the real world.

To make matters worse the author tried to write a novel about his escape, but his publishers rejected it for being too frightening. In a fit of rage the author rewrote the novel as a children's story entitled Alice's Adventures in Wonderland. He has based a character upon me, he has made McKenzie Hatter the Mad Hatter, Archibald Hare into the Mad March Hare and Dr Mouse into the Dormouse. Even the twins have been mentioned along with the great Tsugoth being referenced with a white rabbit character. Unfortunately, I have now discovered that a person can only be brought here once against their will. But I will have my revenge upon he and his lineage. I swear that I will see them eradicated for making a mockery of my friends and I if it takes the remainder of my life. With the longevity granted me by New London that gives me all the time in the world.

7th September 1976

I rule New London alone now.

*McKenzie is an enemy to me. He still believes
that what we do is wrong but without a mirror
to return to the real world he is trapped here
and no threat to me. Archibald has gone insane
and lives alone in his Cathedral atop the hill. I
have not spoken with him in several years, but I
often hear him howling and screaming with
madness. My dear friend Thomas is now dead
too, killed by one of the shadow creatures when
he came to visit me at the hospital several
weeks ago. I have his mirror safely hidden
alongside mine.*

*The twins stay here now, and I journey back to
the real world alone. I have finally become
married to an attractive young widow by the
name of Margaret. We have a daughter upon the
way and when she arrives, we will call her Alice
after my first wife unbeknownst to Margaret.*

23rd January 2021

*Hello again journal. It strikes me as odd when I
look at the dates on the pages where I have
made entries. I seriously feel little older than my*

middle forties, but I am in fact over two hundred years of age now.

And once again bad luck has struck against me. Recently my wife began to get ill but try as I might she would not come and join me and my daughter in New London, where I hoped that the effects of the cancer might be made null and void as her lifespan was extended. Giving in to her pleas I arranged for her to attend a hospital where she was to eventually lose her life at the hands of an incompetent surgeon mere hours after the operation to remove her tumour.

I have also now discovered the identity of the last of the line of Charles Dodgson and they will soon become part of the hunt along with the surgeon responsible for the untimely demise of my beloved Margaret. To add to the numbers on the hunt I will be adding several people that have been brought to my attention of late; a serial killer who is currently in prison serving life for the abuse and murder of over a dozen young women, a pair of journalists who are asking questions regarding my wealth and my past, and an occultist who is scouring the magic shops and markets of the real world making enquiries into the manuscript which came into my possession so very long ago. The prisoner has had a bounty put upon their head which I intend to collect and as for the other three, I cannot allow them to continue asking questions. Soon the hunt will begin again in earnest. May Tsugoth find their deaths worthy.

Chapter Twenty-Three

"Well, well, well" Karl muttered as he closed the journal, shaking his head as he looked up at me, "That was interesting wasn't it."

"Oh my God," Tori shook her head, uttering a laugh which lacked humour. "You are not about to tell me that you believe all of that stuff!"

Turning to face her, I met the woman's gaze, seeing the fear that was filling her eyes.

She believed it whether we did or not.

"So at least we know why we are here," Andrea nodded and let out a shaky sigh. "We know why this man has brought us all to this damn place!"

"We only kind of know," I pointed out, meeting their confused gazes as they looked at me. "Sure, he stated why he wanted us all brought here but we don't know which of us is which do we...that still a fucking mystery."

"Well, I am pretty certain that the surgeon he mentions is me," Andrea sounded as if she was going to be sick, her features pale. "That would explain the memory that came to me when I saw the photograph of them standing together...I must have killed his wife."

"It would also explain how you knew what the medicines were in the first store," Karl added.

Letting out a shaky gasp, Andrea turned and sat down on the surface of the desk, placing the brass ring of keys down and putting her head in her hands. "Oh my God."

"Don't start crying." Tori gave what sounded like a snort of disgust but as I watched she placed an arm gently about the shoulders of Andrea. Wonders will never cease.

"So, which one of the hunted do you think you are Morgan?" Karl asked and frowning I looked at him as he sat staring at me from the chair, my mind racing as I considered his question.

Which one was I indeed?

As much as I did not like the fact that Andrea was upset it stood to reason that she was the surgeon that had been mentioned within the journal, the one responsible at least in his own eyes for the death of his bellowed wife. That left the descendant of Charles Dodgson more commonly known as Lewis Carroll, the serial killer from the prison, the pair of journalists that had been enquiring into the past of Oliver Queenheart and the occultist that was after the manuscript that he owned. I nodded in realisation as I remembered that Amber had got a memory back while we had been standing about the man on the end of the noose back in the asylum, a memory which suggested that she was the descendant of the author Lewis Caroll. That left the killer, the occultist and the hacks. I frowned then, glancing down at my hands, studying the lines upon them in silence. Had these killed before? Could I be the serial killer? The monster that had abused and murdered over a dozen women in cold blood.

Was I capable of such a terrible set of crimes? No, maybe...yes?

Who knew? Certainly not me.

I raised my eyes to find the black man still staring at me and I shook my head. "I don't know. You?"

Karl gave a chuckle and smiled, rising slowly to his feet. "I have no idea either Morgan...but I doubt we will have to wait for long before we find out who is who on the list."

"Meaning?" Tori asked, her arm still draped protectively about the shoulders of Andrea as both women looked at the black man. "How will we find out?"

He gave a laugh then, his brown eyes seeming to sparkle as he looked at first them and me. "We are all slowly getting our memories back my dear...we all now know our names...Andrea and the young woman with the make-up have both remembered something from their past...soon we will all know who we are, and the fun will begin in earnest."

"Fun?" I grimaced. "You think this is fun?"

"No," he smiled. "You know what I mean."

I nodded.

He was right after all.

Soon we would all know our true identities and whereas the thought of that had previously excited me, now it just filled me with a foreboding sense of dread that I could not shake no matter how hard I tried to do so.

"There is another problem," Andrea muttered, and I turned my face to look at her as she rose from the desk to stand beside Tori, her eyes wide behind her glasses. "In the journal it states that there are six people he has brought here for the hunt: the two reporters, the serial killer, the surgeon...me, the descendant and the occultist or magician or whatever"

I nodded and beside me Karl frowned. "And?"

She heaved a heavy sigh. "Seven of us awoke back in the asylum."

There was a moment where the four of us all exchanged shocked glances and curses of shock and then I shook my head. "So, which of us is the seventh person?"

"Who indeed?" Karl grimaced. "Who indeed?"

Chapter Twenty-Four

For several moments we all stood staring at each other in a mixture of shock and suspicion and then Andrea raised her open hands. "Hey, it's not me...I am the surgeon by the look of things, right?"

I nodded at her, throwing a quick glance at Karl and Tori wondering briefly if the mysterious seventh person was one of them or even me. The truth was that until our memories returned, we would not know which of us the seventh was.

Besides, I was more worried about the prospect of one of them or even me being the serial killer than the person that Oliver Queenheart forgot to mention in his journal. Sighing I met the gaze of each of my companions. "I wouldn't worry about who this seventh person is...if anything Queenheart simply forgot to add them to the journal, or they were a late addition...we should be concentrating on finding help before the people hunting us do so."

"And where are you hoping to find this help from?" Karl asked me, an amused tone to his voice. "We are in another dimension...an alternate world to the one that we were born in...who do you think will help us?"

Grimacing, I fell silent, and he nodded, his features grim. "Exactly...there is no-one who can help us but ourselves."

"What do you suggest we do?" Andrea asked him and he turned to face her, smiling coldly. "We do the only thing that we can. We take the fight to Queenheart and retrieve these mirrors that he has. Once we have them, we can speak our names into them and return home to the place where we belong."

A heavy silence fell over our small group as we exchanged glances once again and then I was shaking my head. "You are proposing going to war with him?"

"Do we have another choice?" Karl chuckled dryly. "Do you think that perhaps if we ask him for the mirrors, he will simply give them to us and allow us to escape?"

"I don't think Morgan was saying that!" Tori snapped and I threw her a surprised look as she continued. "If we go head-to-head with this man, we will end up fucking dead and that is not something I want!"

Instead of replying Karl stayed silent, staring past my head and then he was stepping away from us and the desk, backing towards the door, his voice grim. "If you want to avoid a confrontation with him and these twins of his then I suggest we leave this place at once!"

As the two women gave each other scared looks, I frowned and turned about to stare behind me, the hairs on the back of my neck rising. "What are you staring at?"

"That lantern was lit when we entered the room" his words had me glancing up towards it, my stomach lurching as I realised that he was correct. "Which means that whoever lit it...probably Queenheart himself, was here not too long before our arrival which means..."

"Which means he might come back at any moment." I finished for him, cursing and hurrying back around the desk to join the trio that now stood in a huddle at the room's door. Karl was right and we needed to get out now.

As if hearing my thoughts, the black man turned and opened the door, the rest of us following him through it and out into the wide corridor. I paused long enough to shut the door behind me and then we were heading back down the corridor towards the door which we had entered through earlier, my heart pounding. "Shit," Andrea stopped mid step, turning her face back towards the room which we had just been in. "I have left the keys on the desk." "Damn it," Karl snapped, throwing his hands in the air. "I have left the journal and the bottle of acid upon the desk as well...he will know we have been there."

"It's too late to worry about that!" I shook my head, taking another step on towards the door, my voice insistent. "We have to go now."

"But the journal!" Karl began to argue, and I frowned as I saw the mania in his eyes as he continued. "Who knows what secrets I might be able to discover if I were to take the time to study it properly!"

"You are the occultist!" I muttered, a jigsaw piece clicking into place and for a second we stood there in that abandoned hospital corridor in silence, my blue eyes locked to his brown ones as he nodded and shrugged at me.

"Does it matter?" his deep voice answered, a strange smile upon his features. "You have seen what Oliver Queenheart has done to this realm…he doesn't deserve the power that he and his Order stumbled upon!"

I took a step back, the women going with me and I raised an eyebrow. "How long have you known?"

Karl Mackal shrugged, a smile on his face. "Not long…it was while I was reading the journal"

"What now?" there was fear in Andrea's voice as she spoke, "Does this mean we are enemies?"

His laugh was rich and genuine as he shook his head and held her gaze. "Why should it mean that? You wish to return home, I wish to replace Oliver Queenheart. Surely that makes us allies."

I was about to answer, to demand that he told us all that he knew or there was no way that we were any such thing when Tori gave a short, high pitched scream, pointing over at the closest of the three doors on the right of the corridor and as one we all turned to look. For a moment, I could see nothing but the shadows beyond the door but then my stomach lurched, and I felt as if I had hundreds of spiders in my hair beneath the hood of the rabbit costume as I saw what she had seen. In the open doorway the shadows were moving, swirling together like oil in water, becoming something solid and then elongating once more, stretching out towards us across the floor of the corridor. Time seemed to slow as I watched the shadows split, becoming two and then again until four of them were headed our way, thin tendrils of black energy lancing out towards us. Tori screamed again, smashing the dreamlike state that we had all descended into and together we turned and raced for the door, none of us daring to look back at the onyx nightmares behind us.

Chapter Twenty-Five

Rushing out of the front door of the hospital, my three companions close on my heels I turned and paused, eyes searching the shadows of the doorway, seeking some sign of the dread creatures that we had seen pursuing us all.

"Don't stop running," Andrea urged out as she passed me and then stopped, shaking her head, her eyes wide behind her glasses as she glanced back at me. "Come on we need to run!"

"She is right Morgan!" Karl was suddenly at my shoulder, fear on his face. "We need to get away from here now!"

But instead of running I stayed where I was, watching with grim fascination as the shadow creatures suddenly moved into view, swirling and rising as they climbed the door frame, spreading themselves out along its edges.

"Oh my God!" Tori nearly screamed from somewhere behind me with Andrea. "Look out, they're coming!"

"No, they're not," I shook my head, my eyes narrowing as I stared back at the onyx creatures as they shifted and swirled about the door frame like solid smoke, never crossing the wooden threshold out into the daylight.

"They seem scared of the sunlight," I muttered turning to throw my companions what I hoped was a reassuring smile. "We are safe from them here if we stay in the sunshine."

"Not for long," Karl stated, his voice grim. "We are only safe for as long as the suns are out." Feeling sick as the truth of his words dawned on me, I looked up at the twin orbs of fire in the grey sky above us, wincing as I saw that they were both lower in the west than when we had entered the hospital. As the celestial bodies began to fade slightly in intensity, a shudder coursed through my body as a patch of shadow fell across me. In the doorway there was a flurry of activity as the creatures suddenly seemed to thrash about, merging and passing through each other before separating once again but they came no closer, still held back by the power of the strange twin suns but not for much longer.

"How long do you think we have before they are able to get out of there?" Tori asked, sounding as if she was going to be sick and I shook my head as I turned to her, not having any answers. "I have no idea."

"About an hour," Karl stated, meeting my gaze calmly as I cast him a look. "No more than that."

For a moment I wanted to rage at him for knowing that he was the occultist that had been mentioned in the journal but not mentioning it until I had guessed but somehow held my tongue. Shouting at him would achieve nothing. But if he were the occultist it left only four more people that I could be, the two journalists, the serial killer and the unmentioned individual. Grimacing I stepped back away from the building, casting the shadow creatures a grim look and then turning to the others. "Where shall we go now?"

"We were headed to the Cathedral," Tori stated.

"But that is no longer a safe option," Karl pointed out, frowning as he spoke. "The journal said that one of the Order of Shadows lives there...the priest...Father Hare."

"Fuck it," Tori cursed, striding away for several steps before turning back to stare at us. "Where do we go?"

Were we back in the real world, the world that we knew, then we could try and find help or at least a phone to call the police and tell them that we had been abducted! But here in the realm called New London we were alone.

Alone and in danger.

Shaking my head, hating the fact that once again everyone seemed to be looking to me for suggestions as to what we should do, I turned away from them, my mind racing as I tried to come up with a sensible plan. From the top of the hill that the asylum had sat on we had been able to see across the entire land and the only buildings that we had noticed were the hospital and the two small buildings beside it, the Cathedral, the tower in the distance and the ramshackle shanty town in the East. My stomach lurched as that thought occurred to me and heart skipping a beat, I spun back to the others. "Fuck."

"What is it?" Andrea stepped closer, placing a hand on my right arm. "What are you thinking?" The other two of our party moved to stand either side of her, curious expressions upon both their faces as they stared at me and I swallowed hard, trying to keep myself calm. "What's wrong Morgan?" Karl asked me and grimacing I met his gaze, shaking my head as I did so, mind racing as I stared into his eyes. "Don't you remember what it said in the journal about the shanty town in the north east?"

He paused, eyes narrowing as he cast his mind back and then Tori was answering for him. "It said that it was now filled with the people that they brought here."

"That's right," Andrea nodded, grim faced. "The journal said that they are now cannibals."

"Dear God," Karl muttered, eyes widening as he realised what I was getting at. He turned then and cast a look to the north east before turning back to wince at me and both the woman shook their heads in confusion, still not understanding. "What?

"Yeah, what are you two panicking about?"

I paused, letting out a shaky breath then I grimaced as I faced the pair. "That's where Craig, Amber and Ian went."

Chapter Twenty-Six

"Think this through, Morgan," Karl shouted at me some ten minutes later as I was hurrying across the sea of dead grass in the direction that I knew the shanty town lay in, the black man snaking out a hand to grab my wrist and spin me about to face him. "This is madness."

Despite the sudden urge to argue with the man and defend my actions I stayed silent, glaring back at him. After all he was right.

The moment that I had explained to our small party what the matter was, I had turned and begun heading off towards the place which the other members of our former group had headed too earlier. In truth I had no idea exactly what I planned to do when I got to the ramshackle town. After all they had begun walking towards it the same time that we had begun making our way towards the Cathedral on the other hill. The chances were that they had reached it.

Hell, by now they could already be chopped up ready to go into the cooking pot or whatever the cannibals used. My stomach turned over as the thought occurred to me and I shook my head, looking back at the black man. "I have to go and find them...maybe I can reach them before they even enter the area."

He shook his head then, his brown eyes narrowing as he studied me. "You don't really believe that Morgan. You know as well as I do, they are already dead."

"No," I shook my head, guilt touching me as I wished that I had suggested that we all stay together, instead of splitting and going our separate ways. "Don't say that."

He nodded at me. "You know it's the truth. Let it go now...there's nothing you can do to help."

"Damn you," I snapped at him then, the anger rushing from me in a wave, and he took a step back, turning to glance at the stunned and concerned faces of Andrea River and Tori Rice as the pair of them stood nearby, watching us. Then he chuckled, raising an eyebrow. "Damn me? How has this turned out to be my fault?"

"You could have told us who you were sooner," I glared at him, shaking my head. "I am not buying this shit about you only getting your memory back while you were reading the journal. You have known since the asylum, haven't you?"

The smile slid from his face then and he licked at his lips as if they had suddenly gone dry, then he was tilting his head to one side as he stared back at me. "Suppose I had…what difference would it have made? Tell me that!"

"You knew what this place was!" I snarled, surprising myself with the level of anger in my voice. "You knew all this time and you said nothing. You could have stopped them from heading off alone, but you never did you."

"No," he shook his head, shrugging. "But that doesn't mean that you can't trust me. We can help each other!"

For a moment I stared at him in disbelief, unable to believe what I was hearing. "Listen, I don't want to get caught up in your private little war with this Queenheart guy OK Karl, I just want to get me and the others home to the real world, our world, fuck you and this place!"

Karl stayed silent as he glared back at me, the anger on his features like a physical force.

But then he shook his head. "So noble now eh Morgan, but what about back at the asylum when we first awoke and were ready to go through that first door."

"What are you talking about?" I glared at him.

"You told us that it was nothing personal but that you were running and that you suggested we do the same, you said that you are the most important person."

Wincing as I recalled saying those very words, I nodded at him. "Yeah, I said that, but things change. We are all in this together and I don't want to leave anyone behind or have them get hurt because I chose not to help."

"Even the serial killer?" Tori asked as she moved over to stand beside Karl, her expression grim.

"Yes" the black man smiled. "Even them?"

"We don't know who the serial killer is!" Andrea pointed out as she came to stand at my side, the action filling me with strength by her presence.

"Ah but we know who one of them is!" Karl chuckled and nodded. "Dear sweet Amber is the descendant of Charles Dodgson...Lewis Carroll, which means that it could be one of the other two. Craig or Ian could be the serial killer."

"So, could I," I muttered throwing him a grim smile. "So could Tori here, until we know, I am not leaving them behind."

To my surprise he nodded and smiled, taking a step back and gesturing with an arm. "Then pray continue on this path of foolishness Morgan, I won't stop you."

"What are you up to?" I shook my head at him.

"Why so suspicious? I am merely bowing to your will. If you want to rush off and save the lives of complete strangers, feel free. I wish you luck."

"You are not coming?" I asked and he laughed.

"No, no I am not. I am heading off to the tower in the East, I have other business to attend to."

"You're leaving us?" Tori sneered at him, taking a step away, her face suddenly angry. "You king-size shit."

"And you my dear are an utterly loathsome whore," he smiled at her, nodding slightly at her shocked response. He turned then throwing me a final smile and then he was striding off across the dead grass, heading towards the towering white monolith on the horizon, the bottom half hidden by the green of the trees and bushes that surrounded its base. I frowned, wondering if that was the park the mysterious McKenzie Hatter had taken possession of and I cast my mind to the letter he had written us, hidden in the copy of Alice's Adventures in Wonderland. Was he there now?

Hiding in the tower?

Shaking my head, I moved forwards and stood watching for several minutes as the large white rabbit strolled away from us across the grass and then I glanced back at the two women with me. "You could have gone with him if you wanted. You didn't have to stay with me."

Andrea shrugged. "I'd rather be with you."

I blushed, feeling stupid and then turned to look at Tori, frowning as I saw her staring past me and the woman with the glasses, her mouth hanging open as if she had been about to scream but changed her mind. With dread in my heart, I turned about, cursing as I saw the two figures standing some distance away, the pair of them watching us intently as they stood side by side.

"Oh my God," Andrea muttered as she turned her head and saw them herself, one hand crossing herself as she backed over to join me and Tori. "Who are they?"

Gritting my teeth, I stared at the figures, each standing nearly six and a half feet tall and as wide as a door at the shoulder, both dressed in bowler hats, Wellington boots and leather aprons over cheap grey suits. Then my eyes dropped to the weapons that they were holding in their hands; the figure on the right wielding a large sledgehammer and the one on the left holding a chainsaw and I shook my head. "It's the Dumbdee twins."

Chapter Twenty-Seven

Time seemed to grind to a halt as the three of us stood staring back at the two huge men as they stood not twenty feet away, hefting their weapons in their large hands and I felt dread course through me as I saw the impassive expressions upon their fat faces, one framed by large mutton chop sideburns and the other wearing a large 'Village people' moustache.

The truth dawned on me then.

They were not excited at the thought of killing us.

They were devoid of all emotion and doing a job. For some reason that made it seem even worse. Letting out a shaky breath I took a step back, casting a glance over my shoulder in the direction that I knew the shanty town lay in and then looking back at the twins. I had no idea just how far away the cannibal filled town was from where we stood but I was equally sure that if we turned and ran now there was no way the hugely overweight Dumbdee twins would be able to keep up. Keeping my eyes on them, I turned my face towards my two female companions, lowering my voice. "On the count of three we run and don't look back, just run!"

There a barely audible mutter from them both and then I began to count. "One…"

With a scream that sounded as if it was torn from her very soul Tori turned and raced off across the dead grass in the direction that Karl Mackal had taken several minutes before, hands waving frantically beside her. For a fraction of a second I stood and stared at her in complete and utter shock as she hurried away from us and then I shook my head. "What a bitch"

"I can't believe she has left us," Andrea sounded as shocked as me, her voice a gasped whisper.

"Well, well, well," there was a chuckle from opposite us and I snapped my face forwards to find the twins now standing only fifteen feet away from where we were, the one with the sideburns shaking his head as he cast his twin a smile, his Cockney accent strong. "Looks to me like they weren't expecting that to happen, brother."

"You're not wrong brother," the twin with the moustache replied, chuckling. "They seem most put out don't they."

With a grimace I took another step away from them, nearly jumping a mile in the air as Andrea suddenly grasped at the hand nearest her, holding it tight and before us the twins moved forwards, Sideburns hefting the sledgehammer that he was holding in his big hands. "Come on now...let us not be playing silly buggers."

"Silly buggers?" I shook my head, confused and frightened by the bizarre way that they talked.

"Quite," Moustache gave a nod. "Don't you be running off...there's no need to be silly is there!"

"Silly?" Andrea echoed him, shaking her head.

"Am I speaking English, brother?" Moustache threw his twin a grim look at her echo of his words, his cheeks flushing crimson with anger.

"Indeed, you are brother of mine," Sideburns nodded. "It seems that these silly rabbits don't know the rules of the game. A travesty that is brother, a bleedin' travesty!"

"A travesty for certain brother," Moustache grimaced, turning back towards us and fixing me and Andrea with a grim smile. "The rules are simple...you don't make us run too much, and we kill you nice and painless like."

"Nice and quick" Sideburns nodded agreement.

"But if you run that's a different kettle of fish...if you run and make us run...well...," Moustache left the sentence unfinished and blew out a whistle, shaking his head as he faced us.

"A nasty business and no mistake," Moustache winced, his head shaking. "Quite unpleasant." Sideburns nodded at his brother's words and turned to us once more. "Quite...if you make us run, we will make sure it hurts!"

More than anything I wanted to laugh out loud and ask them how they expected to be able to kill us 'nice and painless' with a chainsaw and a sledgehammer but I figured it was probably not the right time right then. When faced with a well-dressed Leatherface and his hammer wielding twin, pissing them off was probably not the best option that we had open to us.

Or maybe it was.

Fixing the twin with the moustache, I forced a smile and raised an eyebrow. "Yeah, I bet you wouldn't want to run with all that weight you are carrying right?"

"What?" he snapped, eyes narrowing as he stared back at me, fingers tightening on the chainsaw. "What?"

"You heard me...you and your brother," I smiled, taking a small step backwards as Moustache and Sideburns exchanged furious glances, leading Andrea with me. When they turned back in my direction I shrugged. "Hey, don't be blaming me...it's your fault...look at the state of you both...have you seen each other?"

Again, they exchanged grim looks and again, me and Andrea took another couple of steps away from them. When they turned back towards us this time though my stomach sank as I saw the grim look in their eyes, the voice of Moustache bubbling with anger as he spoke. "I do believe this one needs to suffer brother."

"Agreed brother," Sideburns shifted the weight of the sledgehammer in his hands as he stared hatred in my direction, addressing his twin as he spoke. "And make them suffer we will."

I flinched as the bowel loosening roar of the chainsaw starting up broke through the air and then me and Andrea were turning and running, desperate to put as much distance between us and the huge lunatics as quickly as we could. We had gone less than twenty steps before the deep voices of the Dumbdee twins reached us as they began to sing. "Run rabbit, run rabbit, run, run, run..."

Chapter Twenty-Eight

We ran for at least fifteen minutes, arms pumping by our sides, sweat bathing our bodies beneath our costumes, before the land before us dipped slightly and the ramshackle shanty town that we had been heading towards came into view. I slowed then and risked a glimpse back over my shoulder, stopping as I saw what I had hoped to see, a wave of relief flooding over me. Far back from where me and Andrea now stood, the Dumbdee twins were now not only little more than dots in the distance but they also seemed to be headed away from us, moving off across the sea of dead grass towards the east.

A stab of concern touched me then as I realised that instead of pursuing us, they were heading after Tori and Karl. But then I grimaced, the concern leaving me in a rush as I recalled how they had both gladly deserted me and Andrea. Heaving a heavy sigh, I turned and gave my only remaining companion a weary smile. "I think we are safe...for the time being at least!"

Instead of appearing even remotely pleased by our escape from immediate danger, Andrea let out a groan and dropped down to a crouch, her head in her hands. Frowning, I stared down at her in silence, unsure what to say, unsure what the matter with her was. Then she was looking up at me with a haunted look in her eyes, her face pale. "What have we done to deserve this Morgan? Why is this happening to us?"

I shrugged, smiling at her grimly. "I guess we each pissed off Oliver Queenheart in our own individual way"

She winced then, her eyes going sad behind her glasses as she held my gaze. "I killed his wife."

What could I say to that?

After all, not only had the journal of the man that had abducted us stated that she had been responsible for the untimely demise of his wife, but her memories had supported the claim.

What could I say to change that?

Nothing I said would change how she felt.

So instead, I turned and looked in the direction that we had been heading, my eyes drifting over the roughly built buildings that lay in the distance, the majority no higher than one storey. I frowned as I saw a plume of smoke coming from what appeared to be the centre of the area and then I shifted my gaze, seeking a sign, any sign that there was life in the dirty township.

I knew by some strange manner that we were walking north-east and if we kept heading to the town, we would reach it in half an hour.

But how?

What secret knowledge did I possess?

"Can you see them?" Andrea's question had me turning towards her as she rose, and I frowned.

"Sorry?"

"Craig, Amber and Ian...can you see them?"

I shook my head, turning back to gaze at the distant town, my stomach sinking. "No, not yet."

"Are we too late?" she asked, her voice wavering. "Do you think the cannibals have got them and killed them?"

Grimacing, not ready to give up on the trio I shook my head and tried to smile. "No, have faith Andrea."

But then my eyes fastened upon the plume of smoke once again and I felt my insides knot at the thought that perhaps the three people that we had come here to save were in the flames.

"It's getting dark," Andrea muttered beside me and I raised my eyes, cursing as I saw the pair of suns were now hanging much lower in the sky.

"Damn it all," my curse was bitter as it left my lips. "As soon as it's dark the shadows will be able to leave the hospital."

"Do you think they will come after us?"

I sent Andrea a grim glance at her question and nodded slowly. "Yes, yes I do. They will come after us for sure."

The woman swore, turning and casting a look back in the direction that we had run, before turning to look at me, a soft chuckle escaping her lips and I frowned at her in confusion. "What?"

"We are stuck in a strange world, hunted by two giant fat men, some creatures made of shadow and some cannibals. It sounds like some badly written novel."

I laughed, nodding. "Yeah, I guess it does."

She gave another chuckle, her head shaking once more. "I have an author friend. He writes about this guy that can turn to a demon. One of the novels had his character visiting an Alice in Wonderland world. He'd love this."

"More memories?" I smiled and she nodded. "I'm getting little bits...you?"

I shook my head, not wanting to tell her that I seemed to know my way around. "No, not yet."

We stood together for a moment in silence and then I gave a heavy sigh and turned back towards the ramshackle town, eyes narrowing as I studied it once more. "If we are going, we best make a move now before it gets dark. Maybe we can find somewhere to hide there for the night and hope that the others have done the same."

"You really think they are still alive?" she asked me, and I flashed what I hoped was a confident smile and nodded, turning away from her again. "Of course, like I said just now, have some faith." Overhead there came a sudden rumble of thunder and my companion sighed. "Oh no...that sounds like rain."

I laughed. "Damn, that would ruin my day."

Chapter Twenty-Nine

It was rain.

By the time that we reached the outskirts of the ramshackle town that was our destination we were both drenched, the cold and dampness seeping through the material of the rabbit costumes that we were wearing, our boots caked in thick clumps of wet mud and grass. We had paused on a small rise to the south of the town, our eyes searching peering through the fading light, seeking some way to enter without being seen by the inhabitants only to discover as we crouched and stared that the town seemed to be absolutely deserted. I had noticed as we had made our way towards it that the plume of smoke in the centre of the town had slowly begun to diminish until it was finally extinguished although whether it had been doused by the rain or by those that had lit it remained to be seen.

When we had realised that there seemed to be no-one about, we had slowly begun to creep forwards, cloaked as best as we could be in white rabbit suits by the cover of darkness, creeping carefully through a hole in some broken boards in the side of the building we had reached, the pair of us overjoyed to be out of the foul weather but on edge due to our location. The town of cannibals.

Shuddering as a cold gust of wind blew in through the gap in the boards I ducked down and sat with my back against another wall, Andrea dropping down beside me, shivering like I was. Out of instinct, I reached over and put my left arm about her shoulders, pulling her against me and with a sigh, she rested her head back on the wall, closing her eyes. For a moment we sat there in our wet costumes, drawing some comfort from the closeness of each other and the miniscule warmth that provided. Then she was turning to face me, her features only inches from mine and I felt my stomach somersault as I looked into her big brown eyes. Swallowing hard, I tried to smile. "Are you OK?"

She nodded, her eyes still locked to mine, a faint smile on her lips. "Yes, thanks to you Morgan."

Feeling embarrassed, I shook my head, looking away. "I haven't done anything special Andrea."

"You have kept me safe from harm," her voice was soft like velvet and I closed my eyes, fighting the urges that suddenly ignited deep in my core, making me shudder with barely contained lust. "I owe you so much."

"Don't be daft," I told her, unable to look back at the woman for fear of what I would do if I saw the same look in her eyes that I was feeling. "Whatever," she gave a soft chuckle, snuggling in against my arm some more and supressing a groan as I felt the swell of a full breast push against me, I forced myself to focus upon our surroundings, desperate to calm down. The room that we were in was barely large enough to deserve such a name, the far wall being less than five feet from the end of my stretched-out legs and the side walls the same if I were to stretch my arms out wide. The floor beneath us consisted of lengths of broken planks pushed together to make a solid base but weeds and undergrowth were growing up through the gaps, some climbing the haphazard planks that made up the walls, reaching for the uneven ceiling overhead. Turning my attention on the walls, I frowned as I saw that some of the boards were secured together with ropes and string, others held in place with bent nails and others still being propped up with other pieces of wood. As I studied the building about us, the rising wind gave another howl, the heavy rain which had drenched us to the skin, hammering down on our refuge and I winced as the walls creaked and swayed slightly, appearing as if they were ready to collapse in upon us at any moment. Holding my breath as I watched the building moving around us, I cursed, wondering how people lived like this. But then they had no choice. If the journal had been correct, they had all been abducted from the eighteenth century of the world which me and Andrea had been taken from. Abducted and dumped in a foreign dangerous realm simply for the shadow beings to hunt and consume. It was a miracle they had survived at all. Shaking my head, I took a deep breath and tried to force any pity that I felt towards the town's inhabitants away.

The journal had said that they had become cannibals. If that was true, then my new friends that had mistakenly ventured here in search of help could be in big trouble. Frowning I tried to work out how long it had been since we had seen them, estimating that it could not have been more than a few hours. Maybe they had managed to avoid trouble and stay alive in the same manner we had. Closing my eyes, I tilted my head back to rest on the wall behind me, trying to picture the three of them hid down somewhere in this sprawling woodpile of a town, hiding from the elements and the cannibals in the same manner as me and Andrea. A slight smile creased my features as I pictured Amber and Ian being terrified and the broad guy with the ginger beard and the rectangular glasses, Craig, taking care of them, keeping them alive. Not that there seemed to be any of the dreaded cannibals about.

Were they too hiding from the storm?

Even as the thought occurred to me, I corrected myself. No, they were hiding from the shadow creatures; the creatures that they had been brought here as prey for.

Experience had no doubt taught them that the creatures hunted at night and so they were laying low. That meant that we were relatively safe until the morning. Hopefully, Craig could keep the others safe until then too.

He seemed the sort of guy who would protect others if he had too and I smiled as images of the man putting a supportive arm about the shoulders of a sobbing Amber back at the asylum returned to me. The smile slid from my face as I considered the fact that the friendly man might be the vile serial killer responsible for the deaths of twelve young women.

He certainly had the physique to be able to dominate women and overpower them with ease. I frowned then as I recalled how he had seemed too close to the young woman, Amber, all the time, always near her, always taking every opportunity to touch her, someone that was a stranger. Had Craig been merely a very tactile man or were his actions towards Amber something far more nefarious?

If he was the killer, Amber was in trouble.

Which meant Ian was too.

I turned my head towards Andrea as she yawned, matching her sudden embarrassed smile with one of my own and then she was looking deep into my eyes again, making me catch my breath. "Penny for your thoughts."

My insides twisted at her question and I felt the smile waver upon my face but then I was forcing it back, not wanting her to know what I had been thinking for risk of scaring her. "I was just thinking about the others."

A strange expression flickered over her face.

Was it hope?

"You think they are still alive?"

I nodded. "Yeah, I do. We are...why not them."
Her face split with a broad grin then and she
leaned over to kiss me upon the cheek. As I
blushed, she began to move her head away, then
stopped, her full lips barely an inch from mine,
her breath hot on my face. I honestly have no
idea who moved to kiss who first, suffice to say
that suddenly our mouths were locked together,
our tongues fighting furiously and then we were
lying down on the uneven wooden floor, me
atop her. I cursed as my fingers moved to the zip
at the front of her costume and found it as
immobile as mine had been earlier but then we
were kissing once more as I moved to lay beside
her. She groaned aloud as my right hand
reached up, grasping at first one large breast
and then the other, squeezing firmly, feeling the
hard nipples beneath the wet material and then
she was arching her back as my hand slid down
to rub at the heat between her open thighs,
rubbing at the material of her costume. As the
rain and wind beyond the small building began
to increase in intensity, a fair amount blowing in
through the gap that we had entered through,
the pair of us lay in the darkness and gave

ourselves over to as much pleasure as our
rabbit costume shaped prisons would allow.

Chapter Thirty

I awoke with a start, blinking against the cold grey sunlight which was shining in through the gaps in the walls and ceiling of the building in which we had crawled the night before. Wiping a hand across the drool which had run from my mouth I lay there on my back, Andrea snuggled in tight against me and I considered what had happened between us the night before, smiling as I did. Then I was flinched and sat up in a rush as I heard the mumbled mutter of voices close by, somewhere beyond the makeshift walls of our temporary refuge. For a moment there was nothing but silence outside and I nearly relaxed, blaming the sound upon my nerves. But then the voice sounded again, somewhere to my left and I turned my head towards it, watching as the light that was seeping through the cracks stopped suddenly as someone passed the wall. "I reckon old Bert was wrong," a deep guttural voice suddenly rasped, barely five feet from where I sat. "There ain't nothin ere but mud an that's a fact!"

"Stow ya complain," another voice replied, making me turn my face to stare at a spot several feet to the left of the first voice. "He ain't steered us wrong yet as he?"

There was a disbelieving grunt from the first voice followed by the sounds of movement. A soft thud sounded, and then the first voice came again, pained and angry. "Hey...wha'd ya bleedin hit me for Charlie?"

"Shut it is what I'm sayin to ya Bill," the second voice snapped. "Stop second guessin Bert or it'll be you that ends up in the soup an no mistake!"

This time the voice of the first man, Bill, was softer, chastised and I could almost picture him nodding at his companion. "I suppose ya right."

There was a chuckle from the other man, Charlie, and then he spoke the words that chilled my blood. "Good, now keep lookin...Bert said he saw rabbits comin to the town this way last night...we needs to find them."

As I sat staring back at the wall before me in abject terror there was a soft groan from beside me and yawning, Andrea sat up, throwing me a smile. Heart racing in my chest, I grasped hold of the back of her head with one hand, clamping my hand over her mouth. Stunned by my actions, eyes wide, she began to struggle, her eyes growing wider still as beyond the walls of our refuge, Charlie spoke. "What was that?"

"What?"

"I just 'erd something!"

Silence reigned for an eternity then Bill was speaking once again. "Are ya sure?"

"Yeah...it was in there I tell ya."

Gritting my teeth, realising that I no longer needed to keep my hand across my companion's mouth, I rose to my feet and gestured for Andrea to do the same, wincing as the light rays coming through the gaps in the wall shifted again. Then Bill was chuckling, the sound like dry leaves blowing in the wind. "Well, there ain't nothing there now is there eh! Come on, let us try the next street."

Standing beside Andrea, I followed their movement away along the side off the small building by the way the light rays moved as they passed between the wall and the sun and then they were gone, the sound of their idle chatter reaching me as they headed away down the dirty street. As their voices finally faded away, I turned to throw Andrea a grim look. "Fuck me that was close!"

She nodded, heaving a heavy sigh and then she was tilting her head to the side. "Cannibals?"

I nodded, remembering how Bill had threatened the other man Charlie with ending up in the soup. "Yeah, I think they were. And they were hunting us."

"What?"

"Apparently someone called Bert saw us enter the town last night...he sent the pair of them looking for us."

"Is he their leader?"

I frowned at her question, finding it odd that a society that had devolved to the extent that they had become cannibals could have anything as structured as a society and a leader. But then they had to have one, right? He was no doubt the strongest and nastiest of them all.

Looking back at Andrea I nodded, "He must be."

"Did they mention the others?"

"No," I shook my head at her, smiling sadly. We held each other's gaze for a moment and then she nodded, stepping forward and putting her arms about my waist, resting her head on my chest and out of instinct I placed my arms about her shoulders. She looked up at me then, brushing her lips against mine. I flinched and spun to the side, Andrea going with me as the wooden wall behind her suddenly seemed to cave inwards with a crash and cursing we fell back down to the uneven boards that we had slept upon last night, staring up at the two dirty bearded men that were now stood in the gap.

Chapter Thirty-One

From my prone position upon the ground, my right arm trapped beneath the weight of Andrea's body, I stared up at the pair of cannibals in grim fascination. Both were dressed in old style clothes, like working class people from the Victorian times, and both were bearded and dirty, both carrying a hungry look in their eyes. As I glared up at them, the biggest of the pair gave a grim chuckle and shook his head. "Did ya think ya could hide from us?"

"I told ya I 'erd something din't I, Bill!" the smaller man grinned, the few teeth that he still possessed black and crooked. "I told ya there was rabbits in 'ere!"

Bill gave another chuckle, nodding as he brought both hands up before his broad chest and cracked his knuckles. "That ya did Charlie me old mate, that ya did!"

They were still metaphorically patting each other upon the back when I pushed Andrea from my arm and surged to my feet, spurred on by some previously unknown anger and confidence. Charlie cursed as he saw me rushing forward and Bill, having been in the process of casting another compliment to his companion turned his face back towards me as if in slow motion, eyes wide with panic. He grunted as my right fist struck him square in the face, the cartilage of his nose crunching beneath the blow but instead of falling backwards he gave me a grin, his mouth awash with blood from my attack upon him. "My turn little rabbit!" He had barely finished speaking before he gripped me by my arms and lifted me effortlessly from the ground. One moment I was dangling there staring back at his bloody face in shock and then the next I was flying, smashing painfully through another of the wooden walls to land hard in the muddy street beyond, pieces of broken board falling about me. Even as I struggled to rise, he was advancing on me, his powerful arms smashing aside the rest of the wall as he stepped out into the cold grey sunlight, a sneer on his bearded face. "You broke my nose rabbit...now ya pay!" "Fuck you," I spat back as I tried to rise, my own nose bleeding courtesy of my painful exit from the building and the large cannibal named Bill laughed across at me. That was until with a creak, the building behind him collapsed in upon itself, the two undamaged remaining walls folding and the roof dropping down upon those still within the building. There was a shout of alarm from the other cannibal and a scream from Andrea. Then silence.

Cursing, Bill the cannibal started to turn in the direction of the ruined building, his voice concerned. "Charlie?"

The word merged into a grunt of shock and pain as I rose quickly behind him with a length of wood in my hands and struck him hard across his broad shoulders. Off balance, he staggered forwards and I followed him, hitting him twice more before he spun suddenly, his outstretched arm catching me straight in the throat, knocking me back to the ground. As I landed hard, the beam of wood flew from the fingers of my right hand and wide eyed, I gasped and choked as the bearded face of Bill the cannibal loomed over me, his eyes promising nothing but death.

"Time to die, little rabbit," he spat down at me, my stomach turning over with revulsion as a big droplet of his saliva and hot blood splashed down onto my face. He chuckled at my reaction, grinning down at me. "Don't like blood eh? Well, ya gonna see lots more before ya end up goin in the pot! You and the other rabbits once we catch them all!"

"Other...rabbits," I gasped, blinking back the tears in my eyes that the choking had produced. He gave another grim chuckle, holding up two large fingers. "Two...two little rabbits ready for the pot...an ya gonna join them!"

So that meant that at least two of the others were still alive, even if they were captives of these bastards. I grimaced up at him then, an idea coming to me as I felt my fingers brush against something and wide eyed, I stared past his broad body. "Andrea hit him!"

He twisted at the waist as I had expected, glancing back towards the building and with a roar of anger I sat up fast, burying the two-foot-long splinter of wood that my fingers had found in the mud, deep into his groin. He screamed as the sharp point punched through the material of his trousers, pushing deep into the soft flesh of his scrotum and then up into his abdomen. Wide-eyed and red faced, he reached down trying to fasten his large hands about my throat and with a snarl I twisted the splinter of wood, turning his scream to a piteous howl of pure agony. As hot blood gushed down over my fingers, I gritted my teeth and wrenched the splinter to the side, snapping it in two, one half in my hand and the other deep inside his body. Grim faced I somehow managed to find my feet and with a bestial roar, I buried the jagged length of wood that I was still holding deep in the side of his neck, coating myself in hot blood as his jugular was ruptured.

Chapter Thirty-Two

Time seemed to slow as I stood there in the middle of the street, my formerly white rabbit suit now coated in dark blood and thick mud, as I stared into the eyes of the large, bearded cannibal on the end of the splinter that I was holding. For a second, he grasped at my hands, trying perhaps to free them from the makeshift weapon and gritting my teeth I did so, stepping back. Pain filled eyes staring back at me in utter hatred, Bill the cannibal gripped one hand to the shard of wood in his neck, his hands becoming quickly coated as his lifeblood pumped out over his fingers and then with a feral snarl he reached down with his other hand, fingers digging into the raw wound in his groin. I watched in a mixture of horror and disgust as with painstaking slowness he dragged the bloody splinter of wood out of his scrotum, twitching and jerking as he did so.

Finally, it came loose, a torrent of blood pouring from between his legs to splash down on the mud at his feet, making him look like a pregnant woman whose waters had just broken. Then with another snarl he tore the other splinter of wood from his neck, holding them both before him like gore encrusted knives as he fixed me with a look of hate, bloody lips moving silently. Then he dropped to his face in the muddy street with a loud squelch, farted once and lay still. Shaking my head, I stared down at his corpse, my body beginning to tremble as the adrenaline brought on by the fight began to leave my body and with a groan I dropped to my knees, sinking several inches in the mud. Only then did I raise my eyes to stare back at the remains of the small building that me and Andrea had spent the night together in and with a curse of horror, I forced myself to rise on shaky legs and hurry towards it. Reaching it, I began to dig with my hands, tearing at the fallen beams and planks, throwing them aside as I tried to uncover my companion, cursing each time a splinter of nail lanced into my unprotected hands. By the time I moved a board and saw the white material of the rabbit costume that Andrea wore my hands were scratched and bleeding, but I did not stop. I could not stop searching until I knew if she was still alive and well. Gritting my teeth, I shifted myself forwards across the other pieces of wood about me and then grasped the large board that seemed to be covering the rest of her body. I nearly cried out with relief as I cast the board aside and found her looking up at me, her eyes wet with tears behind her glasses, which had managed to not break somehow. Dropping to my knees beside her, I sent her a grin. "Oh my God, are you OK?"

She nodded up at me as best as she could, still partially surrounded by debris and then her eyes widened as she took in the mess upon my rabbit costume and my face. "Are you hurt?"

"No," I shook my head. "Not me...him."

"Is he...?"

"Dead?" I nodded, smiling grimly. "I'd say so."

She sighed then, relief visible on her features and I lowered my gaze, studying the way that her arms were pinned beside her by other pieces of wood, my eyes drifting onwards to study a long spike that was pushing down into the ground only inches from her head. I let out a shaky breath as I considered how that would have punched through her face if she had moved the wrong way and then I was studying the beams above her arms once more, realising that it was these that had stopped the larger sheet of wood from reaching her upper body, crushing her head and chest. Frowning, I studied the beams pinioning her limbs a moment longer and then I was meeting her gaze once again. "I will have you out in a moment, keep still."

She nodded back at me and rising I set about the task of removing the beams and debris one piece at a time, careful not to disrupt them in a manner which could cause them to slip and injure my trapped companion. In a matter of minutes, she was free and standing beside me, brushing at the dust and dirt on her white rabbit costume while I stood there in my blood and mud coated outfit studying her. "Are you sure you are ok?"

Again, she nodded. "Yeah, I will be fine. But where did those guys come from? I thought they had gone!"

I considered her words, remembering how the cannibals had headed away from us and then I shrugged. "They must have decided to trick us. They went off but then doubled back to try and surprise us. Fair play to them both...it worked"

She shook her head. "It nearly worked! You got the better off them Morgan. Where did you learn the skills that enabled you to kill two men with your bare hands?"

For a moment, I frowned at her question then I grimaced, turning to stare back at the debris. "What is it?" she asked, shaking her head slowly. I shook my head. "I only killed one of them. Start digging. The other one is here somewhere!"

Chapter Thirty-Three

"What is goin' on" the bearded cannibal named Charlie opened his eyes with a start and tried to sit up, cursing and dropping quickly back down as I lowered a baseball bat length of wood to rest on his chin from where I stood above him. "No sudden moves," I warned him but in truth there was little he could do to pose me and Andrea a threat. We had found him lying unconscious several minutes earlier and without a means to tie him up we had buried his chest and legs in debris, pinning him to the ground. It was not of course a fool-proof plan of course; fully conscious and with enough time he would be able to free himself from the prison. Which was why I was holding the wood.

The moment he tried to free himself, he was dead. I frowned then, chewing my bottom lip as I considered whether I could beat a man to death in cold blood? Agreed, I had just stabbed the other cannibal to death with two shards of broken wood, but I had been defending myself. This man was unable to fight back.

Wincing as I realised I was not sure I could kill him, I let out a breath that I had been holding and pressed my makeshift weapon hard against our prisoner's chin. "If you try and get free, I'll fucking kill you…understand?"

Beneath the debris the cannibal nodded. "Yeah."

Trying not to let the relief show on my face as I realised my bluff had worked, I glared down at him, trying how best to proceed with what me and Andrea had decided. Then I bit the bullet and went with it. "Where are they?"

"Who?" he shook his head, eyes wet with tears.

"Our friends," I stated, coldly. "Where are they?"

"I don't know," he winced. "I swear."

Gritting my teeth, I brought the length of wood I was holding back and then jabbed him hard on the chin with it, enough to make him curse and cry out, then I glared down at him again, my voice cold. "Nice try…but your mate Bill told me you have caught two of them."

He blinked hard then, suddenly seeming to remember his larger friend and then his eyes widened as he lowered them slowly from my face to take in the blood and gore that had coated the rabbit costume I was wearing.

"Bill?" he muttered, fear in his eyes as he stared back at my face. "Wha'd you do to 'im!"

"What do you think?" I stated, giving a dry chuckle purely for theatrical purposes. "He's dead…do you want to join him or are you going to answer my questions?"

Instead of replying the bearded man closed his eyes and shook his head. "Bill…dead…no."

Despite myself I felt a touch of guilt creep into my core as I saw his expression seem to crumple and I cast Andrea a quick glance as she stood beside me, her face wearing an expression of remorse. Then I was cursed and stepped back as the man suddenly snapped his eyes open and snarled up at me, spittle flecking out onto his beard. "Murderers! You ain't meant to fight back…rabbits is meant to die and go in the pot!"

"Fuck you," I snarled, anger coursing through me suddenly and taking a step to the side I brought the length of wood back and swung it like a golf club, striking him hard in the side of the head. There was a soft thud and he cried out in pain, his face twisting away. "Tell me where they are!"

He spat out blood and several black teeth. "No!"

"Tell me," I ordered him, staring down with disgust at the thick line of dark blood that was running from his right ear. "Tell me or I will do some damage that you won't be able to heal!"

"No...fuck you," he snarled as he turned to look back up at me and I grimaced at him and stepped back, my head throbbing with anger, heat flushing up and down my neck in waves. Fine, he wanted to play it tough.

Which meant that we were going to use B plan.

Turning I gave Andrea a grim look. "Do it."

She nodded. "Which one?"

"The left," I stated, turning to stare back down at the dirty bearded man as he in turn moved his eyes to watch Andrea as she made her way to stand by his left side, crouching and dragging a few of the beams away. Before me, upon the ground the cannibal named Charlie made an odd grunt and eyed me suspiciously. "What are ya gonna do to me...let me go!"

Shaking my head, I moved to stand beside the upper arm that Andrea had uncovered, I stared down at the limb, my eyes drifting to where we had buried his forearm and hand in the mud and piled debris atop it. Then I looked back at Charlie. "Tell me where my friends are."

"Never," he snarled but he did not sound sure.

I shrugged then, holding his gaze for a moment. Then I was raising the wood that I was holding in my hands above my head, ready to bring down on his exposed arm only to pause as he cried out. "No...wait!"

"Where are they?" I asked without looking at him, suddenly scared that if I saw how scared he was I would not be able to follow through with it.

"I can't tell ya!" he shouted, "Bert'll kill me!"

"Wrong answer," I muttered, feeling my stomach lurch as I brought the wood down onto his unprotected arm. It struck him a fraction of an inch above the elbow. The arm seemed to jump with the impact, the arm jerking and rolling, and I grimaced and stepped back as the elbow dislocated, the force of the blow dragging his forearm and hand free from its prison.

"Oh my God," the voice of Andrea was shocked beside me and turning to look at her, I found her features pale, one hand cupped over her mouth.

"I warned him," I stated angrily, suddenly feeling that I had to defend my actions and spinning back to face the bearded man I found him sobbing in pain, the dislocated arm jerking awkwardly every time he tried to move it. For a moment I stared down at our prisoner then I gritted my teeth. "Uncover his other arm."

"Morgan?" her voice was barely audible, scared.

"Just do it," I told her, cringing as I felt rather than saw the look of horror upon her face. Taking a steadying breath, I stood and watched while she did as I had asked, uncovering the limb and then stepping back, her eyes downcast, avoiding mine. Swallowing hard, I moved to stand above the arm, my eyes drifting to settle upon the sweaty, pained face of Charlie the cannibal. "Do I need to ask you again?"

"Please," he sobbed at me, the word little more than an animal howl of agony and terror. "Don't do it!"

Gritting my teeth, I held his gaze, raising the wood above my head once again and then he was screaming, his voice barely articulate. "I'll talk…I'll talk…just don't hurt me anymore!" Lowering the wood, I turned to cast a grin at Andrea, hoping she would be pleased. But instead of a triumphant smile she was regarding me with fear on her face and the smile she attempted never seemed to reach her eyes behind her glasses. Sure, I had won and got the information but what had I become to do so?

Chapter Thirty-Four

"Are you sure this is the right way?"

I stopped walking and turned my face to look back at Andrea as I heard her question, nodding at her. "Yeah, this is the way that he said. We shouldn't be too far away now."

She nodded back at me, smiling weakly and I felt my stomach knot. Ever since I had beaten our captive with the length of wood and dislocated his left elbow, she had been acting slightly off kilter with me, fear evident in her bright eyes. In truth, I could not blame her.

Or could I?

We had come to the shanty town with the express purpose of trying to save our new companions from being eaten by those that resided within it. I had learned from the big cannibal named Bill in the moments before I had stabbed him that his people had managed to capture two of my three friends and the only way to discover where they were being held prisoner had been to do what I had done.

Did I regret dislocating the man's arms and smashing him in the face with the wood?

Yes, without question.

Would I do it again if I needed to?

Yes, without question.

Because as violent as my act had been and as much pain as I had caused the man there was one thing that made me feel much better about what had done to him. He and his companion had been fully intent on killing me and Andrea, taking us back to their brethren and sticking us in the pot that they had both mentioned.

So, with the threat of having his other arm smashed, our prisoner had sung like a proverbial canary and told me everything.

Yes, he and his brethren *had* captured two of our friends as prisoners, a man and a woman.

Yes, they were intending to eat them.

No, he had no idea where the other man was. They had only found the two rabbits.

No, the man they had did not wear glasses.

Yes, he would tell us where they were held.

He had cringed when I had asked about the man named Bert, the colour draining from his already pale face and he had shaken his head, begging me in a whiny nasal voice not to tell the man that he had betrayed him. So, I had given him a grim smile and told him that I would if he did not tell me everything there was to know about the man that ruled over the cannibals.

So, sobbing, Charlie the cannibal had begun to spill the beans on the man that scared him so. And what I had learned had not been good. According to my prisoner, Bert was over six feet tall, broad as a bear and five times as nasty even though his right eye was made of glass and that a rusty metal spike protruded from the ruin of his left wrist, a reminder of the attack by the two fat men with hats.

I had nodded at his words, realising that he was referring to the Dumbdee twins and then I had asked him how many people were in his little fucked up community. Which was when his demeanour had changed slightly, and he had given a dry chuckle. "I don't know me numbers, but Charlie says its five hands worth and then some...and they all gonna be comin' after ya!" I had stood frowning down at him for a moment, my eyes locked to his as I tried to work out if five hands worth meant twenty-five or if he was perhaps talking about pairs of hands. The thought of facing off against just twenty-five of them was enough but fifty? Feeling sick I had shaken my head, hoping that he was mistaken, and he had uttered a laugh. "Ya gonna die."

His laugh had ended as I had struck him again on the side of the head with the wood, knocking him out and throwing Andrea a grim look I had gestured for her to follow me as I headed out of the ruins of the building. Now nearly an hour later the pair of us were nearing where it was that Charlie had told us his people were holding our companion's prisoner. In truth we had not travelled that far, the journey probably only taking twenty minutes had we walked normally. But with the threat of death and capture at the hands of the cannibals ever present we had taken to creeping along through the streets, hugging to the shadows and keeping as low and out of sight as we possibly could. Three times we had frozen on the spot, my heart racing in my chest as I had waved Andrea back into hiding. Then we had sat or crouched in silence, watching as small groups of figures passed by, their eyes scouring the streets, their dirty hands filled with crude weapons and lengths of rope. They were hunting us.

Just the same as Charlie and Bill had been. Their leader had seen us enter the town before nightfall and had sent them all out to hunt us down. The irony of that fact had struck me as we had travelled on each time, the grim truth that they had been brought here to be hunted by the shadow creatures but had in turn taken to hunting those placed in the rabbit costumes.

But that was the trouble with rabbits.

Everything is a predator.

So far, we had Oliver Queenheart, the Dumbdee twins, the shadow creatures and now the cannibals after us. Hardly fair odds at all.

But then the hunts weren't supposed to be fair. We were supposed to die; simple as that.

Sighing, I forced my thoughts on the present as Andrea moved to walk past me, giving me a smile as she did so. "Come on Morgan."

Nodding, I joined her, creeping along down the dirty street that we had entered several minutes before and then I froze, my eyes raising skyward as I cursed. "Damn."

"What it is?" she muttered, eyes wide as she stopped walking and allowed me to draw level with her. "What?"

With a shaking finger, I pointed to the grey sky ahead of us above the nearest buildings, the air split by the dark plume of smoke that was rising steadily. "I hope I'm wrong but if you ask me it looks like someone is preparing a meal."

Chapter Thirty-Five

"You don't think..." she left the sentence hang unfinished, shaking her head as she stared back at me. I nodded at her. "Yeah, I doubt they are having a salad."

"Oh my God," she muttered, turning back to stare up at the smoke and grimacing I moved past Andrea and took her hand, leading her in through the open doorway of the wooden building before us, one of the few that was higher than one storey. I paused as we got inside, shuddering as the shadows of the interior wrapped about us and I grimaced as I remembered the creatures from the hospital.

Were they now somewhere in the town?

Had they made their way here when the suns had gone down the night before?

Were they lurking close-by, ready to ambush the unwary, like a spider in a web?

Gritting my teeth, I pushed the dread thoughts away and cast a look about our surroundings, nodding to myself as I saw a rough hole in the boards that made up the ceiling above us and a series of nailed blocks of wood upon the wall beneath it creating a crude ladder. Gesturing for Andrea to follow me as I moved towards it, I crept closer to the hole, trying to keep as silent as I could just in case there was someone upstairs on the next floor only to cringe as my companion trod on an uneven board behind me. As the creak sounded loud in the confined area I spun to about, my eyes on her but my ears straining to hear any sound from above. Minutes seemed to drag by as we stood in the gloomy room, eyes locked on each other's and then I sighed, relaxing slightly as I realised that we were alone. Then I was passing Andrea the length of wood that I had been carrying, ignoring the grimace she made as her eyes drifted to the gore covered end. Turning away from her, I reached up with my right leg, placing my foot on the lowest of the wooden blocks nailed to the wall while my hands reached higher, fingers gripping those a few feet above my head. With a jerk I straightened my leg and pulled with my arms, hauling myself up and then I was climbing the haphazard ladder up and through the hole in the ceiling. As soon as my waist was through the hole, I was bracing myself with my left arm and reaching down with my right, gratefully accepting my weapon as my companion passed it up to me. Moments later and I was crouched above the hole, weapon held ready as Andrea clambered up through it to join me, her face pale amid the white fur of the rabbit costumes hood.

"What are we doing?" she whispered, her voice sounding loud amid the silence and I cringed. "We need to see that that smoke is all about," I told her in a hushed voice. "If they have already killed Amber and Ian then there is no point us risking ourselves"

"You think they are dead?" her eyes widened behind her glasses, just as they had when Charlie the cannibal had told us only those two of our companions had been captured, shaking her head as she had asked me if that meant that Craig was dead. As I had then, I shook my head at Andrea and shrugged, smiling weakly. "I don't know anymore, and I don't want to guess." Without another word, I moved away from her, creeping to the side of the building that the smoke had been emitting from, dropping to my knees beside it. I turned my head to watch as Andrea moved to join me, lowering herself down to kneel at my side and throwing her what I hoped was a reassuring smile, I studied the wall before me, seeking a large enough hole to look through. Like every other building we had passed since being in the ramshackle town, our current location was devoid of any type of window, though the reason for this was architectural decision was lost on me. Nodding to myself, as I found a hole sufficiently large enough to look through and near enough to where I was crouched to not make me uncomfortable, I placed my right eye against it and stared out at the view beyond. For a moment I stayed where I was in silence, my mind racing as I studied the dirty area between the buildings like a town square and then I was staring with grim fascination at the crowd of dirty clothed people that framed it, every one of the men bearded and the few women appearing pale faced and grim. Cursing, I turned from the sight to rest my back against the wall, shaking my head. "Fucking Hell!"

"What is it?" Andrea nearly sobbed. "What?"

For a moment, I sat staring back at her and then I was turning again and looking back through the hole, my eyes once more settling first upon the huge bonfire in the centre of the town square, an equally large pot hanging from wooden scaffolding above it. As I watched, a couple of the dirty men moved forwards from the crowd to throw more wood upon the fire making the smoke that we had seen in the cold grey sky earlier billow with more intensity as it passed the pot. Then with a heavy sigh, I allowed my gaze to return to the large wooden cage that sat some distance from the pot, wincing as I studied the two figures in the rabbit suits which sat within, their heads down, ear's drooping. Amber and Ian; trapped and surrounded by a horde of people who all bore the sole intention of killing them and then eating their flesh as if it was a normal thing.

I grimaced then, imagining how scared the pair of them must be feeling locked in that cage facing the prospect of being cooked and eaten. They must be terrified.

But then who knew what the young pair had already lived through. The absence of the broad-shouldered Craig seemed to serve as an indication that they had already been in trouble. What had happened to him?

As I sat pondering the absence of the man with the ginger beard and the glasses, Andrea gave a sudden grunt of surprise and leaned against me and frowning, I turned to her. "What's wrong?"

I had a second to see the two dirty clothed men that stood there grinning above the unconscious Andrea and then a punch knocked me out.

Chapter Thirty-Six

I was in the foyer of a huge house, the marble floor shining beneath my feet and a large staircase sweeping up before me, curving around to the left where it led to the upstairs of the sprawling property. But despite the bright, intense sunlight shining in through the windows beside the thick oak door behind me, warming my back and shoulders, I felt cold inside. On the stairs, a ginger haired man in a black suit was frowning at me, his strangely cat-like features stern as he shook his head. "You're late."

"I know," I told him, shrugging. "I'm here now."

"Your father won't be happy," the man on the stairs grimaced, taking a step down towards me, his hands clasped behind his back, a sneer on his lips. "You know how he disapproves of tardiness don't you?"

"Listen to me Cheshire." I snapped angrily, moving forward and stopping several feet before him. "Don't try telling me what to do...do you understand?"

He smiled then, his trademark grin filling his face as he nodded, bowing slightly. "Of course, my apologies."

For a moment, the pair of us stood staring back at each other, then he extended a hand to me. "What is it?" I asked, raising an eyebrow as I saw the piece of paper clasped between his fingers. He smiled again, eyes seeming to sparkle in his feline features. "A note…it has your name on it." Taking the paper from him, I held his gaze as I unfolded it and then lowered my eyes to the writing upon it, a frown creasing my features as I realised that it was a single sentence written in what appeared to be Latin. Shaking my head, I looked back up at the man in the black suit, fighting the flush of anger that coursed through me as I saw the broad grin on his cat-like features once again. "Is there a problem?"

"Where did you get this?" I threw Cheshire a grimace, but the thin man shrugged and smiled as if unconcerned by my anger, a hand reaching up to brush back through his ginger hair.

"It was delivered earlier," he gave a shrug, his tone conversational. "One of the maids took it in. Is there some kind of problem? Can I help in some way?"

"No," I shook my head, preparing to screw the strange message up and throw it away. "Where is father?"

"In a meeting," he nodded, holding my gaze, still grinning. "I have told him you are here."

The urge to rant at him for daring to chastise me on my lateness when my father wasn't even ready to meet me, surged up then but I held my tongue, instead lowering my gaze to the single sentence upon the paper I was still holding. Father was having some difficulty lately with people and despite his efforts to hide his concerns, I knew he was troubled by them.

"Might I enquire as to just what the note says?"

Rolling my eyes in irritation, I shook my head at Cheshire. "No, no you cannot."

He nodded at me, dipping his head in a subservient manner once again but that smile stayed on his features. "As you wish...and forgive my forwardness but from the expression upon your face when you read the note, I got the impression that you could not read it"

"What?" I snarled at him, anger coursing through me as I faced him. "Are you saying I am some kind of dullard?"

"Of course, not" he shook his head, having the good sense to remove the smile from his face. "I was just saying that if you could not read it, I am fluent in several different languages. In fact, I believe that it is my proficiency in the art of linguistics that is one of the reasons that your father has employed me…"

Grimacing, shaking my head as the man continued to insinuate that I could not read the sentence, I raised a hand to silence him and then read it out aloud, sounding each syllable as best as I could. As I finished speaking, I threw the man a broad grin, the expression fading from my face as I saw a look of triumph upon his face. Then I was gasping, clasping my hands to my ears as they both popped with pressure and as the room began to spin, I dropped to my knees, staring up in horror at the grinning cat faced man before me. "What…what have you done?" He laughed, shaking his head, his smile seeming to eclipse his head as my vision swam. "I would have thought that was obvious. You are required elsewhere and reading that sentence was the means with which to get you there."

"You're mad!" I managed to gasp, feeling the dark shroud of unconsciousness surging up to embrace me. The last thing I remembered was the amused words of my father's personal assistant, Cheshire, as he gave a hearty chuckle. "We're all mad here."

Chapter Thirty-Seven

"Morgan? Morgan, wake up!"

I snapped my eyes open as the voice called me name, brushing aside the hands that were gripped to the front of my rabbit costume, trying to shake me awake. For a moment, I lay there staring up into the eyes of Andrea as she looked down at me, her eyes filled with concern, right cheek hidden beneath a bruise. I turned my head, stunned to see Amber and Ian looking at me with pale faces and grim smiles.

"Are you OK Morgan?" the young woman with the black make-up streaks on her face asked me, scuttling closer and with a groan I forced myself to sit up, my eyes drifting from her concerned features to study the wooden cage that surrounded us. Beyond the rough timber struts of the cage that held us the crowd had gone ominously quiet, their eyes fixed upon our plight and heaving a sigh, I raised a hand to the pain that was growing in my face from where I had been punched. Then I looked back at Amber and shrugged. "OK is a strong term...I'm alive...that'll have to suffice."

"I doubt we'll be alive long," Andrea muttered, and I grimaced, knowing that she was right.

I wasn't ready to just roll over and die so easy. Groaning I made it to my knees and sent her what I hoped was a confident smile. "We aren't dead yet."

"Yet," she repeated, that single word making my stomach knot and not wanting her to see the fear that suddenly assailed me, I turned away. "Are you either of you hurt?" I asked the others. They shook their heads, exchanging grim looks and then the thin effeminate man winced, his voice filled with dread as he spoke. "Not us...but they killed Craig."

"Oh my God," Andrea sobbed, and I grimaced, turning my face from Ian to glare through the bars at our captors, anger coursing through me. Then I looked back at him. "How did it happen?" As I watched him the young man let out a sigh and raised a trembling hand to his face, "We got here early yesterday afternoon and got pretty much attacked straight away by a trio of these bastards...luckily we managed to get away from them and find a place to hide. Then later just before nightfall me and Craig left Amber in the place that we had been hiding in and went on a quick scout round to see if we could find any help."

He swallowed hard as he finished talking, eyes lowering to look down at his lap and I stayed silent, waiting for him to find the strength to continue. When he did so his voice was tight and emotional, almost childlike. "We spent ages looking about but when it was clear we weren't going to get any help we began to head back to Amber...that is when they ambushed us. One moment, we were walking down a quiet street and the next they were all about us and Craig was going crazy like an animal. He managed to take three of them down with his bare hands before he went down on the ground bleeding badly and the others kept stabbing at him with wooden spears. I ran then, I was so scared. I had only just got back to Amber when more of them appeared and captured us both. It's my fault!"

"Hey, it wasn't your fault," Amber turned then, rubbing at his shoulder nearest her. "You can't blame yourself!"

"She's right," I nodded, meeting Ian's gaze.

"At least Craig managed to go out fighting though right?" Andrea stated, smiling sadly.

Ian nodded. "True. I am amazed at how easily he took those men out though. He was like a fucking maniac!"

I grimaced at his words, thinking that perhaps it was for the best that Craig hadn't made it after all and by the sudden wince on Andrea's bruised face I realised that Ian's remark had made her think the same thing. Craig had been the killer. He was gone now; thank God for small mercies. Sighing, I sat back against the bars of the cage behind me, closing my eyes as I did so, my thoughts drifting to the bizarre dream that had plagued me while I had been unconscious, a strange irritation rising in me as I recalled the smug smile upon the face of the man named Cheshire. I frowned then, shaking my head slightly and opening my eyes I stared up at the grey sky through the bars above me, a shudder running down my spine and through my body as a strange thought entered my head.

Maybe it hadn't been a dream.

Maybe it had been a memory.

After all everyone else seemed to be getting theirs back so why shouldn't I also be beginning to recall my past? As that thought occurred to me, I realised with a strange sense of certainty that what I had envisaged while I had been unconscious was exactly what I believed it was. A memory not a dream.

Grim faced, I sat there, desperately trying to recall as much of it as I could, nodding grimly as I remembered that I had read that strange line in Latin from the piece of paper he'd given me. Hadn't the journal of Oliver Queenheart said that he and his Order had first entered this realm after each reading aloud a sentence which they had found on a manuscript taken from one Dr Mouse's patients at the insane asylum.

Was that what I had read aloud?

Was that how they managed to get those that they hunted brought to New London?

Shaking my head in disbelief, certain that I was right, I sat there grimacing. So, Oliver Queenheart had managed to persuade my father's personal assistant to betray us and give me the sentence required to bring me here.

But why did he want me?

What had I done to deserve this?

I gasped as memories of a life of wealth and social events, of eating good food and drinking fine wine suddenly assailed me, making my head spin and then I was blushing as the face of an attractive woman came to me, naked and dark haired as she lay back in what I knew to be my bed, an arm beckoning me to join her.

Instinctively, I knew that I was not one of the two journalists. No, I was the person that had been omitted from the journal. The person that Oliver Queenheart had seen fit to bring to the hunt but not bother to mention in his writing. Shaking my head, that simple exclusion angering me immensely, I grimaced and tried to dig deeper into my slowly returning memories, trying to come up with a reason why I had been brought here to such a fate only to curse under my breath several minutes later as nothing occurred to me that made any sense at all.

But then I still didn't know everything.

All I could recall was that I had been raised to money and that my father was in trouble.

"Fuck me," I exclaimed aloud, drawing confused looks from my companions. "I know why I am here. This is all to get back at my father!"

"Good for you," Ian muttered. "It'll have to wait."

"What are you talking about?" I shook my head, confused by his tone and he turned and pointed at the large man with the spike for a hand that was now standing between our cage and the crowd, his face set with a grim smile, and excitement in his one good eye. As Andrea and

Amber gave terrified groans, Ian turned back to me and winced, his face pale. "Who is that?" I grimaced then and gave him a nod, shrugging and answering as if it was the most normal thing in the world. "That's Bert."

Chapter Thirty-Eight

"Well, look what we 'ave ere!" the one eyed, one handed, cannibal leader gave a throaty chuckle as he moved over to stand before our cage, his scarred face tilting to one side as he grinned at us, the patch over his right eye and his Victorian clothing making him look like a cross between a pirate and Bill Sykes. "Four fat juicy rabbits, all ready to go into the pot."

At the words of the huge man my three companions all hurried to the back of the cage where I was still sat, all trying to put as much distance between them and him. He laughed then, rising to his full height and lifted his arms skyward as he turned and shouted to the crowd that were watching us in silence. "I think I scared 'em!"

The dirty mob erupted into a chorus of laughs at his words, jeering and shouting at us and I grimaced, shaking my head as I stared back at them in hatred, a snarl on my face as I shouted back. "Fuck you!"

From the front of the cage there was an exclamation of surprise and then the pig ugly face of Bert was peering in as he squatted before it, his one hand gripping to a bar as he met my gaze and raised an eyebrow. "Well, well...it looks like this little rabbit finks it's a dog!"

"Fuck you!" I repeated, my voice grim as I stared at him. "Fuck you and your gang of inbreeds!"

Instead of responding with anger as I had expected, he gave another chuckle. "Fink ya tough rabbit?"

I stayed silent for a moment, not trusting myself to give an answer which wasn't going to get my face smashed in. As much as the prospect of a quick death at the hands of the leader of the cannibals was preferable to being put into the huge cooking pot, no doubt still alive, I simply wasn't ready to give up and die just yet.

Not now I was getting my memories back.

So, I fixed Bert with a grim smile and nodded. "I was more than tough enough to take care of Bill and Charlie."

An expression that I couldn't place passed over his features and I frowned, had it been remorse? Did the cannibal have feelings?

How cute.

For a moment he stayed crouched where he was and then with yet another chuckle he was rising and stepping back from the door of the cage, calling out to his followers. "This rabbit don't fink it's a dog...it finks it's a wolf!"

Once again, they roared and jeered, shouting and hurling abuse at me and my companions. Then Bert was pointing at two dirty clothed men that were stood several feet from the cage wielding wooden spears. "I want that one out 'ere now!"

"Oh shit," I muttered, throwing Andrea a grim look and the colour seemed to drain from her face as she stared back at me, realising the danger I had placed myself in. Then the two men were before the front of the cage, unfastening the cords and ropes that held it shut and lifting the front hatch high, one of them shouting at me angrily. "You rabbit...get out 'ere now!"

For a second, I considered refusing but after my bravado that would only have looked incredibly stupid and weak. If we were going to stand any chance of getting out of this shithole of a town alive then I was going to have to try and show them that I meant business. Gritting my teeth, I moved forwards until I was free of the cage and out in the open, straightening as soon as I was able. At once the two men were lowering the hatch, one of them securing the ropes and cords back into place while the one that had shouted at me to leave the cage turned his spear on me, ensuring that I didn't try anything stupid.

He needn't have worried.

I was far, far too busy staring up at the huge figure that was stood several feet from where I was standing, my eyes wide as I realised for the first time just how big Bert the cannibal was. Charlie had grudgingly told me that the leader of this fucked up town was over six feet tall. Personally, I would have put him at nearer seven feet tall if not more. As I watched him, he stood there grinning back at me and I took the opportunity to study him properly, trying my best to come up with a way, any way to beat him. I have already said how tall he was, but it was more than that. Not only was he the tallest man that I had ever seen but he was broad of shoulder too, a huge gut swelling out beneath his barrel chest making the old dirty clothing that he wore look several sizes too small for his body. As I watched he reached down with his one hand, large fingers scratching at his chest and then his right leg, crushing what was probably dozens of lice as he did so and I cringed and shook my head, my eyes drifting back to his ugly face and his bald head, the scars that covered both a testament to the hardships that he had faced in his violent life.

He looked every inch a killer.

And now I was going to have to fight him.

With a grim chuckle the huge cannibal took a step towards me, raising his fist and his rusty spike before him as he grinned at me. "Ready ta fight me rabbit?"

"On one condition!" I stated, grim faced and before me, Bert frowned and straightened.

"You don't make da rules rabbit," he jabbed a finger at his chest. "I makes da rules not you!"

"If I beat you in this fight then me and my friends go free!" I told him, ignoring his outburst. "If you kill me then you get to do what you like with them."

There was a chorus of alarmed cries from those that I had left behind me in the wooden cage and then Bert was taking another step forward, face furious. "I told ya rabbit...ya don't get to make the rules!"

Despite the urge to turn and run I kept my face as calm as I could in the face of his wrath, and I raised an eyebrow. "Is that because you don't think you can win?"

For a moment, I thought that I had gone too far and that he was going to simply throw himself forwards and beat me to death with that single fist of his but then he was pausing, casting a grim look at the crowd gathered about us and I realised the power that I had suddenly gained. In this community strength was everything. By refusing my challenge or my conditions he was showing weakness in front of those that followed him. Tossing the cannibal, a confident smile, I shrugged. "So...do we have a deal?" Before me, Bert stayed stock still, his one remaining eye locked to my face, his face twisted into a mask of hatred. Then he was chuckling and nodding. "Deal."

I nodded, a smile forming on my features as I realised that I had won a small victory over him. Now all I had to do was stop him from beating me to death. The thought had barely entered my mind when with a roar of pure hatred, Bert rushed me, the spike on his left wrist slashing for my face. With a curse, I ducked out of instinct, the metal jabbing at where my head had been but then I was lifted from my feet as his right fist swung in, catching me hard under the chin. I hit the muddy ground hard, the breath leaving my body in a rush, but I forced myself to rise, making it to my hands and knees before he was rushing in and stamping on my back. With a cry of agony, I dropped back to the ground, pain seeming to surge through every nerve ending in my body and in what felt like slow motion, I rolled over, my eyes staring back up at his one good eye in disbelief as he moved to stand over me. "Time ta die rabbit!"

More than anything I wanted to hurl some witty insult back at him, but my head was spinning, my jaw and back aching and it was all I could do to breathe let alone think of a comedy routine. And so, I lay there in the muck and the dirt like a worm, listening to the horrified cries that were beginning to rise from my companions back in the cage and the excited cheers of the crowd of dirty cannibals that were gathered about us. Bert pointed his spike at my face, a broad grin upon his grim features and then with a speed that belied his size he brought his arm back, ready to drive it through my skull only to pause as above us the sky darkened. All about us the cheers of his followers began to turn to cries of alarm, the cacophony filling the air and as Bert shook his head and took several steps back, I cast a grim look up at the ominous dark clouds which had cast shadows across the town square. A sudden scream of terror made me snap my head to the right as I rose to a sitting position, my eyes widening in dread as I saw the familiar oily black shapes slipping from between the cracks of the surrounding buildings, surging amongst the panicked cannibals and I felt my soul shrivel as I realised what was happening. The shadow creatures had come to play.

Chapter Thirty-Nine

Like a perverse voyeur, I sat on the muddy ground and watched as chaos took over the town square. All about me the dirty clothed cannibals were running in terror, eyes wide as they pushed and pulled at each other in a bid to escape the nightmarish creatures which had appeared in their midst courtesy of the overcast sky. Forcing myself to my feet, I turned my head and stared back at Bert as he stood several feet from where I was, his one good eye fixed on the madness about him. As if sensing my eyes upon him the huge cannibal turned, snarling as he saw me there. Then he was turning and running, his long legs carrying his huge frame across the area of the town square towards the buildings that lay in that direction. I watched in disbelief as he didn't slow his run, smashing bodily through a crude door, crashing through into what lay beyond. Shaking my head, I began to back away as a couple of black shapes drifted across the ground and slipped in after him. "Morgan!"

I spun about as the scream of Andrea snatched my attention, my heart leaping in my chest as I realised that I was standing amid the rushing crowd, in danger of being attacked by both the cannibals and the creatures. I flinched then as amid the heaving bodies I saw one of the nightmarish beasts rushing me, flowing across the ground as if it were coasting atop water, tendril's reaching for my body. With a curse I threw myself sideways, my body screaming as the injuries that Bert had caused me railed against the exertion and gritting my teeth I rolled to a crouch, cursing as I saw that the shadow creature had turned direction and was still rushing towards me. In that instant as I stared into the rushing blackness of the monster, I realised there was nothing I could do. How do you fight a shadow?

But then with a cry of alarm one of the cannibals tripped and stumbled between us and like a dog chasing a ball the creature forgot all about me and leaped on his fallen form, the black essence of its body pouring over the unfortunate man like tar, stealing him from view. Feeling sick with dread, I forced myself to rise, backing away from the sight before me as the black mound seemed to shake and writhe, slurping noises emanating from within. Then I was cursing and grimacing as a hand suddenly thrust through the blackness of the creature's body, fingers searching, desperately trying to grasp onto something solid like a drowning man seeking aid. Then the hand was sliding back beneath the surface once again and I shook my head, still backing away from it. I screamed aloud in shock as hands suddenly gripped at me from behind, fingers pulling at the rabbit costume I wore and cursing, I beat at them until suddenly they released me and with a cry, I fell forwards. "Morgan!" the terrified cry of Amber suddenly seemed to reach me through my panic. "Morgan it's us...help!"

In shock, I pushed myself back to my knees and rose, turning to find that I had bumped into the cage and that the hands had been those of my terrified trio of companions still trapped with it. "Hold on!" I yelled, ignoring my aches and pains as I dropped to a crouch beside it, my fingers scrabbling first at the cord that had secured the hatch shut. "Stay calm, I'll get you out!"

"Hurry!" Andrea sobbed, her face appearing between Ian and Amber at the front of the cage, her eyes on my fingers. "Please Morgan hurry before they come for us!"

"I'm trying God damn it!" I snapped, giving a nod of satisfaction seconds later as the cord came loose for me and I turned my attention to the rope that was tied beside it, trying my best to ignore everything that was happening around me, desperately trying to block out the terrified screams of the cannibals and the insistent requests of my friends that I release them all. Then the knot in the rope came undone and I grim-faced I rose to my feet, lifting the front of the hatch with my hands as Andrea, Ian and Amber hurried out to join me. There was a moment of hugs and thanks and then we were all spinning about as Amber screamed and pointed behind us. "Oh my God...look...look!" Several metres from where we were stood in a small huddle the creature which had thrown itself upon the fallen cannibal was slowly slivering from him and I felt my stomach turn over as I saw the skeleton that it had left behind, what looked like jam clinging to the bones.

It had devoured him completely: his clothes, his skin, his muscles and his internal organs.

All eaten and gone in a matter of minutes.

And now it was headed our way.

Even with the fact that the creatures had no facial features as such I knew without question that it was watching us, readying itself to attack. "Get ready," I told my companions. "We each go different ways and meet outside of the town!"

"Morgan…" the terrified voice of Andrea began, and I shook my head as I met her gaze.

"No questions…just run…it can't follow us all!"

"It won't need too!"

I turned at the grim statement from Ian, my heart sinking as I saw that we were the only humans still standing in the town square, though several others were down upon the ground desperately trying to fend of the attacks of the shadow creatures but to no avail. As I watched, those that had finished sucking the meat from the bones of their unfortunate victims turned towards us, sliding effortlessly and silently over the ground in our direction.

"Quick, get up on the cage!" Andrea cried out, rushing to its side and trying to haul herself up the bars. "Come on!"

But it was too late. Far too late.

Before we had even moved a couple of steps, they were surrounding us like a black tsunami of oil and shadow preparing to sweep us away and grimacing I shook my head, my eyes darting about for a way, any way out of this disaster. Then it came to me.

With a cry of denial, I rushed forwards, dodging to the left as an oily black tendril snaked out from one of the creatures, throwing myself into a forward roll as another tried for me. I came to my feet cat-like before the destination I had been trying to reach, my right hand snaking out to grasp one of the burning branches from the fire beneath the large pot. With a roar of defiance, I spun back around, waving the flaming brand before me like a sword, hoping against hope that they were as scared of fire as they were light. I flinched as a high-pitched whine suddenly sounded, barely audible but enough to make me wince in pain and as I watched the creatures nearest to me reared up and back, trying their best to avoid the fire in my hand. Realising that the high-pitched whine was the creatures screaming in fear at the sight of the fire, I grinned like a maniac and threw the burning branch at the closest of them. The whine increased in intensity as before me the creature seemed to flatten and spread out like rolled dough, a split appearing down its centre as it tried to split in two halves like those that we had seen back at the hospital. Then the burning branch landed in the centre of its black body and with a soft 'whuff' the shadow creature burst into flames as easily as if it had been soaked in petrol. For a fraction of a second I stood there, my eyes locked to the creature as it rolled and twisted, streams of black liquid running from its body to splatter to the ground like paint, its scream of agony almost enough to make me gasp in pain. With shock I realised that the rest of the creatures had all turned towards me, that act allowing my three companions to all clamber up onto the dubious safety of the cage roof. With a rush of movement, the rest of the shadow creatures all moved towards me and I cursed and stepped back, snatching up another burning branch and throwing it at the group, only to flinch as a black tendril snaked out and knocked the burning branch back down in my direction. I cursed as it hit me on the shoulder and bounced down to the muddy ground, resting against the base of the scaffolding holding the huge pot. In that moment of distraction another of the creatures rushed at me and I raised my hands before me defensively, a futile action but one which was more instinct than anything else. Fear gripped me in a stranglehold then as the creature reared up huge before me, body spread out flat and wide like some huge Manta Ray and as I glimpsed the tooth filled maw on its underside, I felt the need to urinate in sudden raw terror. Then the creature that was already alight surged to the side in its death throes, colliding heavily with the one that was threatening to attack me and as one they rolled away, screaming and burning as the flames spread between them. But as lucky as that had been for me, I realised then that I was in deep shit, for with the burning shadow creature having rolled right out of the way the rest were rushing towards me, deadly shadows hungry for flesh. I flinched then as from behind me there came a deep, ominous creaking and with my heart in my mouth I turned my head to stare in shock at the sight of the huge wooden scaffold as it tipped towards me, the leg which the burning branch had fallen against having burned right through. Cursing, I sidestepped as a splash of the water that had been boiling for God knows how long within the pot spilled as the huge metal crucible tipped towards me, off balance and then I was throwing myself sideways, my acrobatics rivalling the best of goalkeepers. With a clang and a hiss, the pot fell from the scaffolding to the ground, emptying its boiling load all over the oncoming shadow creatures and scrambling to my knees I watched with grim fascination as they began to roll and twist, screaming in the same manner as their burning brethren, appearing for all the world like huge black slugs that had been doused with salt. Time seemed to slow as I sat there with my hands on my knees in the mud, breathing hard as I stared first at the shadow creatures which had been boiled alive, watching as one-by-one they ceased their struggles and lay still. Then I was turning to stare in disgust at the blistered and deformed forms of the two shadow creatures which had caught fire, their remains now looking like a pile of melted plastic, the flames having extinguished themselves but smoke still rising from their bodies. With a groan, I forced myself to rise, shaking my head as I studied the devastation in the town square, the area being littered not only with the bodies of the shadow creatures but also by at least fifteen skeletons, each sucked dry of flesh by the monsters themselves. I turned as from atop the wooden cage, Andrea called out to me, her voice thick with emotion. "Morgan...can we go now?" With a grim laugh that I couldn't hold back, I nodded, and smiled. "Yeah, why not, I think we've caused enough trouble here don't you?"

Chapter Forty

"Hey I'm sorry Morgan"

I slowed my walk at the sound of Ian's voice and turned to look back at him as he strode along beside Amber, a frown creasing my face as I regarded the young man in confusion. "What for? What have you done wrong?"

He winced, casting his eyes down to the ground before him and shrugged. "For not helping you in the fight."

Laughing softly, I turned away. "Don't worry about it."

"But it wasn't cool." he continued, obviously disturbed by the fact that he and the two women had stayed upon the roof of the cage and not joined me in fighting off the shadow creatures. "I should have done more to aid you."

"Now I feel shit too," Amber grumbled from where she was walking at my back. "Sorry."

Again, I shrugged, shaking my head. "It doesn't matter. All that matters is that we make it out of this town."

"Where are we going when we do?" Andrea asked and frowning I turned towards her, not having given it much thought. Our original idea of heading to the Cathedral upon the hill in the far south was now out of the question seeing as the journal claimed that the insane Priest Archibald Hare was still in residence.

So where did that leave for us to head to?

It made no sense at all for us to head back to the Asylum and both the hospital and this town were both far too dangerous for us to consider as places of refuge. That left only the large garden and the huge white tower that rose into the clouds as possible destinations for us.

But how safe where they?

When Karl had left us yesterday, he had said he was heading east to the tower and Tori had followed him when the Dumbdee twins had arrived. Had they made it to the tower safely or had the overweight huntsmen caught them.

Or had Karl and Tori turned on each other?

I grimaced as I recalled how the pair had been at each other's throats verbally at the hospital. Surely, they had not continued their arguments once they realised that the twins were following them. Surely, they had bonded to face the threat.

For some reason I wasn't confident.

I had seen the strange look in the eyes of Karl. He was here for his own ends, intent on usurping Oliver Queenheart and his followers from New London and taking control of the mysterious land for himself.

Could he be trusted at all?

Could any of them?

"Hey, where are the others?"

I stopped walking at the question from Amber, frowning as I realised that in the excitement and stress of our reunion and our imprisonment and subsequent escape, we had not had time to explain what had befallen us since we had last seen them and Craig. Sighing, I shrugged, explaining how me, Karl and Andrea had changed our minds and headed towards the hospital while Tori had carried onto the Cathedral, then continued with how the irritating woman had re-joined us and together we had found the journal. I had fallen silent as Andrea took over from me, telling them about the journal that we had discovered in the drawer and what had been written inside its pages, me adding details she had forgotten like the fact that Karl was the occultist mentioned.

"Who am I?" Ian shook his head, "A journalist?"

I nodded. "It looks that way, both you and Tori. Andrea is the doctor, Karl is the occultist, Amber is the last surviving descendant of the author

Lewis Carroll or Charles Dodgson, I am the person not mentioned in the journal and Craig was the serial killer."

Ian sighed. "So, I am one of the journalists and Tori is my friend? This day is getting worse."

As Amber and Andrea chuckled at his dramatics, I picked up the story again, telling them about the shadow creatures that we had seen in the hospital and how me and Andrea had decided to head to the town to save them upon realising that was where the cannibals that the journal had mentioned lived. Ian had raised an eyebrow again at my words, his effeminate features split with a grimace as he picked up on the unspoken sentiment of my words. "Hold on...Karl and the bitch were happy to leave us to die, right?"

"Just Karl." I corrected him. "Tori only decided to run off and leave us when the twins turned up on the scene."

"The twins?" Amber paled, head shaking as she stared at me. "I don't understand...what twins?"

"The Dumbdee twins," Andrea explained, her attractive face grim. "The pair of fat maniacs that your descendant rewrote as Tweedledum and Tweedledee."

"You saw them?" her voice was barely more than a whisper. "What were they like?"

"Insane," I stated grimly. "Totally insane."

"Did they follow you here?" Ian suddenly cast a quick glance about at the buildings around us.

"No, they went after Karl and Tori," Andrea explained and beside Amber, Ian gave a laugh. "Good...I hope they catch them. It'd serve them right for leaving us behind, right?"

I shook my head then, frowning. "But Tori is a friend of yours in the real world...aren't you worried at all?"

"No," he answered, meeting my gaze. "I can't remember her at all. As far as I am concerned, she is a stranger"

For a moment I paused, shaking my head as I faced him, finding the fact that he had got no memories back very strange indeed and beside me, Andrea frowned at the effeminate young man. "You still can't recall anything?"

"No," a look of infinite sadness crossed over his features then. "I have no idea who I am except for the fact that I must be a huge coward. I keep staying out of the fights."

"Don't beat yourself up over that," I told him, pushing my momentary doubts regarding him aside. "If running works then keep doing it. There's no point dying a hero."

"Better that than living as a coward surely?" he asked, and I shook my head, feeling bone tired. "No, just stay alive," I stated. "Deal with everything once we are out of this damn world"

There was a moments silence as the others let my words sink in and then Amber was regarding me strangely. "Hey, didn't you say back in the cage that you knew why you were here Morgan...you mentioned your dad!"

My eyes widened as once again, I recalled what I had seen while I was unconscious, and I nodded at her. "Yeah, a memory came back to me of my former life. I was in a large house; my home and I was late for a meeting with my father although Cheshire pointed out that he was still in a meeting anyway."

"Cheshire?" Andrea frowned. "Who is Cheshire?"

"My father's personal assistant," I grimaced, a wave of anger surging through me as I remembered how I had been betrayed by the man. "It is because of that constantly smiling piece of shit that I am stuck here!"

"I don't understand," Ian shook his head. "It is the fault of Oliver Queenheart that we are here isn't it?"

"Maybe but Cheshire gave me the piece of paper with a Latin sentence written upon it...and when I read it, I got dizzy and passed out. The next thing I knew I was here in the cell with no memory and dressed in this damn outfit."

There was a soft grunt noise from Andrea then and as I turned to look at her, I found her staring down at the muddy ground, nodding slowly. Then she was looking up at me, her eyes narrowed. "I remember now...I was at home too...the postman had just been, and I was sitting down upon my sofa opening my mail. There was a letter from the Hospital Trust saying that I was being sued by them for a breach of trust...that the police were being called in over the fact that I had been heavily medicated when I operated upon the patient that died...the woman named Mrs Queenheart. I remember dropping the letter to the carpet, crying...my life was over...I would be struck off at best, jailed at worst. Then...then I opened the second envelope and took out a small card within...it had a sentence upon it...I remember starting to read it..."

"And then nothing," I finished for her.

"Shit...you killed a patient because you were high?" Ian was shaking his head, surprise upon his face. "Really?"

"It was an accident," Andrea snapped, her face colouring with embarrassment and anger. "You have no idea of the number of hours that we had to work with no rest...I needed something to keep me awake...I never meant..."

"Hey come on!" I raised my voice, moving to put an arm about her shoulders, throwing Ian an irritated look. "We are not going to start arguing and falling out OK?"

The effeminate man raised his open hands, shaking his head as he winced back at me. "Hey sorry OK, I was out of line with that statement. I'm sorry Andrea, really."

She nodded at his words, inserting a finger behind her glasses to wipe away a stray couple of tears and then I turned to look at Amber as I realised how quiet she had gone. "Are you OK?"

"Yes," she nodded, following it up with a heavy sigh and a shrug. "I mean I think I am. I can remember reading a sentence like that too. As far as I can recall I was in a second-hand book shop in Oxford...my book shop. I can remember a man coming in, a man with silver hair and broad shoulders. He spent ages looking about and then he turned and gave me a strange little smile. Then he left. Not sure what he had been up to I went to the window and looked out, but he had gone, and I turned back around. That was when I saw the envelope sticking out of a bookcase with my name written upon it."

"And inside was a piece of paper with the sentence on?"

She nodded at my question, fear in her eyes and sighing I extended my other arm, allowing her to move under it and accept a hug of support. For several moments I stood there loosely embracing the two women, rubbing their outside arms and then I was looking back up to find Ian watching the three of us. "You OK?"

He nodded, a smile creeping to his face, "Yeah, just a little left out I guess."

Laughing softly, I released the woman and nodded at him. "Feel better now?"

Ian gave a chuckle and for a few precious moments the four of us stood smiling at each other, relaxing slightly. I felt rather than saw the danger approaching me from behind and as the eyes of Ian and Amber facing me went wide in terror, I pushed Andrea out of harm's way to the muddy ground and spun to face the threat. The punch struck me hard in the side of the head as my vision blurred, I was thrown to the side, my face feeling like a bomb had gone off against my right cheek. Then I was staring up at the furious figure of Bert the cannibal as he loomed over me, my voice shaky as I called out to my companions. "Ian...get Andrea and Amber to the tower...I can deal with this!"

"But..." his terrified voice began. "I can help!" Several feet before me, the huge cannibal began to turn towards the trio, a snarl emanating from his throat and feeling sick with dread I shouted back at the effeminate man. "Stop fucking arguing and go now...take them!"

For a moment there was silence but then I sighed as I heard the slapping, sloppy sounds of feet running away through the mud off the street and gritting my teeth I forced myself to rise and stand before the huge angry cannibal. "You an me got us some business!" he growled, spike raised before his body and I nodded back at him, my aching face set with a grim smile.

"Yeah, we do...but first you have to catch me"
Then I was turning and running in the other direction, the furious howl of the monstrous ruffian breaking the deathly silence in the street as he gave chase.

Chapter Forty-One

Not bothering to look back at the lumbering maniac that was hot on my heels, knowing without doubt that he wasn't going to stop chasing me until I was dead, I reached the end of the muddy street and turned left. Ducking in through the open doorway of the first building, I turned and crawled straight out of the hole in its back wall. Pausing only long enough to take in my surroundings, cursing as I found myself in yet another of the wooden building lined streets of mud, I charged away to the east. I had gone less than fifty feet before there came the furious snarls of my pursuer and glancing back, I flinched as I saw one of his feet kick through the hole that I had crawled through, trying to make it large enough for him to do the same. Twisting about I searched for a hiding place, realising that within seconds he would be out in the open and able to see me. Hope surged through me then as my eyes settled upon a block nailed into one of the walls of the low wooden buildings, much like the crude ladder that me and Andrea had climbed to reach the second floor of the house that we had been ambushed in. Without even pausing to give my actions anymore thought I surged towards the block, jumping to catch the edge of the low roof and pushing with my right leg as my boot touched the nailed in chunk of wood. Then I was up and onto the flat roof of the building, my eyes widening as the town was laid out before my view. Frowning, I turned and looked about, nodding as I saw the two-level buildings back where the town square sat, some distance off to the north and then I was twisting about to look in the direction of the south east, my eyes fixing to the towering white monolith, its size immense even at this distance. Chewing my bottom lip for a moment I frowned as I studied the distance between me and the edge of the town nearest the tower, my heart sinking as I saw that there were many, many more of the crude wooden buildings and narrow dirty streets between it and me. I cursed and dropped flat in shock as the deep voice of Bert roared out from down in the street. "Where are ya little rabbit!"

I struck the wooden roof of the building hard, cursing as it gave way beneath the weight of my body and then I was crashing through to the room beneath, my back screaming in agony as I struck the ground hard. Beyond the rear wall of the building in which I had fallen the roar of the cannibal grew louder. "I hear ya rabbit!" Cursing beneath my breath, trying to focus past the pain, I forced myself to stand and rushed back out into the street beyond through the open doorway. Then head down, arms pumping by my side I simply ran, desperate to put as much distance between myself and my pursuer as I could, all the while hating the fact that I was heading away from the direction the tower lay in. Time seemed to pass by in a daze as I charged around the labyrinthine streets of the ramshackle town, changing direction every time I caught sight of one of the other cannibals or heard the angry shouts of Bert drawing close once again. Luckily, each time I had one of these encounters the cannibals turned tail and rushed back in the other direction. Perhaps they had seen me take out the shadow creatures back in the town square, perhaps they were just cowards by nature. I didn't know and to be honest I didn't care. If they didn't try to capture me once again, I was happy.

So, on I ran, beginning to feel that my luck was starting to change for the better as each time I looked up into the sky to the south east, the portion of the tower that I could see above the roofs seemed slightly bigger than before.

Then it all went wrong.

I had just turned into a wide street that I hoped was going to bring me even closer to the side of town that I was trying to reach when I cursed and slid to a halt in the mud. Ahead of me Bert the cannibal was stood in the centre of the street, the rusty metal spike on his left wrist raised to the sky as he roared in anger. "Rabbit!" Eyes wide I stood and stared at the back of his head, hoping against hope that he didn't turn around and see me. Then I rushed to the left and ducked through a hole in the wall of a building which looked more damaged than many of the others. Dropping to a crouch in the shadows of the far wall, I held my breath, hoping against hope that should my pursuer come looking he wouldn't see me hiding in the darkness with my costume as caked with blood and mud as it was. For what felt like an eternity I stayed where I was, not daring to move, my breathing shallow as I tried to make as little noise as possible. Then with a heavy sigh I relaxed as I heard the roar of Bert sound once again, much further away than it had been before. I rose on shaky legs then, my head slowly beginning to ache with the stress of the chase and cursing I clasped a hand to the side of my face, wincing as I touched the cheek that Bert had punched. Grimacing, I shook my head, probing the aching area with a finger before finally deciding that he hadn't fractured my cheekbone after all. Shaking my head, I began to walk into the next section of the roughly made building, my thoughts on the man responsible for damaging my face. "Fucking hillbilly cannibal mother fucker!"

"Stop fucking swearing"

I screamed as the voice spoke, my heart nearly leaping out of my mouth and in pure and utter panic I turned, stumbling as my feet caught on the uneven floor and then I was sitting with my back to one of the walls staring in disbelief at the bloody figure before me. For nearly a minute I stayed silent, my face twisting into a grimace as I saw the copious amounts of blood staining the front of the rabbit suit that they were wearing and then I was clearing my throat, shaking my head as I spoke. "I don't understand...Ian said you were dead!"

Craig laughed then, the sound turning into a coughing fit as blood bubbled between his lips.

For a moment he seemed to choke but then he wiped a sleeve of his costume across his mouth, clearing the scarlet fluid away and he grinned at me with bloody teeth. "That doesn't surprise me...he was the one that did this."

Chapter Forty-Two

For a moment I stayed sat where I was, legs out before me, eyes fixed to the bloody mess on the front of his costume. Then I was shaking my head and forcing myself to my knees, frowning as I forced my eyes to leave his wounds and meet his gaze. "What are you talking about?" He gave another chuckle at my words, bringing on another bout of coughing, flecks of blood hitting the floor. "What do...what do you think I mean Morgan?"

I cursed and glancing back down at his stomach, I noticed the bloody handle of the screwdriver that Craig had taken from the table back at the asylum protruding from the front of the suit. "He stabbed you?" my voice sounded weak childlike and on the other side of the gloomy room, Craig nodded, his features twisted in pain. "Several times."

I shook my head again, his words shocking me. What was going on? This made no sense at all. Ian had said that Craig had been stabbed to death with spears by several of the cannibals. Yet here was Craig, alive and although not well, he was telling me a completely different story.

Taking a deep breath, trying to steady the shake which had begun in my hands I shuffled forwards across the floor until I was crouched just beyond the man's feet, still not being willing nor ready to take any chances with the man. Perhaps Ian had been telling the truth. Perhaps when the effeminate young man had fled the fight, Craig was not quite dead and had managed to fight off his attackers before crawling in here to die. Frowning I looked at his face for a moment, holding his gaze as his eyes stared back out at me over the top of his glasses, the lens of one spider-webbed with cracks. He gave a chuckle then, shaking his head as I stared at him. "What's the matter Morgan...you don't believe me?"

"Why should I?" I asked, shrugging slightly. "Ian told me that you and he were attacked by a group of the cannibals...he told me that you went crazy and killed several before they knocked you down and stabbed you to death."

"Well, that's obviously not true," he glared back at me, anger in the eye that I could see. "I am still alive."

My gaze dropped to the bloody mess of his stomach and I winced. He might well be but that would soon change without medical aid.

And to be honest I wasn't sure that he deserved any such help. Heaving another sigh, I looked back up at him. "So…tell me your side of the story…tell me what happened."

Once again anger flared in the eyes of the man with the ginger beard and broken glasses but then he groaned and rested his head back upon the wooden wall behind him, one hand gesturing weakly at me. "What's the point. You aren't going to believe me…just go and leave me here to die in fucking peace."

"You're not going to die," I told him, hating the lie for some reason but he laughed at my words. "Don't talk soft Morgan…I have covered war zones…I know what a mortal injury looks like. I am surprised I have survived the fucking night"

One of my eyebrows arched then and I fixed him with a confused stare. "War zones…what do you mean you have covered them?"

"Me and Tori," he groaned, giving a nod. "We are freelance journalists…we have been to Iraq, Somalia, Afghanistan…you name it…we have been there, in the thick of the fighting, taking photos, getting the story."

"You remember Tori?" I stared at him in horror, the realisation of just what he was saying clicking into place in my mind. "You got your memory back...you and she are the journalists?"

"Yeah, I can remember," he chuckled bitterly. "I go and survive being shot at by all manner of soldiers and then die after getting stabbed by some weedy little woman hating serial killer...just my luck."

My stomach knotted at his words, "How do you know there is a serial killer?"

He seemed as surprised as me, his eyes widening. "You knew there was one too? How? What's going on?"

I paused then, realising just how much there was he didn't know but doubting he had the time to hear it all. Sighing I tried to condense it down as best as I could. "We found a journal belonging to Oliver Queenheart and inside it stated how he was bringing various people here to be hunted to their deaths."

"Fuck me," he grimaced, forcing a smile. "Like Predators...that was a shit movie."

I nodded, smiling sadly as I watched him fall into a fit of coughing, waiting for him to regain his composure before I continued. "The bottom line is that we aren't in the world we knew anymore. We are in a different dimension and nothing is what it seems. The journal said that he had brought us all here for various reasons. Karl is an occultist, and he is trying to take over Oliver Queenheart's land. Amber is the descendant of Lewis Carroll like she said, Andrea is a surgeon or doctor that killed Queenheart's wife by mistake and I thought that Tori and Ian were the pair of journalists that were trying to delve into Queenheart's personal business...and I thought you were the serial killer that he had accepted the contract on...I guess I was wrong."

"How do you know I am not lying?" his voice made me cringe then and I found him smiling at me with bloody teeth. "How do you know I am not the serial killer?"

I stayed silent for a moment, eyes fixed to his and then I sighed and shrugged. "Because you knew about the journalists and the serial killer before I told you..."

"Maybe Ian told me," he shrugged, wincing as the movement sent a jolt of pain rushing through him. "Be careful Morgan...don't trust anyone...I could be lying now."

"But you are not," I stated, suddenly becoming one hundred per cent sure that he was the journalist. "If Ian had been forced to fight you off to save himself then he would have told us the truth, not make up some story about you being attacked by the cannibals. Besides, the cannibals that tried to capture me and Andrea this morning said that they only knew of the two rabbits that they caught last night...they didn't say anything about a third...they had no knowledge of you nor any fight."

"How do you know for sure?" he asked me, his voice weaker than before and glancing down at the front of his costume I saw fresh dark blood soaking through it. Then I was casting my mind back to the way that I had tortured the cannibal named Charlie and I sighed and nodded. "If the person that had told me about the captured rabbits had known about you, he would have told me."

"Good," he smiled, nodding slightly, his features deathly white. "That's sorted."

"How did you know about the serial killer?" I asked him. "How did you end up like this?"

He held my gaze for a moment, lips tight together and I winced as I saw his eyes seem to stare through me as he cast his mind back to the day before. Then he shrugged. "One minute we were walking along through this building and then Ian asked me if he could borrow the screwdriver. I gave it to him, I had no reason not too...then he was just on me, stabbing me. Before I knew what was happening, I was sat down here on the floor, too weak to stand and bleeding out."

He paused then, swallowing hard and groaning in pain slightly, then he was meeting my gaze once again. "As I was sat here in agony, that arrogant bastard stood there where you are crouched...telling me how he didn't know how he had got here but that he was glad he was free. I told him he was mad, that I didn't know what he was talking about and he laughed, shaking his head, telling me that it didn't matter...that he had got me out of the way and now he was going to have fun with the bitches."

I grimaced as I imagined how it must have been to sit there in agony and have some maniac saying such stuff and then I was looking back at Craig as he spoke once again. "Then he went even stranger...shouting that none of them ever listened to him, none of them ever gave him any respect...not the bitches here or the bitches back where he was from. He told me he had already taken care of fifteen of the whores...that he was looking to up his tally...then he stabbed me again and left the screwdriver inside me."

I grimaced, lowering my eyes again to the gore covered handle of the tool which was still embedded in his stomach and I sighed heavily and looked back up to his face. "How do you feel? Do you think you can move?"

He gave a grim chuckle, looking at me through heavy lidded eyes, his face pale. "I don't think I am up to dancing if that's what you are asking me, Morgan."

I smiled, shaking my head and then he was grimacing, the smile slipping from his face. "I feel so cold."

"Just try and keep still," I told him, smiling weakly. "OK?"

"Who are you?" he asked me suddenly, shaking his head slightly. "You never mentioned who you are?"

Shrugging, I held his gaze. "I wasn't mentioned in the journal that we found but I think I was brought here because of my father."

"Your father?" he frowned, his voice barely audible as he stared back at me, his brow furrowed in confusion. Then as if a light had come on in his head, his eyes widened and he stared back at me with the weight of knowledge behind those sparkling orbs, bright against the almost deathly pallor of his face. "I know you…"

"What?" I was stunned, the breath leaving me in a rush as I bent forwards, staring back at him in confusion. "Tell me Craig…tell me what you know! Who am I?"

But there was no reply.

Craig Musdye was dead.

Chapter Forty-Three

For some time, I stayed there beside the body of the man that I had only just met the day before, changing my position so that my back was against the wall, my legs stretched out before me in a mirror of how he himself had been sitting when he died, my hands on my lap.

I knew that I should be trying to get out of the town. That I should be making my way south to meet up with my companions before Bert managed to track me down and murder me.

But things were no longer that simple.

Ian was not the journalist that I had assumed. No, instead he was the brutal serial killer that had been responsible for the deaths of a dozen innocent women. No, that wasn't right.

Craig had told me shortly before his death that Ian had boasted of killing fifteen unfortunates. That meant that there were five women attacked and killed back in our world that hadn't been attributed to the effeminate man. How could five women be murdered and yet have nobody miss them? Or maybe they did have people mourning for them, but the police had simply not put two and two together and pinned the crimes on Ian. I would change that.

If I ever got back to the real world, I would make sure people knew how many women he had really killed. I grimaced at the thought of the others then, my mind conjuring up all manner of scenarios as I considered what Ian might have done to them given the chance.

Had he upped his tally from fifteen?

I let out a shaky breath as I pictured the make-up-stained features of Amber twisted in agony and the pale features of a murdered Andrea, her glasses broken as she lay staring up at the sky above with dead eyes. Cursing myself, refusing to give up on saving the two women if I could, I forced myself to rise and headed to peer back through into the room with the open door, frowning as I saw it was nearly dark outside.

I needed to be gone from this town before night fell properly and any of the shadow creatures that still lived emerged from their hiding places to hunt me down. Frowning slightly as I stared at the fading light beyond the open doorway, I shook my head, realising that we had been in this accursed place for over a day now and yet I wasn't hungry or thirsty at all, not one single bit.

How on Earth was that possible?

I nodded, grimacing as the answer came to me.

We weren't on Earth anymore.

We were in New London.

Maybe here there was no need to eat and drink. But then I was shaking my head as I recalled the storeroom back in the hospital that had been stacked with canned food and bottles of drink. Who was it all for if you didn't need to eat and drink while in this world? Then there was the glaring fact that the people living in this dirty shithole of a town had turned to cannibalism in order to survive, feasting upon human flesh. Why would they do that unless they needed to? What would make a man decide to consume another if he didn't have to do so?

Unless they were already mad.

Perhaps the journey through to New London from the real world had not been as relatively painless as it had been for me and my companions. And by the sounds of it they had been here living in this insane little world for decades if not centuries. Even considering time passed differently here it must have been an ordeal. Cursing at yet another problem I didn't understand I turned from where I was stood and stared back at Craig, a tight cold place opening up in my soul as I realised that he was never going to return back to the real world.

Would that happen to me?

Would I end up dead and forgotten in a dimension that most of the real world had no idea even existed?

Grimacing at the thought, I shook my head and spoke aloud. "No, not me"

Moving to crouch back down before the dead man, my eyes lingered upon his pale features for a moment before travelling down his body to stare in grim fascination at the handle of the screwdriver that was still protruding from the bloody centre of his rabbit costume. Grimacing I reached out with my right hand, my fingers hovering around the handle for a moment before with a soft curse, I gripped it, trying not to gag as I felt the thick blood slide at my touch. For a moment I stayed still, grasping lightly to the handle of the tool and then I was tightening my grip and dragging my arm back slowly. Letting out a shaky breath, I watched as the tool began to slide free from the wound, dragging the material of the rabbit costume with it where the blood had dried the white flock and the metal of the screwdriver. Then with a soft pop the shaft of the tool came free of the wound followed by a small river of blood which ran down over the costume and began to pool in his lap. Gagging, shaking my head at the smell, I moved to the far side of the gloomy room and stared back at the dead man, wishing more than anything that I had time to at least bury him. Without a shadow of a doubt, I knew that before long the cannibals that inhabited this town would stumble across his body and consume him like a free meal. As I stood staring at the man, the wrongness of such an act seemed even viler as I realised that Craig looked like he was sleeping, his head tilted back against the wooden wall behind him, and his eyes closed. But time was something I no longer possessed. Somewhere out in New London, Ian was alone with Andrea and Amber, if they were still alive. With a heavy sigh, I nodded at the body of the dead man with the ginger beard and glasses, smiling sadly and headed out into the night.

Chapter Forty-Four

By the time the twin suns had dropped beneath the distant skyline and dark had fallen across the mysterious land know as New London, I was nearly half a mile away from the shanty town where I had nearly died countless times.

Upon leaving the building I had clambered back up onto the low rooftops, making my way cautiously across their surfaces, dreading crashing through them like I had earlier.

As I travelled, I kept my eyes locked onto the distant tower, its white surface visible even through the darkness, guiding me like a beacon. Each time I came to a street dissecting my rooftop travel I crouched and waited in silence, refusing to allow myself to fall prey to an ambush by either the cannibals or the shadow creatures. Each time there had been naught but silence and with gritted teeth I had dropped down to the muddy ground of the street and raced across, before hauling myself back up. And so on, and so on until finally I had been dropping down to the dead grass that made up the huge open area beyond the town and hurrying away as I fast as I possibly could.

I paused as I reached the top of a slope, turning and casting a grim look back at the town of cannibals, the town where the unfortunate Craig Musdye had lost his life. Again, the wrongness of leaving his body behind to be discovered and consumed by the cannibals struck me like a physical force but there had been no other choice open to me that I could have taken. But that didn't mean I was fine with what I'd done. Luckily though I knew the blame behind the entire situation lay not with me but with the effeminate Ian, the serial killer within our midst. Anger flared through me then as the darkness became almost complete about me, the only light being that from a needle thin crescent of a red moon that hung low in the north, another celestial abnormality of this bizarre world. Sighing, shaking my head as I considered what might have happened to Amber and Andrea since I had last seen them, I turned and began to walk across the dead grass once again, still guided by the almost luminescent glow of the white tower. With my mind a storm of emotion, I strode on through the night across the sea of dead grass, the hours seeming to drag by in a blur as before me the huge white tower grew larger and larger. I paused atop another small rise, staring down at the strange sight which lay spread out before me, the view illuminated both by the red crescent moon and by the soft glow that the tower seemed to be giving off. Then with a shake of my head, telling myself that I shouldn't be surprised by anything I saw in this strange world anymore, I began to make my way down from the top of the slope towards the huge park before me. I had seen many parks like this before in London, the majority exclusive areas for residents in deluxe locations of the capital city where big money talked loudly. Like these areas that I had seen before, the park before me was fenced off with a head high spiked iron fence and as I reached the large ornate double gate, I saw the plaque, which was fixed to it, declaring it as, 'St Alice's Park'. Standing on the outside of the metal fence, I stood and stared through the gaps, trying desperately to see if there was any sign at all my friends within but even with the light from the strange moon and the tower there was no way that I could discern anything properly.

Try as I might I could not shake the feeling of dread that had snatched at my stomach the moment that I realised that I was going to have to enter through the gates and make my way through the obviously well cared for bushes and trees but there was nothing I could do. From the top of the slope, I had seen that the base of the tower was set slap bang in the middle of the huge park. If I wanted to get to the tower, I was going to have make my way through the park. Frowning, I cast a look up at the tower, my eyes travelling over its ivory surface and I closed my eyes, trying to recall all that I had heard about the place and the park from the journal of Oliver Queenheart that me and the others had read back at the deserted hospital. Then I nodded as the words I had read returned to my mind. According to Queenheart when he and his Order had first arrived in the land, they would come to call New London they had found the asylum, the hospital, the Cathedral and the park before which I was now stood, each location seeming to fit with one of their number, places which they had each adopted as their own. The park had been taken by McKenzie Hatter, the man having been a landscape gardener back in the real world, back in eighteenth Century London.

If the journal had been correct and so far, everything it had stated had turned out to be true, then it had been McKenzie who had allowed the author Charles Dodgson, Ambers descendent, to escape from this mad realm. It had also stated that the man was trapped here without access to a mirror and had gone completely insane.

I frowned as I considered those facts.

On the one hand an enemy of Oliver Queenheart was more than likely a friend of ours.

After all, hadn't he been the one to leave the book with the note inside it for us to discover back at the asylum, telling us that he would aid us if he ever got the opportunity to do so.

But on the other hand, he was insane.

That was never going to be a good thing no matter how one tried to look at it.

And his desire after so long in this place had to be to escape back to the real world surely.

Could we trust him? Should I trust him?

I had trusted Ian with possibly disastrous consequences. Sparked into action as the thought of the effeminate man entered my head, I stepped up to the double gates and pushed them gently with my hands, cringing as they swung inward, creaking on their rusty hinges. Stepping inside and pushing them shut behind me, I turned slowly about, staring wide-eyed at the scene before me. Despite the darkness of the night now that I was within the iron fence that ringed the park, the scene before me was clearly visible in the faint light from above and I stared like a child in wonder at the numerous animals and shapes which had been created from the carefully pruned bushes which seemed to fill my view. Shaking my head, the urgency of my mission momentarily forgotten, I smiled as I saw familiar shape after familiar shape amongst the greenery; giraffes, bears, elephants, squirrels, peacocks, and more, made with a care and attention which was clear to see, the love of the artisan shining through each creation. Then sighing, forcing myself to move, I began to walk forward only to pause as I stared down at the crunching gravel beneath my boots. Cursing beneath my breath, I grimaced. If anyone else was in the park hiding, then they were going to hear me long before they saw me approach. Shrugging, realising that there was nothing I could do to alter the problem I slowly began to continue down the path, my breath coming in quick nervous gasps, certain that somebody was going to ambush me at any moment from behind one of the countless bushes or bends in the gravel path. Rounding the large shape of a bear, I gasped, swore and took a step back in dread as I saw the two figures standing staring at me from the shadows to my right, the lack of ears atop their head telling me at once that it wasn't one of my companions. Gritting my teeth, I took another step away from the pair, readying myself to turn and run if they made even the slightest move towards me, my mind racing at the same time as I tried to figure out who they might be. Like I said they were not one of my companions, not unless they had managed to get out of the rabbit costumes they were wearing, and neither figure was big enough to be one of the huge overweight Dumbdee twins. "Oliver Queenheart" I muttered, my right-hand folding back, fingertips probing the elasticated sleeve cuff until the screwdriver that I had taken from Craig slid down and filled my grip. "It's you isn't it?"

As I spoke, I took a step forwards, anger giving me courage and I let out a sigh of relief and an embarrassed laugh as above me the light of the moon seemed to shift, and I saw who the mysterious pair of figures really were.

Bushes; carefully sculpted pieces of topiary. Shaking my head, I pushed the screwdriver back into my sleeve, letting the elasticated cuff come taut again, trapping the tool there, then I was continuing down the path, my mood somewhat lightened by my scare. But then the good mood was fading and the smile slipping from my face as I stopped dead on the gravel path, my eyes fixed to the white leg that was protruding from beneath a skilfully sculpted bush in the shape of a horse. Taking a deep breath, trying to control the shaking that had begun in my hands I slowly turned my head, ears straining to listen for any sound of danger in the park about me, my eyes peering through the gloom.

But there was nobody there.

Or at least nobody moving.

Taking another deep breath, I moved my fingers as before, releasing the screwdriver down until the handle filled my palm and then I began to advance on the leg. In moments I was crouching beside it, my eyes once more searching the shadows and darkness about me, realising that if an ambush was to come then it would be now while I was on my knees and distracted. But still there was no movement or sound in the park that surrounded me. Swallowing hard, I returned my gaze to the leg, grimacing as I realised that it was covered in the same material that my rabbit suit was made from, the black boot on the end of the leg matching those which I had awoken to find on my feet. Then I was peering into the darkness beneath the bush, grimacing as I saw the white clad figure which lay there.

Chapter Forty-Five

Gritting my teeth, knowing without question that this was one of my companions, I reached down and stabbed the screwdriver down into the soft earth beside the gravel path. Then I grasped the leg and boot with my hands and dragged backwards, trying to haul their body clear of its hiding place. For a moment there was minor resistance, the body no doubt stuck on some part of the undergrowth in the darkness beneath the bush but then it came free and cursing I fell to my rump. Then I was staring at the body in the rabbit costume which I had dragged from beneath the bush, the chill touch of fear suddenly gripping at my heart as I realised that I was about to find out which one of the people that I had been transported here with had now joined Craig. Taking a deep breath, I rose to my feet and stepped over them, cursing as I saw that they were lying face down on the gravel path. This wasn't going to be easy. It was then as I stood staring down at the body that I saw that the hands of the person were white, the palm and fingers much smaller than mine. That meant that it wasn't Karl Mackal lying at my feet but one of the other three, Tori, Andrea or Amber. Or maybe it was Ian. Maybe they had realised his nefarious intentions and somehow managed to fight him off as he attacked them. Perhaps this was the serial killer lying dead at my feet. But then I shook my head, realising that made no sense. If it was Ian, then why would they hide him? The answer was that they wouldn't.

That meant that it wasn't the effeminate man that was lying on the ground as much as I wished it was. Shaking my head, steadying myself for the grim task I was about to perform, I crouched back down beside the body and took hold of the white rabbit costume with hands. Grimacing I rolled it over to its back, my eyes fixed to a spot before me on the bush as I psyched myself for the task of identifying them. With a curse, I lowered my gaze, hands resting on my knees as I stared down at the terrible wound in their stomach, my own turning over as I glimpsed the wide jagged tear that went from their left hip up across their stomach to their right collarbone, the breath leaving my body in disgust as I glimpsed the bones within the gory wound. I was no specialist in injuries or weapons but if I had to make a bet, I would have said this was done by something powerful, something that tore and ripped as much as cut. Grimacing as I recalled the chainsaw that one of the Dumbdee twins had been holding when me and Andrea had met them, I nodded in disgust. That'd do it.

With a final sigh, I turned my eyes to their face. "Holy shit," I muttered, my eyes travelling over their features, grimacing as I took in the sunken eyes and the bloated oily texture of their pale skin, several strands of black curly hair having slipped from the confines of the rabbit hood and stuck to her right cheek. With a groan I shook my head, my mind racing as I wondered just who the woman might have been when alive. She was certainly not one of my companions. Eyes still fixed to her slowly decomposing features I rose to my feet and let out a shaky breath, realising that she must have been one of the victims of previous hunts just like the men that we had found hanging from the rope and strapped into the chair back at the asylum. Damn that seemed so long ago now.

A thought occurred to me then and frowning I dropped to my hands and knees and peered back under the bush, my hands feeling about, fingers brushing the floor. I gave a grunt of triumph as my fingers touched what I had been looking for and then I was rising once again, holding the small piece of card up before me. Just like the two cards which we had discovered near the bodies of the other rabbits, this one had writing upon it, no doubt another humourless little poem detailing the woman's unfortunate and ultimately painful demise. Unlike the other pieces of card though, the ink upon the one that I was holding in my hand had run through exposure to the elements making the words illegible. With a grimace I cast the card aside and then returned my gaze to the woman lying at my feet. Remorse and guilt touched me then and I winced, shaking my head. Remorse that yet another person had died as a result of the twisted machinations of the mad Oliver Queenheart. Guilt that I was pleased it was her, whoever she might have been in life, and not one of my newfound companions.

I cursed then, my eyes rising to stare at the dark sky above me as a streak of lightning flashed through the night. The last thing I wanted was for it to rain again with me stuck out in the open as I was. As skilful as Mackenzie Hatter had been when he had sculpted the topiary of his huge park, he had obviously never made them for sheltering beneath during a bad storm.

With a curse of surprise, I glanced up at the huge white tower, still some distance across the park from where I was standing, my eyes travelling up its white body to stare in shock and confusion as a bright light suddenly shone out of it again, the beam nearly lost amid the mist that lingered around its upper reaches. The words that McKenzie Hatter had written upon the note that he had hidden within the book that he had left for us returned then and I nodded as I repeated them softly. "Look for my light and I will guide you to me"

Crouching, I collected my screwdriver from where I had stuck it into the earth and placed it back inside my elasticated cuff. Then I was striding forwards down the gravel path once again, heading for the ivory tower that awaited me amid the darkness and a meeting with the man behind the legend of the Mad Hatter.

Chapter Forty-Six

It took what felt like an hour for me to traverse the huge park, making my way around the countless bushes and trees each sculpted to look like living things. Twice more on the journey I stopped in dread as I thought I saw figures standing watching me, twice more I had felt foolish upon discovering they were nothing but bushes. In all honesty I would have gotten lost if it weren't for the fact that I was using the tower that was looming over me as a compass, always checking how close I was to it before choosing which path to make my way down. Finally, just as I was beginning to think that perhaps I might never find my way to the tower I emerged from between two topiary lions to find myself standing in an area which had been formed into a semi-circle by a stand of huge conifer trees and ahead of me at the centre of the curving edge sat the entrance to the tower. For a moment I stood between the pair of huge green lions, my eyes drifting over the scene before me, studying the marble plinths either side of the towers entrance, each bearing a statue and then I studied the centre of the clearing, frowning at the item which sat between me and the tower. It appeared to be a small stone table, the soft glow from the tower and the light from the moon above reflecting off something upon its surface and frowning I made my way over to it, raising an eyebrow as I saw what had caused the reflection of light. Set into the surface of the table were hundreds and hundreds of shards of broken pottery of various colours, each finished off with a glaze which was causing the light to reflect into the sky above.

As I stood there staring down at the shards which seemed to be set together in a completely random manner, I let loose a gasp of surprise and shook my head as I realised that they made up a picture of a huge white rabbit sitting against a star filled sky of brilliant blue.

I blinked hard as I stared down at the image, narrowing my gaze as before my eyes the rabbit seemed to yawn, his body relaxing, sinking lower to the ground. Cursing, shaking my head, I moved back a step, glancing at the image once again only to discover that it was how it had been when I had first discerned the rabbit shape. Biting my bottom lip slightly, I stayed staring at the small mosaic, waiting for it to move once again but the pieces stayed still and

laughing bitterly, cursing my need for sleep I moved my gaze to the outside of the stone table, noticing the word carved there for the first time. Reaching out with a finger of a hand I traced the letters, my lips moving as I did so. "Tsugoth." I snatched my fingers back as a tingle of energy seemed to run up through them, buzzing around my hand and making the joint of my wrist pop slightly and I yawned, feeling the urge to sleep washing over me once again. I blinked again, raising a hand to rub at my face trying to wake myself up, I took another step away from the stone table, realising in some detached way that there was something about it and the image upon it which was making me feel so tired. Shaking my head, trying to clear my senses, I turned back to face the huge white tower, tilting my head back to stare up at it as it rose into the dark sky above me. I frowned then as I realised that there were no seams or brickwork visible upon its white surface, appearing to all intents as if crafted from one single piece of stone.
How was that possible?
Lowering my gaze, I studied the width of the tower before me, estimating that it was at least

twenty-five foot across. There was no way that it could have been made from just one piece. But then this was New London, I had already learned that anything was possible here. Why should the tower be any different?

I glanced up as above me there was another flash of light from the upper reaches of the tower, giving it the illusion of being some strange landlocked lighthouse for a moment before the light winked out once again, making the park seem darker with its absence. With a heavy sigh I took a step towards the dark open entrance at the base of the tower, my eyes drifting again to settle upon the pair of marble statues, one either side of the door, an eyebrow arching as I realised that they were sculptures of the rabbit creature from the mosaic. Pausing, I frowned at each of them, stifled another yawn and headed forwards into the tower.

Chapter Forty-Seven

I shuddered as I stepped within the darkness beyond the door, not from cold but from warmth that spread through my body like a wave, making me sigh heavily. Then I was turning, my eyes fixing upon the white stairs which began to my left, hugging the wall as they wound clockwise up through the tower leaving the central area empty. Shrugging, realising that if I was going to get any answers at all from the mysterious McKenzie Hatter, I was going to have to climb the stairs and meet him, I made my way over to their base and placed a hand on the wall to steady myself. Instantly I withdrew my fingers, a look of surprise creeping onto my features as I stared at the white wall. Then I placed my fingers against it again before withdrawing the screwdriver from my cuff and tapping the wall with the shaft of the tool. "Wow," I muttered, returning the screwdriver to my sleeve and raising an eyebrow in surprise. The wall of the tower was constructed of metal. Again, I raised my eyes, peering up into the circular hole between the stairs, wondering once again how on Earth it had been built using what appeared to be one piece. Then with a heavy sigh, I began to climb the stairs, keeping back beside the wall as I did so for fear of tripping and tumbling down through the centre void. I had made my way around the walls twice before I discovered a lit torch in a sconce upon the wall beside me, the flames flickering as I stopped before them. For a moment I considered removing the torch and taking it with me up the tower but then I decided against it, my eyes fixing to the soft glow emanating from around the curve of the steps above and before me. Leaving the torch where it was, I edged towards the centre void, leaning out slightly as I peered up the tower, realising just how well-lit it was. Moving back from the gaping hole, I began to climb the stairs once again, leaving the torch where it hung upon the wall, my decision rewarded moments later as I found another fixed to the tower some fifteen metres later. And it went on, me climbing up through the tower, keeping away from the centre as I practically hugged the wall, trying not to let the growing dizziness that the circular journey was having on me affect my climb. Time seemed to slow for me then and before long I was out of breath, my calf muscles aching and my vision beginning to blur. Cursing I lowered myself to sit down upon the steps, wanting more than anything in my life to just lay down and sleep but the fear of rolling and falling through the centre hole in the stairs kept me awake. Frowning, suddenly curious, I leaned to my right, edging closer to the hole and peering down into it. I cursed as I saw how high I was, the ground seeming to be little more than a dot of white in the distance and sitting back up I leaned against the wall and shuddered. If I fell from this height, there was no way whatsoever that I would be able to survive the fall.

Not a chance.

Groaning, cursing my decision to enter the tower in the first place I rose unsteadily to my feet and began to move once more, determined to get to the top of the mysterious white metal tower as quickly as I could. I cursed out loud then as the toe of my leading boot struck the lip of the next step instead of moving atop it, the curse quickly turning to a scream of alarm as I staggered to the side and struck the wall beside me hard, the impact rocking me backwards in the other direction. With bowel loosening certainty I realised that I was going to fall down the hole and with a cry borne of pure denial I threw myself to the side, spreading my body wide to try and land face down upon the stairs. My head jerked back as the edge of a step struck me hard upon the chin, another mashing me hard in the kneecap and then I was slipping as the right side of my body came down on empty space. Screaming as I fell, I snatched out with my hands, fingers grasping to the edge of the stairs, the weight of my body jerking hard on my wrists as I dangled down into the centre void. For a moment I hung there in shock, my legs swinging below me, my body aching from my hard impact with the stairs. Then with a grunt I began trying to haul myself back up to where I had fallen from, the muscles of my arms burning with fire as they strained within the confines of the rabbit suit. Cursing, I allowed my arms to go to full stretch once again, realising with a cold dread that I was too weak, too tired to drag myself back up over the lip of the stairs above me. Panic flared through me then, making my heart pound in my chest like a wild animal seeking escape and as my hands began to ache above me, I realised that I didn't have long before I fell. Grimacing, teeth gritted together I lowered my head to stare down past my hanging body, wincing as my split chin brushed against the material of the rabbit costume. For a moment I could see nothing but my swinging legs and then I was cursing in horror internally as I saw the drop below me. Strange thoughts entered my head then and I frowned, closing my eyes as I tried desperately to force the questions which I didn't want nor need to know the answers to from the forefront of my mind.

How long would it take me to fall?

Would it hurt much when I hit the bottom?

Would I pass out with shock on the way down?

With a grim shudder I opened my eyes once more, again staring down at my swinging legs and I felt a surge of hope as the sight sent an idea rocketing through my consciousness, forcing all other thoughts aside. Letting out a shaky breath I began to move my legs myself, tucking my knees up behind me as they came back before extending them again as they swung forwards once more. Above me I felt my fingers begin to slip slightly upon the smooth edge of the stairs, the sweat that was by now coating my digits doing me no favours whatsoever, but I forced myself to ignore them, concentrating on purely swinging my legs, building as much momentum as I could. A bout of fear induced giggles washed over me then as I imagined the reaction of any that stumbled across me now, looking for all the world like an entrant in a fancy-dress gymnastic event. The giggles left me in a rush, replaced by a scream of horror as above me my fingers suddenly came loose and I began to fall, heart and stomach leaping to my mouth. Then I was crying out in pain as my back landed hard upon the stairs beneath the part where I had fallen from, the inertia of my leg swinging having carried me under the lip of the overhang. For a moment I lay there, groaning in agony, my head and neck hanging back over the edge of the steps and then I was laughing, my limbs shaking as the adrenaline began to leave my body. With tears of relief in my eyes, I sat up and twisted about on the stairs until I was sitting once again with my back to the wall, my eyes closing as I leaned back and sighed. For nearly five minutes I stayed sitting there, my thoughts on what had happened to me. Then with a shake of my head I opened my eyes and rose to my feet as I began to climb the stairs once again.

This time though I was fully awake, the horror of my near death having forced the dangerous fatigue from my aching body.

Chapter Forty-Eight

With a groan I stepped onto the landing at the top of the stairs and dropped to my knees, my hands resting on the floor beneath me as I groaned. "Fuck that!"

Dropping to my face, resting my right cheek against the cool white surface of the floor, my arms stretched out beside me. A distant part of my brain expressed surprise that like the walls and steps of the tower, the floor also seemed to be made entirely from metal, but the rest of my body was far too exhausted to pay it any attention whatsoever. For what seemed an eternity I lay there, my haggard breathing slowly regulating itself and then with another groan I rolled to my back and stared up at the domed ceiling high above me, eyes closing once again. With a curse I pushed myself to my feet and stared about, my eyes widening as the realisation of what I was seeing dawned on me. The circular room about me looked to be some fifty foot in diameter if not more, dozens of lit torches hanging in sconces illuminating not only this area but also the corridor that began on the east wall and headed off into the distance.

But how was that possible?

How could a fifty-foot room sit at the top of a tower which had been no more than twenty-five foot across? As I had stood looking at the tower from outside there had been no visible enlargement but perhaps that had been hidden by the mist around its uppermost regions. But then even if that was the case, even if somehow the top of the tower was wider than its base that still didn't explain how on Earth, there was a corridor leading away from it. Cursing, hating the confusion that I was beginning to feel now at every turn, I shook my head and turned to cast a look back at the stairs, considering heading back down them and back out of the tower. Except as I stood there staring back, I found myself at the bottom of a set of white stairs and not at the top. Grimacing, shaking my head I moved closer to the bottom of the stairs and peered up, cursing as I saw the inner void towering above me. "Fuck this," I muttered, turning from the stairs, refusing to waste anymore of my time on the bizarre tower of its mysterious architecture. Pausing only long enough to ensure that the hallway ahead of me was illuminated by torches I headed into it, moving my hand so that the screwdriver slid down into my right palm as I did so. Treading as softly as I could, trying not to let whoever it was that was ahead of me in the tunnel know I was coming, I followed the curve of the tunnel, marvelling at the smooth seamless construction of it, occasionally tracing the fingertips of my left hand along the cool metal. Then abruptly the tunnel ended, and I found myself standing at the entrance to another large white room almost identical to the one which had been at the top...no, the bottom...of the stairs that I had climbed.

Frowning I studied my surroundings, my gaze drifting from the six white columns which stretched from floor to ceiling scattered about the area, then I was frowning as I saw the window on the far side of the room, a covered lantern before it upon the windowsill. Casting another look about, I frowned in confusion as I realised that whoever it had been that had been flashing the light from the window, presumably McKenzie Hatter, was nowhere to be seen. Gripping tight to the screwdriver, ready for trouble, I began to edge my way into the room, staring carefully at each of the columns, fully expecting an attack to come from behind one of them. But much to my surprise I reached the window and the lantern untroubled, realising on route that there was no-one else in the room with me after all. Stepping alongside the window I discovered that it was devoid of any glass, instead appearing to just be a hole in the metal wall of the tower, the edges smooth and rounded. Curious, I leaned on the windowsill with one hand, placing the screwdriver down with the other and uncovering the lantern. The gasp that escaped me then as the beam shone out over the land of New London was one which I had no power to control and for long minutes I stood there in the window, my eyes travelling over the sights that I had seen from the hill outside of the asylum. The difference was that from up here in the tower everything seemed to small and distant, like a child's toys laid out before me on a table. In the north the huge bulk of the cannibal town was hunkered down low and dark against the landscape, not a single light daring to shine within its borders. Wincing as the memory of how I had left Craig's body alone there returned to me I moved my gaze onwards, spying the lonely shape of the asylum in the distance before moving my eyes to stare at the familiar shape of the hospital and the two buildings beside it. I frowned then, my head tilting to one side as I glimpsed what appeared to be a light in one of the buildings windows and for some time I stayed still, trying to figure out what side of the building I was looking at, a small part of my mind wondering if what I was seeing was the lantern within the private office of Oliver Queenheart. I tensed as I pictured the man seated behind his desk, my brow furrowing as I tried to imagine what he was thinking. Was he aware that one of our number had already perished? Did he have some way of knowing? It didn't seem likely, but this realm was full of surprises. Forcing myself to turn away from the light in the window I moved my gaze to the large shape of the Cathedral atop the hill in the far west and I frowned, remembering how the journal had claimed that the priest Archibald Hare was still in there, howling and cursing each night. Shaking my head, I leaned forwards slightly, angling my head to one side as if I could hear his mournful wails but there was nothing but the howl of the wind rushing past the window. Chuckling, shaking my head I lifted the lantern then, turning it towards the dark sea that I had glimpsed from the hilltop, suddenly curious as to what it looked like from a closer if a little higher perspective. Wide-eyed I stood staring at the large black waves as they crashed and rolled together, the white foam of their collision spraying high up into the night air.

I cursed aloud, my heart skipping a beat as I caught sight of something huge and monstrous amid the waves, a thing of biblical proportions, a mess of thrashing tentacles, too many to count. Then I was taking a step back, certain that in the brief sighting of the creature it had seen me back, its eyes boring deep into my very soul, hungry and yearning to taste my flesh.

"That is Shal'ep."

I cursed in terror as the voice spoke, close behind me and dropping the lantern to clatter to the ground I spun about, my empty hands raised before me in shock. I had the briefest of moments to raise my eyebrows as I saw the man in the dirty purple suit and top hat that was standing, smiling. Then he hit me with a chair.

Chapter Forty-Nine

"Wakey-wakey, rise and shine."

I jerked awake at the sound of the cheerful voice, my body lurching as I sat and stared in shock at the man that was bent at the waist before me, staring at my face. I hadn't been sure off what I had been expecting to see when I finally met the man that the character of the Mad Hatter had been based on, thinking that perhaps he might resemble Johnny Depp's version or even that of Andrew Lee Potts, the geeky nerd from the TV series called Primeval. But no, the man that was stood before me resembled neither of those two actors, instead looking much more like a living human version of the character that Disney had devised for their film Alice in Wonderland. His hair was wild and silver, poking from both sides of his large top hat in huge sprouts, and beneath his large bulbous nose his mouth was twisted to the side with a daft smile upon it, the mania in that expression mirrored in his bright eyes, one green and the other blue, which sat nestled beneath thick black eyebrows. As he saw me staring back at him, the man's daft smile turned to a huge grin and he straightened, his hands clapping before him like an excited child. "Ooh finally you are awake...just in time for tea."

"You have to be fucking kidding me," I muttered, shaking my head as I stared back at him and he gave a shrill chuckle, shaking his head from side to side as he hurried away to the other side of the room. Frowning I listened as he began to potter about, the chinks and clatter of cups and cutlery reaching my ears and then with a flourish the bizarre little man in the purple suit and hat was spinning back to face me, a tray balanced on one hand as he virtually skipped the distance between us. Eyes wide, I watched in disbelief as he dropped to the floor beneath my chair to sit with his legs crossed and set the tray down on the white floor in front of him. From my vantage point above him on the chair, I stared down at the dirty tray and the two broken cups upon it, one little more than half its original shape and both completely and utterly empty. Then with another broad grin, the man selected the cup nearest him and raised it before him, his little finger poking out to the side as he threw me a wink. "Bottoms up." Dumbstruck I watched as he sat there, the cup tipped to his mouth, his throat swallowing as he drank, then he was lowering the cup once again and wiping his free hand across his mouth with an exaggerated sigh of contentment. "Ah that hit the spot."

"What did?" I grimaced, regarding him wearily. Another chuckle escaped his lips as he tilted his head to one side, eyeing me as if I had asked the stupidest question ever and he raised the cup again. "The tea!"

For a moment I held his gaze in silence and then I shook my head. "There's nothing in the cup."

"I know," he gave a chuckle. "I just drank it."

Resisting the urge to rant at the man before me, seeing that he was clearly not the full package, I turned my eyes from his face and studied our surroundings to find that we were still in the room with the window, the lantern now sitting back on the sill beside my screwdriver. Movement dragged my eyes back upon the strange man and I found him now sitting drinking from the second cup, the broken china cradled in his hands as he slurped and sighed, completely unaware that I was watching.

"Where are my friends?" I asked suddenly and he jerked to his feet, eyes wide as he glanced guiltily down at the china he was now holding.

"Oh, I am so sorry...did you want to drink this?" Letting out a controlled breath, I closed my eyes as it dawned on me that the only way to get any sense out of the man would be to play along, to accept his mania as reality. Then I opened them once more and forced a smile. "No thank you, you are welcome to finish it."

"I can?" his smile was huge, reminding me momentarily of the smile that the traitor Cheshire had given me as I had collapsed to the floor back in my father's home, back in the real world. Keeping the smile on my face, I nodded at the man in the top hat and purple suit.

"Of course, feel free. Waste not want not."

"Indeed," he gave a chuckle and tipped the cup back to his lips, eyes bright above the broken china in his hands. Focusing upon his face, I watched as he drank, my mind wondering just what he must have endured during his time trapped in this alternate world all alone. After all I had only been here for nearly two days and I was already beginning to feel the stress of the ordeal. If the journal of Oliver Queenheart was to be believed then the unfortunate wretch before me had been trapped here since Charles Dodgson, the author Lewis Carol, had taken his mirror from him back in 1862. Before me, McKenzie Hatter bent and placed the broken cup back upon the filthy tray, rising and carrying it back over to where he had got it from. Then he turned to face me, a curious smile upon his face. "Ask it again."

"What?"

The question you asked me," he grinned, moving back over to stop before where I was tied. "Ask me again."

I frowned for a second and then recalled what I had asked him. "Where are my friends?"

"Your friends?" he raised an eyebrow, shaking his head as he held my gaze. "I'm quite sure I don't know."

"What do you mean you don't know?" I grimaced, feeling my temper slipping. "They were headed here."

"They were?"

"Yes...three women and two men...have you seen them?"

McKenzie Hatter frowned for a moment, one long finger tapping the side of his nose and then his eyes widened, and he clicked his fingers. "Ah those people...friends of yours? How odd."

"Odd?" I asked, confused by his words. "How is it odd they are my friends? What are you talking about?"

The smile he gave me was a grim one. "I wasn't aware you were allowed to have rabbit friends."

I was about to ask what he meant when his other choice of words sank into my head and I blinked. "What do you mean by that?"

"Which part?" he smiled, his cheerful demeanour returning as he scratched at the tip of his nose, blinking in confusion. "Eh?"

"You said you weren't aware that I was allowed to have rabbit friends...that implies that you know me."

"Maybe I do know you," he grinned, tilting his head to one side. "Maybe that's why you are tied up in the chair."

"What the fuck are you talking about, you crazy little fucker?" I snapped then, shaking my head and glaring at him angrily. "I have never seen you before in my life!"

It was his turn to look surprised, both eyebrows raising to vanish beneath his top hat. "You haven't? Well that certainly is odd!"

"Who do you think I am?" I snapped at him angrily and he jumped in shock and hurried back several steps, eyeing me in confusion. "Who do you think you are?"

I grimaced. "Why do you have to answer every one of my questions with another question?"

"I am?"

"Yes," I shouted, feeling giddy as the blood rushed around my head. Heaving a heavy sigh, I closed my eyes, trying to control my temper and then I opened them as McKenzie Hatter spoke. "So...who are you?"

"I'm Morgan," I told him, feeling weary. "My name is Morgan...Morgan Carew."

"Morgan Carew," the man repeated the names several times, letting each syllable roll around his tongue as if he were savouring an extremely fine wine. "How odd."

Shaking my head at his last statement I held his gaze. "I have no idea what I am doing here on this hunt, but it has to be something to do with my father...I'd bet my life on it. You have to help me...I need to get home!"

A look of fear crossed his face then and he shook his head. "How can I help...I'm just an author?"

That took me by surprise, and I frowned. "I thought that you were a landscape gardener?" His laugh was high and heavy with genuine mirth. "No, no, no...I am fond of gardens for certain, but I am not one for messing about in them. No, I write books."

I raised an eyebrow, my stomach knotting. "So just for the record...what is your name again?" The man before me grinned and performed a small bow: doffing his top hat slightly in my direction as he spoke, his voice proud. "My name is Charles Dodgson."

Chapter Fifty

"Wait a minute," I shook my head, frowning at him. "You can't be Charles Dodgson…he escaped from this place, didn't he? I was under the impression that he took your mirror and got the Hell out while he could!"

Before me, the man in the top hat began to shake his head, chuckling with amusement but then he paused, and the smile slid from his features. Still tied to the chair I winced as the man suddenly seemed to be crushed emotionally and mentally before my very eyes, his sad gaze lowering to stare down at the ground. Then he looked back up at me, eyes wet with the promise of tears, "I don't understand, why would he do that to me…I thought that we had become friends…I told him all about the mirror and then he just left me here to rot!"

Despite my anger with the man for first hitting me with the chair and then tying me up like a prisoner, I felt a wave of sympathy for him wash over me and I frowned, watching as he turned from me and made his way over to stand beside the window and the lantern. Not sure what else to say to the obviously troubled man I stayed silent, sitting on the chair and watching him carefully. For long minutes he stood there framed by the window, sobbing gently, his arms wrapped bout himself and then slowly but surely, he began to calm down, the sound of his crying slowly dwindling, replaced by silence. When he finally spoke, his voice was thick with pain and confusion. "So...so I am McKenzie Hatter...is that right?"

"Yeah," I nodded, aware that he couldn't see the gesture. Once again, the man in top hat fell into a bout of silence and in the chair, I felt a shroud of dread settle about me as I realised that in his confused and distressed state he might jump from the window. If he did that then I would be stuck tied as I was in the damn chair. I had a good feeling that due to the natural laws of this realm I wasn't in danger of starving to death or dying of dehydration, but the fact remained that there were far too many people hunting me for me to want to remain tied up and helpless.

"Are you OK?" I asked him, feeling awkward and with a whirl of his purple suit jacket he spun about to face me, clapping his hands before his body excitedly once again as he grinned, his eyes wide as if seeing me for the very first time.

"Excellent, you are awake…just in time for tea!" He was halfway back towards the dirty tray and broken crockery when I shouted at him, having had enough of the madness. "No…no tea. I want to be untied now!"

He frowned then, shaking his head as he began to walk back towards me. "No…that won't do…I cannot untie you I am afraid…it's completely out of the question."

"Why?" I snapped, stamping my foot as best as I could from where I was sat, the effort only causing a small tap, leaving me feeling stupid.

He winced. "You could be dangerous."

That took the biscuit. "Me…dangerous? Are you mad? You're the one that hit me with a chair!"

The man before me shrugged, his expression going serious again. "Well, I couldn't take any chances, could I?"

"With?"

"With you being you know who?"

"Who?" I suddenly shouted at him, hurting my throat in the process. "Who the fuck is it that you think I am? I told you my name is Morgan Carew, and I am here looking for my friends; two men and three women!"

"Friends?" he gave me a surprised look, shaking his head. "A man and a woman arrived here not long ago!"

I scowled, stunned by his admission. "Why didn't you tell me when I asked?"

"You never asked," he was indignant, throwing me a look of amusement as he folded his arms across his chest. "If you had asked me, I would've told you, wouldn't I?"

"Is this some kind of a joke?" I grimaced, holding his gaze with a grim look. "If my friends were here then where are they now? What have you done to them?"

"Nothing," he smiled, spreading his arms and shrugging. "Why would I have done something to them?"

I took a steadying breath, my top lip curling as I tried to stay calm. "Well...let me think...you hit me with a fucking chair and then tied me up...why not them too?"

"Oh yes," he nodded, still smiling. "Yes, I tied them up."

"Where are they?" I asked and he gestured with a hand towards the back of the large room. "Over there."

For a moment, I stared at the wall which he had pointed at and then I was looking back at him in disbelief. "What are you talking about? There's no-one there!"

As I watched he gave a chuckle and shook his head, taking several steps back towards one of the white columns which rose from floor to ceiling, a hand sweeping down over the smooth surface. There was a soft click and then I flinched and turned my head as I glimpsed movement out of the corner of my eye.

"Ta dah!" the man in the top hat exclaimed, gesturing with both hands as the wall I had been staring at, my eyes following it as I swung backwards to reveal the two figures in rabbit suits that were tied to wooden chairs like I was. For a second I held their gaze, seeing their eyes widen in surprise as they in turn saw me watching them, then I nodded at them and forced a weary smile despite the fact we had parted on far from friendly terms. "Karl, Tori...fancy meeting you here."

Chapter Fifty-One

"Morgan!" Tori cried out, tears in her eyes as she stared back across the white room at me. "I thought you were dead! Where have you been?" I resisted the urge to point out she had left me and Andrea to face the Dumbdee twins alone and forced a weak smile. "Surviving."

"Are you OK?" Karl asked, brown eyes fixed to mine as I turned to meet his gaze. "Did you save the others?"

"The people that you couldn't be bothered to help me try and rescue? Those others?" I grimaced and he lowered his gaze and nodded. "I admit I was wrong to turn my back on them"

"Damn straight, you were!" I snapped and he shook his head, raising his eyes to stare at me. "So, did you...did you save them?"

I paused before answering, my mind running through a list of everything that had occurred since I had last seen the black American and then I shrugged, deciding to go with the quick answer. "We saved Amber...and Ian."

"What about the other man...Craig?" Karl asked, the grim look of horror in his eyes showing that he had already guessed why I had omitted him.

"He's dead," I stated, shrugging, turning my gaze to a stunned Tori as she sat listening. "Before he died, he got his memories back…he told me that you and he were partners…you and he were the reporters Oliver Queenheart had transported here because you were trying to uncover some dirt on him and his activities."

She winced then, shaking her head as she stared back at me. "I…I don't remember him from before…I can remember being a journalist now, but I had no idea which of you was my partner."

Nodding, I turned back to find Karl studying me intently, his expression grim. "How did he die?"

"Ian killed him."

There was a gasp of shock from Tori then Karl was shaking his head. "Ian killed him? Why?"

"Why do you think?" I asked, shrugging. "He is the serial killer. And I let him go off with Andrea and Amber."

"Are you insane?" Tori shouted across at me, her eyes wide. "Why would you do that Morgan?"

"I didn't know he was the serial killer at the time." I snapped at her, losing my temper. "We had just got away from the cannibals and the shadow creatures…Ian had told us that Craig was already dead, killed the day before by other cannibals. Then we were attacked again and told Ian to get Amber and Andrea to safety...I thought they would come here!"

A heavy silence descended upon the three of us then, them staring at me and me in turn staring back at them. If it hadn't been for the fact that I was tied to the chair I would have leaped out of it as the face of the man in the top hat, McKenzie Hatter suddenly appeared alongside me, his tone conversational. "Would you like some tea?"

"No" much to my surprise my tone was even and calm as I answered him. "No...I would not like some tea!"

For a moment he looked mortally offended but then we were both turning to look back at Karl as he spoke. "So, if Ian is the serial killer and Craig was the other journalist then that leaves you as the mystery person, doesn't it Morgan?"

I nodded, holding his gaze with no shame or guilt. "Yes, it does. I can remember being at my father's house and being tricked into reading some sentence upon a sheet of paper...then I was here. Queenheart must be using me to punish my father!"

I turned my face towards McKenzie Hatter as he gave an amused chuckle. "What now?"

"Nothing!" he raised his open palms and backed away once again, smiling innocently, "I don't know you and you don't know me remember, we are strangers!"

I was about to pursue the matter when Karl spoke again, his deep voice low as I turned back to him. "Perhaps you are the serial killer Morgan...perhaps the others are all dead and this is just a trick so you can kill us too."

There was another gasp of shock from Tori, and I sighed, too tired and weary to continue playing games with people, "Fine, if that is what you think so be it. I really don't fucking care anymore...I just want to find Amber and Andrea and get the Hell out of here!"

"You need mirrors to get out of this place," the grim voice of McKenzie Hatter had all three of us turning towards him as he leaned back against one of the columns, his face ashen grey as he seemed to look past us all into the depths of his memories. "You won't be able to go anywhere without a mirror. You'll just be trapped here like me...alone and betrayed."

Karl frowned. "By Dodgson or Queenheart?"

"By them all!" the man in the top hat suddenly snarled, his formerly jovial expression switching to one of hatred as he clenched his fists by his sides. "One led me here to this barren land of nightmares and the other stole my only means of escape...and after I tried to help him too."

Frowning, I kept my eyes on the disturbed man a moment longer then cast a look back at Karl, seeing the curiosity in his eyes as he grimaced. "Is that why you have tied us all up?" he asked then, drawing the attention of our captor towards him. "To stop us from betraying you like Charles Dodgson did?"

McKenzie Hatter paused before answering and I cringed as his eyes settled on me for a tad longer than I would have liked before moving back to Morgan. "Yes...that is one of the reasons...it never pays to be too careful here!"

Karl grinned back at the man, his smile both charming and supportive. "I understand completely. Trust just isn't what it used to be anymore, am I right?"

McKenzie nodded: his features etched with anger. "Oliver never wanted to hear my side of the story!"

Karl smiled then. "So, tell us what really happened. It doesn't look like we are going anywhere for some time."

Chapter Fifty-Two

"It was 1858 when it finally all began to go wrong," McKenzie Hatter smiled sadly, meeting the gaze of each of us in turn, his head nodding slightly as he spoke. "Oliver had started accepting contracts on people and we were making big money. Me, Archibald and Thomas were against the idea at first but eventually Oliver won us over to his way of thinking. He always seemed to have that power over us. I don't know why but he did. Suffice to say that once we had accepted a contract on an individual, we would send them a scrap of paper with the sentence of power written upon it in the hope that they would recite it and be transported here to New London."

"That's what happened to me," I grimaced and by the looks upon the faces of Karl and Tori I knew that they could now remember falling for the very same trick, just like Amber and Andrea. In the centre of the room, McKenzie Hatter gave a heavy sigh and continued with his tale. "In the beginning it was mainly criminals that we brought here, people that were refusing to become a part of modern society...the trouble was most of them couldn't read and so it took several attempts for them to pronounce the sentence of power correctly. But in the end the vast number of our targets always wound up here unconscious and we would dress them in the white rabbit suits and hunt them half a dozen at a time."

"Why only six?" Tori asked, interrupting the man and he shrugged at her, clearly unhappy with the intrusion to his bit of storytelling. "Oliver said it was best to not have too many rabbits to hunt down."

"Then why are there seven rabbits on our hunt?" I asked and he cast me a look that I couldn't place, his eyes lingering on me and his mouth moving as if he was going to speak. But then he sighed and shook his head. "Do you want to know the tale I was telling? You said you wanted to know!"

"Hey, calm down," Karl smiled, his natural charm again managing to quell the madness which had resurfaced with McKenzie Hatter. "I'm sorry," the man sighed, adjusting his top hat upon his head. "What was I saying?"

"You were telling us how you hunted those that were brought here in groups of six," Karl stated and with a grin, the madman in the purple suit clapped his hands together excitedly again.

"Ah that's right, well like I said, we would trick our targets into reciting the sentence then when they were transported here all disorientated, we would dress them and keep them ready for the hunt. You see not everyone would arrive at the same time and so those that arrived before the others would be kept sedated by Oliver until we had enough people for the hunt to begin."

I nodded at his words, exchanging a glance with Karl, both of us no doubt remembering the store that we had found back at the hospital with the mysterious bottles of medicine in just as I had. Frowning, I took a risk, interrupting him once more. "Is that why the food was in the hospital? To feed the prisoners waiting to be hunted?"

Instead of snapping angrily at my interruption, McKenzie turned to me, shaking his head. "No, no…in New London one doesn't need to eat or drink. For some reason there is no need to find nourishment while in this realm. I haven't eaten for a hundred years or more."

"Then why the store full of food?" Tori asked, shaking her head. "If it not for the prisoners then who was it for?"

"McKenzie turned to look at her then, his face grim. "The food is for Oliver...you see we discovered early on that while we didn't need to eat whilst in New London the moment that we returned to the real world we were all beset with agonizing stomach cramps that would virtually cripple us for days if not weeks. To that end we found that if we had been here for an extended period, then the pains could be avoided by eating and drinking copious amounts in the day before the return."

Karl raised an eyebrow, nodding. "To acclimatise your bodies for the change back to the pressures and physics of the real world...it makes sense to me."

McKenzie Hatter gave a laugh and threw his hands up in the air. "I don't know about any of that. All I know is that if you are returning after a long period here and you want to avoid being in agony then you need to eat. Time changes differently here remember, you might only be here for a few hours but in the real world a month or two might have passed. Of course, that's how it works out for those that come here willingly. For those like you who were brought here against your will, tricked into making the journey, you would return to your own time if you managed to escape from New London."

I frowned at his words, considering what that would mean to us. If we could escape, then we would go back to our own time and not end up years in the future then it would be as if this had never happened. Waiting until he glanced at me again, I raised an eyebrow in question. "Is that what happened with Charles Dodgson? He escaped here and went back to when he was abducted?"

A flicker of anger passed over the face of the man in the purple top hat but then he sighed and nodded, his eyes seeming to stare through me, delving once more back into the depths of his memories. "Dodgson was a total surprise as a selection for a rabbit. I can still remember Oliver telling us who was on the next hunt, reeling of their names and crimes and then he had mentioned Dodgson. To be perfectly honest I was somewhat aghast. I knew of the man as a mathematician, a quite clever fellow who had done extremely well at Christchurch College at Oxford. Not to mention that he was a from a long line of priests, his great grandfather having been a Bishop and his father an Archdeacon.

Poor old Archibald had been furious with Oliver for agreeing to choose such a target for the hunt but as was his way Oliver managed to swing us round through a combination of threats and promises. Oliver pointed out that Dodgson was little more than an opium smoking card cheat who had run up huge debts with the wrong people. It was our duty to make him pay."

"That poor man," Tori winced, head shaking. McKenzie nodded, throwing her a grim smile and sighing again. "To be perfectly honest when I had stood looking at those that would be in the hunt with him, I thought that he would be the first to be caught and killed and I remember thinking that perhaps that was for the best. You see he looked so sickly and pale, even more so when in the white rabbit costume, but it was more than that...he was in with a rough lot."

"A rough lot?" I asked him curiously. "Meaning?" McKenzie Hatter laughed at my question as he turned to grin at me. "The people on the hunt with him...his fellow rabbits...they were all from the lower echelons of society, a veritable who's who of ne'er do wells...a rogue's gallery of miscreants if you get my drift. But somehow, despite his somewhat sheltered existence up until that point Dodgson managed to outwit and outlive the rest of his fellow rabbits, using his considerable intellect and cunning to avoid the deaths which took them all with ease. I can recall his words regarding his fellow hunted in the days when he had taken me hostage, he had a name for each of them you see, a non de plume which fitted well with their characteristics" McKenzie paused then, tilting his head to one side as he chuckled. "Dodgson really was quite a wit. And he used them all in his novel too just like he used me, Oliver and the others...he made us all famous in that respect."

"He put them in the book?" Karl was intrigued, his eyes fixed to our insane narrator, "In what way?"

"One of those who were hunted with him was a wiry little weasel of a man by the name of Tuttle, who had been arrested countless times back in the real world for confidence schemes. He was by his own admission a compulsive liar, a fabricator of the truth. Well, Dodgson added him to the book as the Mock Turtle, a play on the man's deceptive nature and his surname"

"Who were the others?" Tori asked and I turned to see her staring at McKenzie Hatter with an expression of curiosity on her face, her journalistic side getting the better of her.

"There was a man by the name of Piotr, a Russian immigrant who had built up a small empire in the West of London selling opium and other narcotics to those with the money to pay. He was a vile wretch of a man, a buffoon who considered himself an intellectual, always speaking in long streams of words that ultimately made no sense whatsoever. But it was his features that I recall the most; his eyes huge and staring, his face bony and angular much like the carapace of an insect. Dodgson made him into the literary character called the Caterpillar, complete with the pipe that the man kept stating that he was missing. In the end he decided this was all a dream brought on by the drugs that he sold, and he sat down to wait until his head cleared. He was still sat there waiting when the Dumbdee twins found him and chopped him into tiny little pieces."

"He sounds like a charming man," I muttered, and McKenzie gave a laugh, turning to grin. "Believe me...compared to the last three on the same hunt, the Caterpillar and the Mock Turtle were angels."

As me and the others exchanged glances, he grinned and continued. "Remember the Duchess from the Alice's adventures in Wonderland novel? Well in real life she was Betty Cork, an Irish prostitute, a whore, a woman so vile and disease ridden that if we hadn't brought her here for the hunt, she would probably been dead within the year. You see Betty was a low rent, a woman so ugly and horrible that she barely charged for her services as they were. This meant that she got more customers, and each left her with the taint of syphilis, carrying the disease back to their homes and partners. According to Oliver she had given the sickness to a friend of his who had in turn infected his heavily pregnant wife. Needless to say, that the unborn child died, killing the wife when an attempt was made to deliver its corpse in the usual manner. As such Betty Cork was placed on the hunt by Oliver as a personal gift to his grieving friend."

"Who are the last two?" I asked, suddenly as interested as my companions to hear who else in the novel had been based on some Victorian criminal, the fact that I had read the book and seen movie adaptions of it so many times without realising the truth behind it weighing upon my mind. "Who are they in the book?" "The Walrus and the Carpenter," McKenzie stated, holding my gaze before throwing amused grins at Karl and Tori. "Remember in the book how they were two close friends who turned on each other after preying upon the poor unfortunate little oysters? Well in the real world the Walrus was a man named Kendrick Chase, a fat, stinking ogre off a man with a bald head and a huge moustache. Kendrick ruled South London with a fist of iron, running protection rackets and living the life of royalty on his ill-gotten gains, while his personal bodyguard and right-hand man, Tate Talbot, kept things running smoothly through a mixture of threats and extreme violence. You see Tate was as small as Kendrick was large, but he had the advantage over other men. He was a complete and utter maniac and with his reputation for sawing off the legs and arms of those who refused to pay he soon became known as The Carpenter," McKenzie paused then as if for effect and then he was shrugging and shaking his head. "But like in the novel they soon turned against each other, arguing and fighting when the pressure began to increase."

"How did they die?" Tori asked, her voice soft. The man in the top hat grimaced. "The shadow creatures managed to corner The Carpenter in the hospital and sucked the flesh from his bones...and the Walrus...well, he wandered too close by far to the town in the north. Even up here in the tower I could smell him cooking for many a night afterwards."

I grimaced at his description, my stomach lurching as once again I pictured the cannibals finding Craig where I had left him. Then I looked at McKenzie and shook my head. "Well, we aren't like any of them...you have to let us go!"

"So, you can steal my mirror!" he snapped, his face a mask of anger and despite myself I flinched, shaking my head as he approached me.

"No!" the deep voice of Karl snatched both mine and McKenzie Hatters attention. "Oliver Queenheart brought me here because he knew I was a threat to him! I have the knowledge and ability to free this land from his control...but you have to let me out of this chair."

"But if I let you go, you'll betray me," McKenzie muttered, the words barely more than a miserable sniffle. "Just like Dodgson did when I told him where my mirror was."

"We won't," I shook my head, forcing a smile. "I just want to find my friends and go home...you can come with us."

His eyes widened, a lopsided smile creeping onto his features. "Are you telling me the truth? You would let me leave this cursed land?"

I nodded, holding his gaze. "Yes. But you have to let us go and then take us to where Queenheart has the mirrors do you understand?"

He nodded, a frown creeping onto his features then as he stared at me. "But why do you want to escape? Why should I trust you of all people?"

I shook my head, confused by his words, the most recent in a string of comments. "What?"

"You heard me," he repeated. "Why should I trust you one inch when you carry the blood of somebody that has betrayed me before?"

Even though I never moved my eyes from the face of the man in the top hat, I knew without a question of a doubt that Karl Mackal and Tori Rice were staring at me in confusion. Taking a deep breath, the implications of what he was getting at raced through my brain and I shook my head. "No...you are wrong...I am not the last descendant of Charles Dodgson…that's Amber!" The grin that split the features of McKenzie Hatter nearly went from ear to ear, "You really have no idea who you are do you? You weren't lying to me."

"I'm Morgan Carew!" I stated, sounding unsure myself. Before me, the man in the purple suit and top hat grinned and nodded, chuckling. "You keep telling yourself that."

A heavy silence descended upon the four of us then only to be broken by the voice of Tori, her voice hopeful. "Are you going to untie us then?"

"Of course, I am," he grinned at her before dropping down beside my chair, his fingers fiddling with the knots on my bonds. "We have some mirrors to find."

Chapter Fifty-Three

By the time, the four of us were leaving the front of the tower, the twin suns were rising in the grey sky once again, and in the light of the day, the monolith seemed even whiter than ever. After releasing us nearly an hour before, we had all made our way down the stairs, yes you heard me right...down the stairs. By the time we had reached them they had reverted to how they had been when I had first entered the tower earlier that night and with a grim face, I had stared at them in irritation and disbelief, drawing a look from McKenzie. "Problem?"

"You could say that" I had grimaced. "The stairs moved when I was here last...they changed from up to down."

He had nodded, seeming unsurprised by my claim. "This is the Tower of Tsugoth...the God of sleep and change."

I had frowned at his words. "Sleep and change?"

"That's right," Karl had moved alongside me, his face set with a faint smile. "Tsugoth is the deity that rules over this realm...the God which makes all things possible here and his magic is centred on sleep and change. It created locations especially for Oliver, McKenzie here and the others…how do you think it knew what they wanted?"

I had shrugged, holding his gaze. "No idea."

"Because it took them from their dreams, from their innermost desires…Tsugoth is the God who can give everything to those that are willing to worship him. That is why objects here like the stairs and the celestial bodies in the sky do not obey any laws of the physical world that we know…instead changing as if in a dream. But fear not, my research has taught me that Tsugoth is not a dangerous God to those that respect and worship him."

"Worship him?" I had grimaced, shaking my head slightly as I stare back at him. "By offering him sacrifices like Oliver Queenheart is doing. Is that what you intend to do when you take his place as ruler Karl?"

He had chuckled, shaking his head but the smile had not reached his eyes. "Of course not."

"Look, are we going or not?" Tori had asked then, throwing each of us a grim glance. "Please, can we go."

Nodding, I had turned away from Karl to find McKenzie Hatter standing several steps down from the top of the landing, yawning as if he had never slept a single day in his entire life.

"Are you OK?" I had asked, concern touching me as I recalled how my lapse in concentration had nearly brought about my death and he had laughed and nodded at me, stretching his arms.

"Yes, don't worry about me…it is just the caress of the Tower of Tsugoth having its desired effect upon me."

Tori had frowned. "I don't understand."

"This tower is an embodiment of the mighty Tsugoth; he who sleeps and dreams…the magic in these walls is designed to fill those that traverse these stairs with the need to sleep, to lay down and rest their eyes."

"Like a trap" I had grimaced, my head shaking.

"In a way…it ensures that only the most determined will reach the top…or the bottom."

I had stood staring back at him in shock then, shaking my head as I realised that was why I had felt so tired and weary on my climb up through the tower. Then I was nodding in agreement as Karl Mackal had stepped alongside me once again. "Then I suggest we leave before any of us feel the urge to get some shut eye."

Now standing outside the tower beside the other three, I turned to meet their gazes. "I think we need to head back to the hospital as quickly as we can."

"Whoa...wait the hospital?" Tori frowned at me, a look of surprise on her features. "Why the fuck do you want to go to the damn hospital?"

"I thought we were going to get mirrors?" Karl added, throwing me a sideways glance from where he was standing beside a suddenly quiet McKenzie Hatter. Frowning I studied the man in the top hat for a moment, curious as to his behaviour, having fully expected him to become upset when he realised that I wanted to find my friends before we went in search of the mirrors.

"Morgan," Karl muttered my name, irritation in his deep voice, his American accent strong. "Are you listening to me? We need to find the mirrors first, then we can look for the others!"

"Yes, I'm listening," I snapped at him, turning from where I had been staring at the silent form of McKenzie Hatter to glare angrily at the black man. "Were you listening when I told you that Ian is the serial killer and that he has Amber and Andrea with him? God knows what he might have done to them already!"

"They might already be dead." Tori muttered, throwing me a grim look. "There is no point us going after them and placing ourselves in danger if he has already killed them is there?" Dumbstruck by her statement I turned and stared at her in disbelief. "But we won't know if they are dead unless we go and look. Are you suggesting we just assume they are dead and cut our losses? What if they are still alive and we leave them here with Ian...could you live with the guilt knowing that you never even tried to save them?"

She looked down at her boots, her lips clamped together but I saw the answer in her eyes as she did so. She was more than willing to do exactly what I had said if it meant saving her own skin. Shaking my head, I looked at Karl, finding him regarding me with a grim expression. "So...what about you? Are you going to abandon them like you abandoned Amber, Ian and Craig when me and Andrea went back for them? You said up in the tower that you regretted not helping...now you are going to turn your back on people again?"

"It isn't as easy as that," Karl Mackal grimaced, brown eyes locked to mine. "You know what I intend to do. I mean to take control from Oliver Queenheart, and I can't allow the fate of others to stop me from doing that!"

I took a step back, disgusted with him. "What is it about this place that makes you want it so badly eh? What makes it so important that you more than willing to leave people to die a horrible fucking death?"

Anger flashed in his eyes and he jabbed a finger in my direction. "Don't push me...you don't understand!"

"So, tell me," I snapped angrily, knocking the finger away. "Tell me what this is all about!"

Suddenly Tori was between us, shouting and cursing, pushing us both back away from each other, yelling at us to grow up and stop fighting. With a grimace, I nodded and raised my open hands, stepping back away from the angry black man before me. "OK, I'm calm."

"And you?" Tori rounded on Karl. "Are you?"

He nodded, throwing me a grim look. "I am".

"Good...now can we please just find these mirrors and get out of here!" Tori snapped and strode across the small clearing before the tower, rounding the stone table with the pottery mosaic of Tsugoth and stopping between the bushes sculpted to look like lions as she glared back at the three of us. "Well, come on then!" For a moment me and Karl exchanged glances and then we were walking forwards, the black man continuing over to stop before Tori as I paused beside the stone table and turned back to look at McKenzie. I frowned as I found him still standing there quietly with his head tilted to one side as if listening to something, his lips tight together and casting my other two companions a confused glance, I sighed. "What's up with him now?"

"I expect that he just feels let down that you have changed your mind about going for the mirrors first," Karl muttered, a cold smile upon his lips and I flicked him my middle finger.

"Oh, for the love of God, I swear, don't start arguing again," Tori snarled, hands dropping to her hips as she glared at me. "Listen Morgan, if you want to go and find the others then feel free...that's your choice...but me, Karl and McKenzie are all finding the mirrors and getting out of here the first chance that we get!"

"For once I agree with her," Karl nodded and I grimaced, feeling anger beginning to course through me yet again only to snap my head about as I heard McKenzie Hatter begin to chuckle softly. Gritting my teeth, somewhat unnerved by the sound of the mania in his laughter, I moved to stand beside the man. "What's wrong?"

For a moment I thought that he hadn't heard my question as he stood there stock still like a statue but then he began to speak, his voice barely audible, the words uttered in an almost childlike sing-song voice. "Tweedledum and Tweedledee agreed to have a battle; For Tweedledum said Tweedledee had spoiled his nice new rattle..."

My stomach lurched with dread as I stood staring at him as he lapsed into silence but then he turned his head and staring into my face with madness in his wide eyes. "They're here."

Snapping my head towards my two companions that were still stood over near the pair of topiary lions, I shouted a warning and Karl took a step towards us, his face grim. "What did he say? What's wrong?"

I flinched then as the gut-wrenching metallic snarl of a chainsaw broke the silence and then I was watching in horror as Tori suddenly thrust her pelvis and stomach forwards, her arms

flailing wildly at her sides as she screamed in
agony, the huge bulky shape of a man in a
bowler hat standing in the dark shadows behind
her. In front of the unfortunate woman, Karl had
stumbled and fallen to the gravel path in fright
and had now rolled to his back, a hand raised to
protect his face from the torrent of blood that
was spraying from the now gory front of Tori's
rabbit costume, more gushing out as the teeth of
the chainsaw emerged from her chest. As
quickly as it had appeared the head of the
chainsaw vanished once more and with her
screams becoming little more than a choking
gurgle, Tori dropped to her knees and then her
face, a dark pool of blood spreading out on the
gravel path beneath her body. At my side,
McKenzie Hatter gave a terrified squeak and
turned to flee back into the safety of the tower
behind us only to stagger back as I grasped at
his suit and hauled him up against me. For a
moment longer he struggled to get away but
then he was pressing against me, hands
grasping to me like a drowning man to a piece of
wood as we both stood and stared at the two
obese figures which had entered the clearing.
"Hello, Hatter old chum. Been captured by

rabbits again 'ave ya," chuckled the man wielding the gore covered chainsaw, before casting a grin at his twin. "This is gettin ta be a regular thing for him ain't it, brother of mine." Beside him, the fat man holding the extremely large sledgehammer nodded, chuckling as he adjusted his grip on the handle. "That it is brother of mine...that it is."

Chapter Fifty-Four

For a moment, the five of us still alive in the clearing stayed as still as statues locked frozen in a tableau. Then with another chuckle, the twins began to move forwards, Moustache with the chainsaw standing upon the back of the unfortunate Tori as he approached me and McKenzie, while his brother moved to stand above the fallen figure of Karl Mackal, the large man bringing the sledgehammer back over his head with both hands as he laughed aloud. "Karl!" I screamed in warning as I saw the head of the tool begin its descent down but then my view was blocked by the bulk of the huge man that was rushing at me with the chainsaw. With a curse I managed to divest myself of the clinging hands of McKenzie Hatter and push him back out of the way of the oncoming buzzing blades, then I was staggering back against the wall of the tower, the twin and his snarling metallic monster following me. I cried out, wincing as I felt the rush of air brush over my skin as the bloody chainsaw sped at my face. Then I was gasping in a mixture of shock and relief as my attacker suddenly stumbled to the side as something large and purple stuck him in the side of the head and the chainsaw rose and pivoted to the left of my head, missing my face by inches. He hit the ground hard, the chainsaw bouncing free of his grasp as he sprawled upon all fours, the blades still racing as it spun out of control on the gravel. Stunned I pushed myself away from the white wall of the tower, eyes wide as I watched McKenzie rush towards the fallen twin and snatch up his top hat, throwing me a grin as he turned. "The brim is wood!"

"You crazy bastard!" I shook my head at him in disbelief, watching as he placed it atop his head and threw me a grin only for the expression to fade as with curse and a groan, the twin he had felled began to rise, his chubby features now wearing a mask of complete and utter hatred. "You hat wearin' little bastard!"

"Run away!" howled McKenzie.

In a flash he was racing past me and pausing only long enough to watch as the Dumbdee twin reached down to pick his chainsaw up, I turned to follow McKenzie as he ran. Instantly I was cursing as I saw the second Dumbdee twin with the sideburns, bring the sledgehammer back above his head for another swing at Karl Mackal, the black man now grimacing and clasping at his left shoulder with his right hand. Vaguely aware of the fleeing figure of McKenzie as he leaped the body of Tori and vanished between the topiary lions, I gave a roar and charged forwards, throwing my arms about the waist of Sideburns as the sledgehammer swung down. As I struck the obese man, I grunted in surprise, stunned to find that he barely even moved. In response the twin gave a curse and turned to snarl at me, the distraction enough to allow Karl to move beneath the oncoming blow, the sledgehammer mashing the gravel where his head had just been moments before.

"Get offa me!" Sideburns roared suddenly, releasing his grip on the sledgehammers handle with one large hand to shove me back, "Fucking rabbits, get offa me!"

Thrown back by the strength behind his push, I hit the ground hard, my stomach turning over as I glimpsed not only Sideburns turning to face me with the sledgehammer held ready but also Moustache as he turned in our direction, the chainsaw back in his hands. Then with a cry borne of desperation, Karl Mackal brought both legs up high to his chest as he lay on his back and then snapped them out straight once again,

the soles of his boots connecting with the side of
Sideburns left knee. There was a crack like a
branch snapping and then with a howl like a
wounded animal, Sideburns toppled to the
ground like a felled tree, dropping the weapon
as he did so, both hands clutched to his badly
twisted left leg. Forcing myself to rise, I hurried
over to Karl, grabbing him by his right arm and
dragging him to his feet, aware that we were
still in danger of being attacked by the twin that
was wielding the chainsaw. "Come on Karl, we
need to get the fuck out of here now!"
With a nod, he sent me a weak smile and
allowed me to lead him towards the gap
between the topiary lions, both of us pausing as
we reached it to stare back at the scene behind
us. Sideburns was now seated on the gravel, his
good leg bent beneath him and the leg that Karl
had kicked before him, the foot at an odd angle
to his knee as he roared and snarled in agony.
Beside him, Moustache was crouched down on
one knee, the chainsaw switched off as he tried
to calm his twin, face set with genuine concern.
Then he was snapping his head in our direction
as he rose to his feet and started the chainsaw,
the furious pained voice of his brother loud in

the clearing. "Kill them John...kill them!"

Chapter Fifty-Five

"Are you OK?" I asked Karl as we paused against the side of a huge topiary elephant, the pair of us using the shadows before it to hide while we tried to catch our breath after ten minutes of running through the park from John Dumbdee. He nodded at me, sweat on his brow. "I'm fine."

"Are you sure?" I asked, frowning as I saw the way that he was still clutching to his left shoulder. "The arm OK?"

Karl laughed bitterly, shaking his head. "It hurts like Hell, but it was just hit with a sledgehammer by one of the two fattest men I have ever seen."

I matched his laugh with a weary grin. "Well, don't get too complacent...the other fattest guy is still somewhere around here with a bloody great chainsaw."

For a moment, the two of us stood there, grinning and shaking our heads and then he grimaced. "Did you see the mess that he made of poor Tori?"

"Yeah," I nodded back at him, wincing as I recalled the violent death of the woman. Agreed she was far from the nicest individual that I had ever met but no-one deserved to die like that. Well, maybe some people but not her.

Shaking my head as I pictured her lying face down on the gravel path with the wound in the back of her rabbit suit, I cursed, head shaking. Her death had placed more blood on the hands of Oliver Queenheart, along with that of Craig and the countless others that he had brought here to be hunted and killed. Now both the reporters which had posed a threat to him back in the real world were dead and gone and unless one of us made it back to our own reality he would be safe from exposure. A cold place opened in my stomach then as I realised how many must have died on these hunts and the only person to have ever escaped was Charles Dodgson. One survivor out of how many?

"What do you think he meant when he said about your bloodline?" Karl asked suddenly and I turned and raised an eyebrow as I found the black man regarding me with curiosity. He took my silence as a sign that I didn't know what he was talking about and smiling softly he continued. "Back at the tower, McKenzie said he couldn't trust you because someone with the same blood as you had betrayed him before. What do you think he meant?"

"I don't know," I told him honestly. "The journal said Queenheart had found the last descendant of Dodgson and from what Amber had said back at the asylum I assumed it was her that he was referring to."

"Maybe she is mistaken?" Karl offered and I nodded, unsure what to say. If I was the descendent after all then that meant that Amber was the person not mentioned in the journal. Frowning, I shook my head. "But I can recall having a father...in the memory that had returned I had gone to see him when I was tricked into reading the sentence of power that brought me here. If I have a living father, then I can't be the last descendent can I...after all that would make my father a descendant too?"

"Perhaps you are adopted," Karl answered then grimaced. "Perhaps your father is now dead."

He was right. Damn it.

As I stood there pondering the words of the strange little man in the purple suit and top hat, Karl gave a bitter chuckle. "Speaking of McKenzie Hatter...so much for him fearing that we would betray him…he didn't stick around for long did he?"

I grimaced, shaking my head as I pictured how the man in the top hat had fled and left us behind. "No, he didn't. By the time I realised he was going he was gone."

Karl gave a laugh. "I don't think I have ever seen anyone run that fast outside of the Olympics, have you?"

Throwing him a weary grin, I shook my head and then cast another look about. "Do you think you can go on yet or do you need more rest?"

He winced. "Another minute tops…is that OK?"

I nodded, holding his gaze. "I won't leave you."

He laughed at my words. "Touché"

"Sorry?" I shook my head at him, confused.

Karl smiled sadly: eyes locked to mine. "Twice now I have been reluctant to help others and yet you are still willing to wait with me instead of saving yourself."

I nodded and shrugged, not seeing the point in going back over it and falling into an argument with him once again. "It's my choice. Don't make a big deal out of it."

A heavy silence descended upon us then as he held my gaze and feeling uncomfortable, I turned away, studying the topiary around us. "It's my wife, Janet."

"What?" I turned back towards Karl as the sound of his voice. "Your wife? What are you talking about?"

He smiled and turned to look away from me but not before I noticed the tears that were building in the corners of his eyes. "My wife Janet. She is the reason I am so determined to make this world mine to control."

Frowning, not entirely sure what he was talking about I stayed silent, letting him continue. "I have always been interested in the occult Morgan, even when I was a child. That didn't change as I grew. In my life I have gained a Doctorate in Anthropology, I have taught at some of the most prodigious Universities in the United States, I have been through two divorces and I have six children somewhere out there in the world that we know. But through all this my passion for the occult never wavered...not once. But back then it was all just a hobby. I collected papers, information, photographs and whatever I could find on the occult, building up quite a collection of paraphernalia but it was all still a hobby. Then I retired early from work and met Janet, my third wife and without question the one true love of my life."

"OK," I nodded, still unsure what he was getting at. Beside me the black man smiled sadly and shook his head, his eyes still staring off into the distance as he spoke. "We were so happy...but then life decided that we weren't allowed to be. We were at our summer home in Spokane, Washington when Janet first started getting the headaches, complaining of an intense pressure in her skull. Naturally, we arranged for her to see a neurosurgeon at once, a close friend of mine to look at her. Some tests were run and then we were told the news. She has an Anaplastic Astrocytoma on the frontal lobe of her brain, a tumour that is swelling up and affecting the areas in that region, namely her memory and behaviour."

I shook my head, feeling awkward, "I'm sorry." He nodded, turning to face me then and I winced once more as I saw the grief and pain in his eyes. "It is a malignant tumour...she is dying and there is nothing I could do to save her. Or at least that's what the surgeons told us. Our best hope was to spend the last months of her life together and enjoy that time we had"

What do you say to that? How can you reply? Luckily, he was speaking once again, his voice sounding slightly stronger than before, more determined. "Then I found out about this realm and its magical properties. I believe that if I can bring Janet here where time doesn't pass in the same manner then she won't die as quickly as she would back in the real world. She might not even die at all. That is why I need to take control from Oliver Queenheart...that is why I cannot put anyone else first in my plans! I have to do this for Janet's sake."

I nodded, understanding the reasons behind his intentions well enough now but still feeling a touch of dread as I recalled how Oliver Queenheart had written that his wife too had been a victim of cancer. He had hoped to bring her here so that the slow-moving time of the realm would extend her life only to have his requests rebuffed by the woman he loved.

Would Janet be any different?

Would she gladly turn her back on the real world and come and live in this world of madness and mystery? Even with her life as the prize I had a feeling that her answer might very well be the same as the one which Queenheart's wife had given him. For a moment I stayed silent, considering pointing all of this out to the man at my side but then I saw the hope in his eyes, and I knew without doubt that I could not. It was his to discover.

"I'm ready," Karl stated then, throwing me a smile and nodding I stepped away from the topiary elephant, pausing for him to join me. He opened his mouth as he did so, about to say something only for the words to turn into a warning as he thrust out his right arm, a finger pointing behind me. "Morgan, look out!"

Without even thinking, I threw myself forwards into a roll, my heart leaping in my chest as I felt the rush of air as something passed mere inches above my head. Then I was rolling into a crouch, staring in disbelief at the sight before me. Leaning heavily against the side of the topiary elephant, his bulk causing the inanimate creature to bow to the side slightly stood Jim Dumbdee, his Christian name no longer a mystery since he had called his brother John. For a moment I stayed crouched staring up into the furious pained features of the man as he stared back at me, then I was lowering my gaze first to the huge sledgehammer he was still wielding and then to his right knee, grimacing as I saw that the leg below it was bent to the side in a way that nature had never intended. With a snarl the obese man switched his gaze from me to fasten upon Karl as the black man stood further along the elephant, backing towards me until we were side by side once again. Then the huge man pushed himself away from the support of the topiary elephant and took a hop towards us, wincing and groaning in agony as his bad leg bumped the ground as he landed.

A nervous laugh escaped me then and before us Jim Dumbdee gave a snort of fury, spittle hanging from his mouth as he sneered at me and Karl Mackal. "I am gonna crush ya both ta death...!"

"On that leg?" Karl shook his head, his teeth bright against his brown skin. "Only if you can keep up with us."

With a roar, Jim Dumbdee came hopping towards us faster than I would ever have thought possible, the sledgehammer swung back over his left shoulder ready to bring crashing round into us, his face a mask of hatred beneath the fuzz of his huge ginger sideburns. Cursing, I turned to run, colliding with Karl as he did the same and as we reached the corner of the next row of topiary animals we stumbled and fell heavily to the ground. Time slowed then as a huge shadow fell across our bodies and in horror, I looked up to find the furious form of Jim Dumbdee above us, the sledgehammer altering its route to swing down towards us. Despite my horror at the thought of how much this was going to hurt, I flinched involuntarily as the metallic snarl of a chainsaw suddenly sounded right on top of us and with a curse, Jim Dumbdee halted the swing of his heavy weapon and glanced up and ahead, eyes widening.

At precisely that moment John Dumbdee rounded the corner, hollering like a madman only to try and stop as he found his brother before him blocking his path, the chainsaw that he was wielding sliding deep into his twin's huge stomach like a hot knife into a block of margarine. Still stuck on the ground beneath the twins, me and Karl began to choke and gasp as the hot lifeblood of Jim Dumbdee began to pour down over us, splashing into our eyes and mouths, the coppery stench making us gag as above us the mortally wounded man screamed in agony. Mind tilting in pain and terror, the big man lashed out with his sledgehammer, a blow striking the side of his twin's face with a sickening crack and with a grunt, John Dumbdee fell backwards, hands still grasping tight to the handle of his chainsaw as it sliced a bloody furrow up through his brother's chest and throat and exited via his chin in a torrent of gore and organs. Laying down upon the ground, covered in blood and gobbets of flesh, I watched in shock as each twin dropped out of sight in a different direction, then Karl spoke, the pair of us still lying side by side. "Well, that was unexpected."

, "You can say that again"

"Well, that was unexpected"

Chapter Fifty-Six

"Who do you think it was Morgan?"

I shrugged, my eyes still locked to the distant shape of the hospital, occasionally drifting to scan over the two smaller buildings either side of it but then always returning to the largest of the three, my thoughts on the light that I had seen in the window the night before. "Honestly, Karl? I have no idea. It could have been Queenheart...but then it might not have been him at all."

"Do you think it might have been Ian, Amber and Andrea in the hospital?" he asked, throwing me a grim glance from where he stood beside me, the pair of us standing in the sea of dead grass, still some distance from the hospital and its outbuildings. "Maybe it was them?"

I nodded at his words, having considered that myself more than once since we had left the bloody bodies of Tori Rice, the Dumbdee twins, the Tower of Tsugoth and the well-kept park far behind us two hours before. Side by side, both covered in the blood of the obese man that had been known in life as Jim Dumbdee, we had begun making our way across the sea of grass that seemed to cover everything except the park and muddy ground of the cannibal town to the North. As we had travelled, we had discussed our options once again, this time though Karl surprised me by offering to accompany me to the hospital to find out if the others were there. Perhaps he was feeling guilty for turning his back. Perhaps with McKenzie Hatter having deserted us, and the poor unfortunate Tori dead he just didn't want to be on his own again in this dangerous land. I didn't really care. I was happy for the company. But once he had made the offer to join me in heading towards the hospital, I ensured his support by pointing out that perhaps the doors to the Cathedral upon the hill would be locked, adding that if that was the case then we would need the set of mysterious keys that Andrea had left upon the desk of Oliver Queenheart when we had fled the hospital from the shadow creatures. He had nodded at my words, not arguing with me in the slightest and changing the subject we had begun to talk about what had befallen both of us in the time between us parting and then meeting up once again in the Tower of Tsugoth.

As we walked, he listened in silence as I described how me and Andrea had arrived during the storm at the town and had sheltered from it within the rundown shack, omitting the part where passion had unexpectedly taken over us. Then I had told him of how we had been attacked by the cannibals Charlie and Bill and how we had then headed off to find the others only to wind up getting captured ourselves. His silence had ended though as I told him about how I had somehow miraculously managed to fight off the attacks of the shadow creatures, his eyebrows raising as he heard of the weapons' I had used against them. "So, fire and the boiling water affected them? That is good news."

"Good news?" I had frowned and he had nodded. "Of course," he had smiled, his brown eyes sparkling with amusement. "It is always important to know an enemy's weakness don't you think? To know their Kryptonite."

I had laughed, shaking my head. "Kryptonite?"

With a chuckle, Karl had shrugged. "Yeah, guilty as charged. I grew up as a Superman fan. Isn't everyone?"

"Not me," I had shaken my head, frowning in surprise as images of me sitting on my bed reading comics had suddenly returned to me. "I was more of a Batman fan."

"Batman eh," he had nodded at me, a lopsided grin on his face. "That sounds about the right hero for you."

"How so?"

He had shrugged. "You have already shown several times that you are willing to take it to the next level to get things done and save people...Batman."

With that he had turned and begun walking once more and I had followed in silence for a few minutes before he had asked about how I had discovered Craig. Then he had been listening with a grim face as I had told him about the man's last few minutes of life, once again omitting something; the way that Craig had seemed to recognise before dying without revealing what it was that he had known.

We had lapsed into another comfortable silence for several minutes as we had made our way across the sea of dead grass towards the distant hospital and then with a sigh Karl had begun to relate what had happened to him and Tori. Apparently, he had been roughly halfway between where he had left us and the park before the Tower of Tsugoth when he had suddenly realised that Tori was following him, the woman screaming and sobbing that me and Andrea had both been killed by the Dumbdee twins prompting her to flee after him. Karl had shaken his head at that point of his tale, calling himself a fool for believing her claims without going to check for himself but before I could point out that looking out for others was hardly his forte, he had been speaking once again, relating how they had travelled on towards the park and nervously entered it. Night had fallen by then and they had taken the decision to not attempt to enter the tower until the morning, instead taking shelter beneath a topiary horse and cart, trying to stay dry as best as they could from the rain until finally the storm had passed and morning had arrived. He had given a soft chuckle as he had told me how together he and Tori had slowly made their way up through the tower, each coaxing the other onwards as the fatigue and weariness that had assailed me on my journey up the tower, had affected them. Finally, as had I, they had reached the top of the stairs and begun to explore the new location, the pair heading off down the tunnel in good spirits, Tori suggesting that they stay in the tower until help arrived. According to Karl he had been in the process of pointing out to the unfortunate woman how bad an idea her suggestion was when they had entered the large room with the window. He had been afforded the merest of seconds to frown at it and then he had been dropping to the ground as something hard had struck him across the shoulders, a purple blur entering his fading vision as he had passed out. I had grimaced and shaken my head then. "McKenzie Hatter."

Karl had given me an equally grim look and nodded as he continued, telling how he had awoken later that evening to find that he and Tori had both been tied to chairs and that their assailant was now standing before the window, flashing a lantern out into the dark night.

"What do you think he was doing that for?" I had asked my companion, suddenly curious. "Why leave the note in the book for us to find and then shine the light only to take us all prisoner when we climb the tower to meet up with him? Why did he do that?"

Karl had shrugged. "I can only imagine that he was hoping that one of us would be carrying a mirror of some description Morgan. I think as much as he harped on about being betrayed that was his intention for us."

"But what are the chances we would be carrying mirrors?" I had grimaced. "Surely, he would have known that we would be placed in these rabbit suits and stripped of all our possessions." The American had stopped walking then and frowned, biting his bottom lip as he held my gaze before replying. "Unless he hoped that we had found the mirrors that Oliver Queenheart took from him and that Dr Mouse fellow."

I had clicked my fingers in the air, smiling at him. "Which proves that they must be somewhere here in New London doesn't it? For us to have stood a chance to find them they must be in one of these buildings."

For several moment's we had stayed there smiling at each other, then we had turned and continued our journey towards the hospital, our pace quickened as we had begun to formulate a plan. We would search his room once again at the hospital, seeking not only the mirrors but also clues as to where they might be if they were not hidden somewhere there. Our plans were combined now for I wanted the mirrors to return me, Amber and Andrea home and then

Karl could have them to use as a bargaining tool against Oliver Queenheart. Now we were here and ready, standing facing the hospital and I had only just recalled seeing the light shining from within the building when I had been peering out of the tower window the night before. Heaving a heavy sigh, I shrugged and threw Karl a grim look. "Shall we get it over with?"

He nodded. "Why not."

Chapter Fifty-Seven

By the time we reached the front door of the hospital once again the twin suns had made their way almost halfway across the grey sky and were beginning to start their descent once more, the day having passed in a blur of climbing down the tower, fighting the twins and walking across the sea of dead grass. Frowning I stood there staring at the door that me and Karl had entered two days before, finding it hard to believe that we had been in this accursed dimension for that long already. Then I glanced sideways at my companion and forced a grim smile. "Are you ready?"

He laughed and shook his head. "Not as ready as I would feel if we had used our brains and brought the twins chainsaw or the sledgehammer with us, Morgan."

It was the second time he had pointed out the absence of any type of weapon in the last five minutes and I nodded, understanding how nervous he was feeling. I felt it too.

We were about to head into a building where we had seen shadow creatures before, a building that could even now be a hiding place for a deranged serial killer or the stronghold of the man that had brought us all here. The thought of meeting up with any of them was a grim prospect but we had to take the risk and venture inside. With another grim look at Karl, I stepped forwards, entering the hospital for the second time in as many days, shuddering as the chill of the building wrapped about me. Aware that my companion was close on my heels, I turned right in the foyer, pushing open the door to the huge corridor beyond, wincing as the nerve shredding sound of the hinges sounded. "Well, if anyone is here, they know that they have company now," Karl muttered, moving through the second door to stand alongside me, letting it close behind him with another prolonged squeak and a thud. For a moment we stood there in silence as we stared about the huge open corridor before us, my eyes drifting over the empty beds and then on to the doors to the store cupboards that we had checked when we had been here last. I frowned, shaking my head and turning I found Karl meeting my gaze curiously. "Well, it seems that the rooms we opened are still that way."

Suppressing a grim chuckle at the fact that he had said exactly what I had been about to, I nodded. "Yeah, surely if Queenheart had been back here then he would have shut them, wouldn't he?"

Karl made a face as if he wasn't sure, his eyes scanning the area about us. "Perhaps, unless he wanted us to think that he hadn't been here. Then he might leave them open. We need to check his room."

"Wait," I shook my head as something caught my eye on the floor through the open door of the first room that we had checked earlier, and I moved towards it and crouching to pick it up. "What have you found?"

"My hammer," I held it aloft as I turned back to face him, surprised at just how much more comfortable I was feeling now that the tool was back in my hands. Frowning, he moved to my side, eyeing the hammer in my hands curiously and I nodded. "That clinches it. I dropped this after Tori surprised us remember. That means Queenheart can't have been the one that I saw here last night...if he had been back, he wouldn't have left weapons lying, about would he?"

My companion chuckled then and shook his head at me, a smile on his features. "You are forgetting the fact that it was Oliver Queenheart that left the hammer upon the table in the first place along with all of the other items."

I cursed, feeling stupid and Karl frowned, a silver eyebrow rising. "That is one of the things that I don't understand about all of this Morgan. Why leave us items to choose from at all? Why bother doing that?"

"Maybe he thinks it makes it harder for him," I offered, not sure myself. "Maybe he doesn't want easy kills."

"Maybe," Karl nodded, his face grim, "That makes sense."

"But why the keys?" I asked, shaking my head as the thought entered my mind. "The keys open any door and then fade away to nothing...that seems quite a powerful thing to have left us don't you think. Why would he have done that?"

The smug grin that appeared on Karl's features then made me frown. "Actually, the key spell isn't that powerful a trick to replicate Morgan. It is basically a spell created through the manipulation of shadows and the hope of the key user. Nothing too complicated at all."

"You make it sound like you can cast spells."

"I can do various things Morgan," Karl replied, his tone grim. "And I am willing to use everything at my disposal to secure this land for my wife…I need to do it for her."

I forced a smile, nodding at him. "I know and the sooner we can get these mirrors the better."

He smiled as he held my gaze, his head tilting to one side as he chuckled. "You do trust me?"

"Of course," I told him, wishing that I felt as sincere as I sounded. "Is there some reason why I shouldn't?"

Karl laughed again, shaking his head. "Of course not. Most people don't react well when faced with the occult and the supernatural."

"Hey, I have no choice but to believe," I told him, gesturing about me with the hammer. "I am in this fucked up world. How could I not believe?"

"Wise words," he nodded, smiling at me. "Then you agree that I might be better served to face Queenheart than any of the rest of you? Can I ask that you leave confronting the man to me?"

For a moment I held his gaze in silence and then I nodded, shrugging. "Look Karl, I just want to get home. If you and your wife want to make this your own private paradise, then good luck to you but I just want out!"

He smiled, nodding. "So, we are agreed?"

"Sure whatever."

With another grin he turned and headed off down the length of the corridor, angling his route towards the last door on the left-hand side, the door which led to the private room of the mysterious Oliver Queenheart. We paused as we reached it and I frowned, shaking my head. "Wait how will we get in? Last time we needed the keys that Andrea was carrying. The keys we left in there!"

He nodded, holding my gaze. "We will have to hope that when we closed the door as we left it didn't lock."

So saying he reached out with a hand, grasping to the brass handle of the door before looking back at me and turning his wrist. There was a soft click then the door swung open, the glow of the room surging out to meet us as it had before, and Karl grinned. "That was fortunate."

He was still standing there grinning at me when there was a surge of movement within the doorway and then he was staggering back, hands clasped to his chest. Time seemed to slow as he turned towards me, shock in his wide eyes as they met mine and then I lowered my gaze to stare at the red stain that was spreading out beneath his fingers, barely visible amid the blood and gore already coating his rabbit suit. With a soft grunt, his legs gave way and he slumped down to sit on the edge of the nearest bed frame for a moment, eyes rolling in his head. Then he dropped back to the bed and I was turned to stare in a mixture of shock and hatred at the naked figure that stood within the doorway, my stomach knotting as I saw the amount of blood that was coating his pale flesh. They laughed then and took another step forward, brandishing what looked like a letter opener in their hands, the blood of Karl dripping from its blade. As rage surged through my body I snarled at the figure, my hands fists. "Bastard!" Ian Towel gave a chuckle. "Hello Morgan."

Then he was rushing me with the blade raised.

Chapter Fifty-Eight

Cursing I took several steps back, cursing as the frame of a bed behind me stopped my escape and then I was swinging the hammer in from the right at my attacker just as Ian leaped at me with the knife raised to strike. He grunted as the head of the hammer struck him upon the side of his head but then I was crying out as the blade sank into my left shoulder. Locked together by the knife in my body, we tumbled backwards, over the bed and onto the hard floor beyond, a curse escaping my lips as my grip on the hammer was lost as I landed. Breathing hard from the burning pain in my shoulder I forced myself to my knees as quickly as I could manage, only to curse aloud as with a scream of excitement Ian was rushing me once again, my hammer clasped in his hand, the maniac already having made it back to his feet. I lashed out as he reached me, my right fist striking him hard in the face, crunching his nose even as the head of the hammer glanced off my right temple.

As he staggered and fell away from me, one hand clutching at his now bleeding nose, I took several steps back and shook my head, trying to clear my head from the effects of the blow that had struck it. With blurred vision I looked up in time to see him start to approach me once again, stalking me like a cat with a mouse and grimacing I reached up and dragged the blade clear of my left shoulder with my right hand. Brandishing it before me, I snarled at Ian like a maniac. "Come on mother fucker...come on!"

Ian Towel gave another chuckle, but I could tell by the forced sound of it that I had hurt him, perhaps twice. "Brave Morgan...do you really think you can save the day!"

"You killed Craig," I snarled at him in hatred, shaking my head once again, trying desperately to focus on the naked man as he began to step from side to side, the mocking grin on his face one of the only things I could see with clarity.

"Yeah, I killed Craig," he taunted me. "You should have seen his face when I stabbed him. He didn't have any idea what was going on!"

"Is that why you told him about you being a woman hater?" I grimaced, surprised to hear the grunt of shock from the naked madman.

"You spoke to him?"

I nodded, forcing a smile. "Oh yeah I spoke to him. He was alive for ages after you stabbed him. He told me all about what a fucked up little mummy's boy you are."

The last part of my statement had been nothing but a lie, conjured from my memories of Craig telling me that Ian had ranted about how none of the women he had killed back in the real world had any respect for him. Nevertheless, Ian snarled and spat on the ground. "Shut your fucking mouth! You don't know what you are talking about! You know nothing...nothing!"

Blinking hard, rewarded with a slightly clearer vision of the naked man with the hammer I gave a chuckle. "Oh, I know alright Ian. That's why you killed them all isn't it? All those poor women. You killed them all because mummy was too strict with you. I'm right, aren't I?"

Much to my surprise, Ian just smiled. "No Morgan...I killed them because I enjoy raping and killing women..."

He rushed me so quickly that before I knew it, he was upon me, a swing of the hammer numbing my right wrist enough for me to drop the hammer, another swing catching me under the chin and rocking me back from my feet to hit the ground hard once again. I cried out as the back of my head struck the hard surface with enough pain to smash my dizziness into dust and with wide eyes I watched in horror as he moved to stand above me, a grin of maniacal proportions etched upon his feminine features. "Poor, poor Morgan…time for you to die like the others!"

"If you kill me you will never find out how to get out of here!" I told him, trying to stall whatever he had planned for me. "I know how you can get out of this world!"

His laugh was genuine. "Why would I want to leave this place? I am having so much fun."

"Bastard," I snarled, and he wagged a finger. "Now now…sticks and stones…"

Wincing I tried to move, to push myself away across the floor of the hospital but Ian took a step to the side, the heel of his left foot pushing down on where the letter opener had stabbed me in the shoulder, and I cried out in agony until with another chuckle he removed his foot.

"Now before I begin the fun…where is Tori?" he asked suddenly, raising an eyebrow. "Where is that utterly horrible vile fucking whore."

"She's dead, killed by the Dumbdee twins," I stated, grimacing up at him and I was stunned to see the look of utter grief that crossed his features as he sighed heavily, visibly moved by the news. Then he was grinning once again and shrugging. "That is such a shame. I had so much fun lined up for her. Ah well...shall we begin?"

"I won't beg," I told him, sounding braver than I felt and above me Ian gave a hearty laugh.

"That's what they all say...they were all wrong." Then he was stamping down on the stab wound in my shoulder time and time again until I was dizzy with agony. Still standing over me Ian Towel gave another chuckle and tossed the hammer that he was still holding away across the hospital floor before turning his head to glance about. "Now where has that knife gone?"

I sat up so fast that he barely had time to gasp in surprise before he was arching his back and grunting in shock as I clasped the back of his legs with my hands and fastened my mouth about his hanging scrotum, managing to catch his flaccid penis and one testicle behind my teeth as I bit hard. For a moment, I nearly gagged on the sour stench and taste of his sweat and the hairs that were scraping the inside of my cheeks and my tongue but then I was biting harder and shaking my head from side to side, determined to cause as much damage to him as I possibly could. Above me Ian's grunt turned to a high-pitched wail of agony, a sound so pain filled that it sounded inhuman, and his position shifted as if he was going up on tiptoes. I winced in agony as several heavy blows struck me about the head as he desperately tried to dislodge me, but the long ears of the rabbit costume cushioned them and snarling like a rabid dog, I bit harder. My eyes widened as the coppery taste of blood suddenly filled my mouth and then the connection to my opponent seemed to vanish as the testicle and penis between my teeth suddenly fell loose. Gagging, nearly choking on the meaty deposits, I pushed Ian away and spat them out onto the ground, both sticking to it like slugs to a window, joined together not only by saliva thick blood but by a thin string of muscle and skin. My mind racing at what I had done, I forced myself to my feet, eyes focused upon the pale figure of Ian Towel as he continued to back away, still screaming in agony, hands frantically trying to stem the flow of blood that was pouring from his ruined groin. For a moment, our eyes met and then he was turning and fleeing towards the far door with a lurching run, howling as he went. With a heavy sigh I dropped to my knees and shook my head as I stared at the still form of Karl Mackal upon the bed frame. Another one of us was gone.

Chapter Fifty-Nine

I stayed kneeling upon the ground for quite some time, shaking my head as I shifted my gaze between the body of Karl and the items that I had bitten from Ian's body, spitting and gagging every time I viewed the latter. How had I bitten off his scrotum? Agreed he had been about to kill me, and I had been without a weapon but how had I gone to such an extreme? I winced as I recalled how I had butchered the cannibal named Bill back in the muddy streets of the ramshackle little town in the north, shaking my head once again, disturbed at how easily such violence seemed to come to me. Sighing heavily, I pushed myself to my feet and stood looking around for the knife that had been knocked from my hand, cursing after several minutes as I realised that it was nowhere to be seen.

Nodding as I spied the discarded hammer, I walked slowly over to it and bent, reaching for it with my right hand only to wince and straighten up, hissing in pain as the stab wound in my left shoulder flared again with fire. Taking a deep breath, I turned my head and stared down at the wound as best as I could, calming slightly as I realised it didn't seem to be as deep as I had feared, the blood already beginning to congeal about the hole in the rabbit suit. Thank God for small mercies. Reaching up with my right hand, I touched my fingers to my chin where the hammer had struck me and knocked me to the ground, the tips coming away wet with blood from where the blow had reopened the injury I had received while banging my chin of the stairs in the Tower of Tsugoth. Groaning as I felt the ache of the numerous fights and the wounds that I had received in them all seemed to assail me at once I turned and headed towards the open doorway to Oliver Queenheart's office, pausing again to stare down at the body of Karl. I screamed as he opened his eyes, a faint smile creeping onto his face and I crouched beside where he lay on the bed. "Oh, my fucking God!" He smiled weakly. "Where is Ian?"

"Gone," I nodded at him. "Don't worry!"

"How did you beat him?" Karl asked, shaking his head, wincing as the movement hurt him.

"Let's just say he bit off more than he could chew...or rather I bit off more than I could."

"I don't understand."

"Forget it," I smiled grimly. "He isn't a worry anymore."

On the bed, Karl raised a hand and poked at the area where he had been stabbed, gasping and cursing as his fingers touched the wound. Grimacing, I met his gaze. "Does it hurt much?"

"Only when I laugh," he grimaced, reaching out with a hand and grasping it, I helped him to sit. "You are in no fit state to move?"

"I will be fine," he nodded, his expression grim as he answered my question. "I don't think the blade went in too deep. I am afraid to admit that the shock of his attack and the subsequent pain made me pass out. I can't believe he managed to stab me, the little shit."

Shrugging, I pointed to my left shoulder. "I wouldn't beat yourself up over it, Karl, he stabbed me too."

For a moment he sat there nodding, eyes fixed on my wound then he gave a groan as he tried to rise, finally managing it as I stood and helped him to his feet, the pair off us glancing about.

"Is there any sign of Amber or Andrea?" he asked me then and I winced, guilt coursing through me as I realised that in the stress of Ian's attack, I had forgotten about the women. "No, not yet."

As one we both turned and stared at the open door of the office and beside me Karl gave a sigh, his voice tight with dread. "Shall we?"

I nodded at him, holding to his waist as I helped him move forwards to the door only for him to stop and throw me a grim look. "I still can't believe that Ian actually attacked us. I didn't think he'd have the balls."

The chuckle of grim humour left my mouth before I could stop it then and as I stood shaking my head, amused by his choice of words he raised an eyebrow. "Did I say something funny?"

Shaking my head, I gestured to the open office door and forced the grim smile from my features, trying not to picture the testicle that I had bitten off. "No, Karl, nothing at all."

Chapter Sixty

Moments later any humour that might have been left inside me was rushing out to be replaced with grief as I stood beside Karl in the doorway to the office beyond, both our eyes staring down at the pool of blood which was partially visible past the door itself. Letting out a shaky gasp, I cursed. "Fuck...we were too late."

"It might not be them," Karl stated, eyes still locked to the blood. "Perhaps Ian has killed Oliver Queenheart."

"Then where are Amber and Andrea?"

He shook his head and shrugged, having no answer for my question and gritting my teeth I steadied myself as best as I could and stepped fully into the room, Karl moving with me. For a moment, the pair of us stood staring to the left of the door, our eyes locked to the naked figure upon the desk, then both of us were cursing and turning away from the scene of mutilation. Groaning, his head in his hands, Karl moved over to lean back against the large bookcase which ran along the wall just indie the door while I simply stood there staring down at the floor with tear filled eyes. Then with a grimace, I turned back to stare at the remains of Amber.

The face of the unfortunate young woman was turned towards me, her dead eyes open and accusing as they stared straight ahead, the black lines of her make-up still smudging her cheeks and her mouth frozen in a silent scream. Minutes seemed to drag by as I held her gaze, fully expecting her to blink and awaken just as Karl had done outside but then I lowered my gaze to her body, and I knew that there was no chance that would happen. Despite the face of the young woman appearing to be completely devoid of any type of injury, from the neck down it was a different story. As I stood there, I felt a tear roll down my right cheek as I began to catalogue her wounds, keeping my mind busy to stop from vomiting violently upon the ground. The skin of her throat was badly bruised, purple and red in colour and I grimaced as I saw what looked like thumb prints amid the colouring. Forcing my gaze from the discolouration about her throat I looked lower, wincing as I saw that her small breasts bore signs of biting, the nipple and areola completely missing on the right one. "Bastard" I muttered, my face screwing up in anger as I turned from them, focusing instead on the numerous stab wounds in her stomach.

Letting out a shaky breath I stepped closer to the desk, my eyes moving from one stab wound to another, trying for some reason to count them, cursing in disgust as I discovered that some were so close that they had joined together to create wide slits in her flesh. Gagging as I glimpsed her coiled intestines through one of the wide slits, I closed my eyes and turned my head to the side away from the grisly sight only to curse as I opened them once more to find that I was now staring at her badly bruised and bloody legs. A sob of horror escaped me then as I realised that her thighs were open, legs splayed on the desk as if poor Amber had finally slipped into the welcome embrace of death while he had been raping her and he had simply climbed from her and left them that way. Blinking hard against the tears in my eyes, I lowered them to the ground, wincing once again as I caught sight of the badly broken fingers of her right hand as her arm hung off the table, nails missing from every single one of the digits. Movement behind me in the room had me snapping my head towards it then and I sighed as I saw that Karl had moved to stand alongside me, his voice deep and pained as he spoke. "The poor girl...she must have been in absolute agony until the very end." I grimaced at his words, turning away from the grisly sight of her body upon the table. "And it's all my fault."

He followed me with his head. "And how on Earth did you manage to come to that conclusion Morgan?"

"I let her go off with Ian. Andrea and Amber were basically put into his care by me!"

He shrugged. "That doesn't make it your fault Morgan. If you want to blame anyone for her death blame Ian or Oliver Queenheart...don't start blaming yourself for it."

"Maybe," I told him, my voice grim. "Maybe not." He held my gaze for a moment but didn't try to dissuade me from my thoughts anymore, instead he began to make his way around the back of the desk on which Amber was sprawled. I knew that he had been right in a way.

There was no question that Amber's blood should stain the hands of Ian and Oliver Queenheart but at the same time I couldn't shake the feeling that I should have done more. Perhaps I should have headed for the hospital instead of the tower and the park when I had left the cannibal town or perhaps when I had glimpsed the light shining from the hospital window the night before I should have headed straight there as quickly as I possibly could.

A wave of guilt surged over me as I realised that when I had been looking at the light it had been Ian having his twisted fun with poor Amber. "Fuck it!" I snarled, lashing out with a hand, knocking several books from the bookcase.

"Are you OK?" the concerned voice of Karl dragged my gaze to find him standing behind the desk, his hands filled with the remains of a rabbit costume, the white material stained with a mixture of blood and mud. Realising that he was still waiting for an answer to the question that he had asked me, I nodded. "Yeah, I guess." He winced slightly at my answer, still holding my gaze with his deep brown eyes. Then he nodded down at the material in his hands. "Ian must have found the letter opener in one of the drawers and managed to cut the rabbits suits from his and Ambers bodies."

"Any sign of the keys?" I asked him hopefully.

"No, they are gone. The bottle that I left is still here, but I can't seem to find the ring of keys."

Cursing at their loss, I watched him as he gripped at the side of the rabbit costume he was holding with both hands and draped it across the lower half of Amber's body, before bending and rising again with another torn suit, which he placed over her top half as if he was putting a child to bed. I smiled sadly as he did so, touched by the tenderness that he was showing and then he was sighing again, raising his eyes to meet mine. "She was so young...just a baby really." Wincing at his words, I nodded and sighed. "So, the line of Dodgson is now at an end."

He shook his head back at me. "Not necessarily."

"Meaning?"

He chewed his bottom lip for a moment before answering me. "You know what McKenzie Hatter said about you. We still don't know that Amber was right. What if the memory that she could recall wasn't what she thought it was? She must have been mistaken!"

"I don't know," I shook my head, feeling strange talking about her while she was still laying there on the table with her face turned towards me. "I just don't know."

"But you could be the last descendant of Charles Dodgson," Karl stated, moving back around the desk to stand facing me, his eyes searching my face. "Do you know what that means?"

I shrugged. "No, what?"

He grimaced. "The rest of us are here for minor reasons; he fears me usurping him, Craig and Tori were digging dirt on him, Ian was a contract hit and Amber was a mystery. You and Andrea, that's different...you mean something to him. She killed his wife, albeit unintentionally, and you are the last surviving descendant of the one person to escape New London!"

"Oh my God." I paled, my heart lurching in my chest and before me the American nodded. "Exactly...he will want to make you suffer."

I shook my head, features grim as I stepped towards the door, "No, it's not that"

He raised an eyebrow, "What then?"

The words caught in my throat as I uttered them, emotion getting the better of me. "Where the fuck is Andrea?"

Chapter Sixty-One

"Morgan!" Karl called after me, but I was already back out of the office door and heading across the large open hall with the hospital beds, my head banging with the stress of the situation. Behind me the footfalls of my companion sounded, and I knew without looking that he too had left the office and had come after me. Dragging open the squeaking door that led to the entrance foyer, I stepped through and then turned and exited the hospital through the main door. Outside the sky was gloomier than when we had entered, the suns hanging much lower than they had been earlier, and I grimaced as I realised that nightfall wasn't very far away.

I jumped as the door behind me banged suddenly and then I was turning and staring back at Karl as he stood facing me, one hand clutched to the wound in his chest where he had been stabbed. Grimacing, I stood staring at the blood that was running through his fingers and then I met his eyes with concern. "Are you OK?"

"I'll be fine," he told me with a weak smile. "I think rushing after you has re-opened the injury."

I nodded, accepting the chastisement. "Sorry."

"No," he shook his head, sweat beading upon his brow as he faced me. "Don't apologise...you are right, we need to find Andrea. But where would she be?"

"Damn," I shook my head, not really having any idea where I had been running off to. "I haven't got a clue."

Karl nodded back at me, leaning heavily back against the wall beside the door as he winced in pain again. Shaking my head, I stood there feeling helpless as I realised that he was far more injured than he had been letting on.

"Let me take a look at the wound," I told him, starting to step forwards and he gave a chuckle. "Can you remember being a doctor or a nurse?"

"No."

He chuckled again, shaking his head. "Then looking at my wound will do nothing but worry us both. We will let Andrea look at it when we find her Morgan."

"Are you sure?"

He nodded. "Yes. Now let's concentrate on Andrea. Do you think she is still alive?"

Wincing as the thought of the woman that I had grown close to having suffered the same fate as

Amber entered my head, I nodded, trying to sound confident. "Yeah."

He smiled at me. "So do I. Which means she escaped Ian"

"Maybe not," I winced. "Maybe he hid her"

"OK," Karl nodded. "Well, he's run off, maybe he went back to her...did you see where he ran?"

"No," I admitted but then I gestured to the ground and the trail of blood that led away from the hospital door. "But I think we should be able to find him."

Karl's eyes widened as he followed the gesture and saw the fresh blood on the dead grass, then he looked back at me. "What did you do to him?"

"I stopped him killing me," I stated, reluctant to reveal the extent of what I had done to Ian.

"Well, it worked whatever you did. Like I said, I think that if she is still alive then he would have headed off to where she was being held. So, we follow the blood trail agreed?"

I nodded at him, already beginning to move away from the front of the hospital, my eyes upon the ground and with a groan Karl pushed himself away from the wall and began to follow me, the pain that he was in becoming more and more evident as time went by. Pausing I turned to look back at him in concern and he forced a weary smile. "Go on Morgan, the sooner we find Ian the sooner we find Andrea. Then we can face Queenheart."

Touched by his support, I nodded, turning back to the front once again and glancing down at the trail of blood as it ran off before me, rounding the corner of one of the smaller buildings. Turning back to nod at Karl, I gestured for him to continue following me. "This way."

He nodded, waving a hand for me to go on and turning back around I rushed ahead and rounded the building, coming to a halt as I saw the bloody naked body which was lying face down beside a door set into the wall. Grimacing, I took a step closer, a snarl creeping onto my features as I saw the familiar face of Ian turned sideways, his right hand up to the wrist in the ground to the right of the door, looking for all the world like he had died whilst trying to dig something out from beneath the dead grass. Letting out a shaky breath I knelt beside him, my hands reaching out to take hold of the bare skin of his torso, my stomach turning as my fingers slid in the sweat and blood upon his skin and then I was heaving with my arms, rolling him over to lie upon his back. Shaking my head, I stayed knelt where I was, my eyes locked to his effeminate face, wondering just how a person that looked so innocent could be such a monster. Then taking another deep breath I turned my gaze to the injury that I had caused him not that long ago, my eyes widening as I saw his one remaining testicle hanging there shrivelled beneath the gory stump of his penis, like some blood covered walnut. Spitting on the ground once more as the memory of having my mouth wrapped about his groin returned to me in a rush, I grimaced and looked back at his face. "Surprise" he growled at me, his bright blue eyes wide open, his right hand suddenly flashing up towards me, the knuckles striking me hard in the centre of my throat. Gasping, choking as pain flared through my neck I fell to my back, both hands reaching for my throat as I fought to breathe. Then I was staring up at the grim-faced form of Ian Towel as he staggered to his feet and dropped astride my stomach, the jolt of the impact making me wheeze even more and him cry out in agony from where I had bitten him. Desperately I released my throat, raising my hands to try and push the enraged maniac from atop me only to grunt as he batted them aside with ease and hammered a series of punches into my unprotected face. Crying out in shock, still struggling to breath past the pain in my throat, I raised my hands once more, futilely trying to protect my face as the voice of the enraged man washed over me. "You have ruined me...ruined me! How can I ever hurt bitches in the way they deserve now you have taken away my power...!"

His words ended abruptly then and as his blows ceased raining down on my face I stared up through my arms. I nearly cried out in relief as I saw the familiar figure of Karl standing behind Ian Towel, one arm wrapped about his throat and the other grasping at a handful of the naked man's curly blonde hair tilting his head back. "Get the fuck off me old man!" the serial killer choked, reaching up with his hands only to curse as I reached out and grabbed his wrists, pinning his arms before him. Then I watched in surprise as the face of Karl Mackal split into a cold snarl as he removed his arm from Ian's throat, the fingers of that hand reaching to the elasticated sleeve of his other arm. "Did you think you could stab me and not pay the price?"

Before Ian could answer, the black man raised the small bottle that he had taken from the table so long ago to the lips of the naked serial killer, pouring its contents inside his mouth. "Here, have a drink on me."

Atop me, the naked man began to writhe and squirm, fighting to get away and then as Karl released his hold on his hair and stepped back I in turn let go of his arms. With an agonised scream the serial killer rose to his feet, shaking his head like a man possessed as smoke began to pour from his mouth. Cursing, unable to believe what I was seeing I crawled backwards away from Ian, forcing myself to rise, my eyes never leaving the man before me. His eyes were wide now, blinking hard as the smoke from his mouth began to blow into them and then he was screaming even louder as one eye seemed to blacken and bubble as I watched, my stomach lurching in disgust as I recalled that the bottle had held acid. By now Ian was in a bad way, his fingers clawing at his throat as black sores began to appear on the flesh there, more of the acidic smoke exiting through the holes. I gagged as his fingernails suddenly to unsheathe a whole chunk of skin from his throat exposing the blistered and blackened muscle beneath and then his right eye seemed to fold in upon itself, a torrent of black goo exiting the badly blistered socket and running down his cheek, burning the skin beneath. He turned to me then, his one remaining eye staring out at me from the ruin of his blistered features, hands still tearing at his visibly smoking and bleeding throat and for a moment I felt physically sick at the terror within that single orb. But then I was picturing poor Amber as I had seen her upon the desk in Queenheart's office, her body bitten, stabbed and violated beyond description. Blinking back the tears that the memory provoked I watched as before me Ian raised the fingers of his right hand in my direction, his blackened lips moving in a silent plea and I shook my head. "Fuck you, this is for Amber and Craig."

Then he was falling backwards to the grass behind him to lie still, his one eye staring up at the grey sky above. Grimacing, one hand rising to rub at my throat and face where he had punched me, I stared at Ian's body, wishing that he had suffered more before he had died.

"Well, look what we have here," Karl stated, drawing my gaze to find him crouching down beside the door in the wall, his right hand in the hole where Ian's had been. Then he was rising and facing me, the brass ring that Andrea had left upon Oliver Queenheart's desk in his hand, five onyx black keys hanging down from it. Frowning, I moved to his side, staring first at the keys then him. "Why hide the keys here?"

The words had barely left my lips before we both turned to face the door, nodding in realisation and Karl stepped forwards and inserting one into the lock. As before, the key seemed to turn to black flakes and drift to the ground the moment that the lock clicked, and the door swung open wide revealing the interior of the small building. But me and Karl were no longer studying the key. We were too busy looking with relief at Andrea as she lay just inside the door, tied up in her rabbit suit.

Chapter Sixty-Two

"I can't believe he is actually dead," Andrea shook her head, repeating the words that she had already uttered half a dozen times since we had untied the rope securing her wrists and ankles, freeing her from the dark room in which Ian had left her bound, awaiting his return.

"Well, you don't have to worry anymore, he is gone, and he isn't coming back," I told her, the truth of those words making me smile broadly.

"Thank you" she smiled, eyes locked to mine and my heart raced as I saw the emotion in them. Blushing I shrugged. "Hey, it was Karl who took him out not me. I was getting my arse kicked till he saved me"

She nodded back at me, her bottom lip catching between her teeth and I was suddenly filled with the urge to embrace and kiss her, to feel her body against mine. Instead, I stopped walking across the sea of dead grass and stood smiling at her, genuinely overjoyed to find that she was still alive, believing after what had happened to Amber that she had suffered the same fate or worse. "I'm just glad you are safe."

Ahead of us Karl turned from where he was walking towards the dark shape of the cathedral atop the hillside and regarded us with grim amusement. "I am as pleased as you that this monster is dead, and I hate to be a damp squib, but we should save the hugs and kisses until we reach somewhere safer than this."

I nodded back at him, knowing that he was off course right and throwing Andrea a smile I began to walk once again, the bespectacled woman joining me. Sighing heavily as we strode ever onwards, I cast my thoughts back to what had happened since we had discovered Andrea locked up in the small building. Upon releasing Andrea from her bonds, we had spent several minutes checking that she was uninjured before Karl had strode away from the building, gesturing for us to follow him, the key ring clutched tightly in his hand. Shaking my head, I had argued with him that we needed to all get inside the building and rest for the night, to gather our wits and our strength before we went looking for Oliver Queenheart and the mirrors, that we were relatively safe now after all what with the Dumbdee twins and Ian all dead only for him to shake his head in reply. "What about the shadow creatures? OK I understand you managed to fight them off while you were out in the open with a fire to use as a weapon but how will you fight them off if they enter the building?"

"And I can't stay in that building again," Andrea had sealed the deal, shaking her head as she had faced me with tears in her eyes. "I can't do it Morgan...we should head for someplace else." Reluctantly I had agreed and then the three of us had set off across the dead grass towards the cathedral on the hill, slowly making our way through the growing night to where we were now walking through the darkness under the faint glow of the crimson moon.

According to Andrea: her, Ian and Amber had been hurriedly heading towards the tower where I had told him to take them when he had suddenly let out a curse and told them all to get down upon the ground quickly. Terrified they had done as he had requested and then they had all crouched low atop a small rise in the dead grass staring down at the large park which was spread out before them around the base of the large white tower. For some time, none of them had spoken and then Ian had thrust out a finger, claiming that he had seen the Dumbdee twins, lurking amongst the bushes. The decision had been taken by Ian then that the best plan was for them to head towards the hospital in the centre of the dead grass and hide out there until the rest of us found them. Andrea had shaken her head at the idea, reminding him that when she, me, Karl and Tori had been there we had encountered shadow creatures only for the effeminate young man to argue that they were all dead, killed by me in the cannibal town, Amber enthusiastically agreeing with the young man. And so just like I had been outvoted in heading for the cathedral tonight, she had been outvoted in heading for the hospital, the three of them making their way east. Everything had been going fine until they had entered the hospital, Ian groaning and dropping to one knee, clutching at his chest with a hand and Andrea had rushed to his side in concern. She had seen the faint smile on his lips as he had risen then, hammering a punch underneath her chin, knocking her unconscious. Andrea had winced, shaking her head and wiping tears from her eyes as she had gone on to tell how she had awoken sometime later in the small building with her hands and feet tied together with rope that Ian had apparently found there. He had been naked by then and laughing as he had cut the rabbit costume from a hysterical Amber with a small knife before dragging the younger woman towards the building's single door by the hair. Ian had paused then, turning to sneer back at the captive Andrea. "I'll be back to have my fun with you later bitch, get some rest while you can."

The next thing she had heard was the sound of fighting outside the building and she had lain there in terror, hoping against hope that it was the right people who opened the door to her. Done with her story, her questions had begun.

How had we known that Ian was a danger?

How had I managed to escape the cannibals?

Where was Tori?

Was Amber OK?

Had we saved her too?

One by one we had answered her questions and she had listened in shock to my words as she walked beside me. The black man had watched me as I told her what she wanted to know, perhaps thinking I would reveal how he had been reluctant to go looking for her, but I kept quiet, figuring that it wasn't something that she needed to know. In my mind he had more than made up for his previously unsympathetic attitude both with his confession about his dying wife and by his actions. Tears had filled her eyes as she had learned the details of the deaths of Craig, Tori and Amber, and for some time she had fallen into silence beside me as we walked. Feeling depressed with the talk of those that we had lost, I had changed the subject telling her how McKenzie seemed to think I was the descendant of Charles Dodgson, aware of Karl casting me a glance as I had done so.

"Do you think this McKenzie was right?" Andrea had asked me, and I had shrugged in reply.

"I have no idea...he seemed convinced."

We had lapsed into silence then until she had repeated her relief that the maniac that had killed poor Amber was dead.

Now we were heading to find our freedom.

I fixed my eyes to the large shape of the cathedral that was rising rapidly on the horizon before us, the sheer size of it resembling a castle rather than a house of God but then in this realm nothing was as it should be. It was a lesson I was learning fast. But then I was also learning just who was important. Throwing Andrea, a smile as she walked along beside me in the night, I reached out and took her hand in mine. Then together we were quickening our pace as we followed Karl Mackal ever closer to our destination.

Chapter Sixty-Three

Less than an hour later and the three of us were huddled together at the bottom of a high narrow set of stone steps that climbed the Eastern face of the hill, each of us staring up at the colossal cathedral high above. Unsure about taking the direct route to the top of the hill, fearing an ambush should we take that route the three of us had at first some distance to the right of the steps and tried to climb the grassy incline. Each time we had only made it roughly fifteen metres from the ground before our boots had slid upon the grass and we had fallen to our faces and slid back down. Gritting my teeth, realising that we had no other choice but to take the stone steps to the top if we wanted to climb the hill and enter the cathedral, I began to move up them, Andrea and Karl at my back. For some time, I climbed in silence, eyes fixed to the steps before me and then I realised that I was halfway up them I paused and turned my face to glance over my shoulder at the soft glow on the horizon, smiling as I realised that dawn was not far away now. With its arrival, the twin suns would begin their climb into the sky once again, illuminating all New London for us to see, thereby eliminating the immediate threat of an attack by the carnivorous shadow creatures. "It's quite a view isn't it?" the deep voice of Karl had me lowering my gaze to meet his as he stood behind Andrea on the steps, some ten feet below me and I nodded, casting another look about before turning back to meet the brown eyes of my companion once again as I smiled. Though it was not as magnificent as the view that I had been afforded from the top of the Tower of Tsugoth, I could see all the way to the asylum in the north, the cannibal town in the north east and to the hospital in the centre of the whole area. "Yeah, yeah it is."

Smiling, Andrea moved to the step below me, her eyes turning to gaze out across the land as the first rays of sunlight began to spread across the sea of dead grass like ghostly golden fingers. "Oh no" the tone of her voice, made grimmer by her Midlands accent had me snapping my head back in the direction she was facing, my eyes following her outstretched arm. "Who is that?" For a moment I stood staring out across the land, trying to figure out just what she was talking about but then my eyes fell upon the person she was indicating, and I cursed in

dread, my stomach lurching. "Oh, fuck me no!"
"Who the Hell is that enormous man?" Karl
Mackal had moved up the stone steps and edged
past me to stand staring in the same direction
that me and Andrea were, his features grim.
For a moment I kept silent, my eyes still locked
to the figure that was approaching slowly from
the north east, their form large and their walk
easily recognisable even though they were still
far in the distance. Then I shook my head and
turned to smile grimly at Karl. "That? That's
Bert...Bert the cannibal..."

Chapter Sixty-Four

"What is he doing heading this way?" Andrea asked, voice thick with fear as she turned to me. "He must be coming for me," I muttered, grimacing as the words left my mouth, hating the way the mere sight of the huge one-eyed and one-handed man made my stomach lurch with dread. If I was right, then that meant that he had followed me all the way from the cannibal town in the north east with the intention of killing me. Letting out a shaky breath, I gestured to the steps ahead of us. "We need to get moving and inside the cathedral."

Without another word of encouragement, my pair of companions were heading up the stone steps, leaving me standing staring out across the sea of dead grass at the small figure of the cannibal. Was he really coming here to finish what he had started back in the town square? I was genuinely surprised to find that he had been brave enough to venture from the safety of the town he ruled with an iron fist...and spike. Then I winced as a thought occurred to me. Perhaps he wasn't the ruler of the town now. Had surviving the fight with him made his fellow cannibals view him with doubt?

Had he been found wanting?

The only reason I was alive now was because the clouds had provided enough cover for the shadow creatures to attack in the daytime.

Had the crazed town folk seen this as some omen against Bert, an omen enforced when he had failed to capture and kill me later that same day in the streets. Had he been cast out?

Agreed he was without question the toughest and meanest of the cannibals that I had seen within the town but that didn't mean anything. Nodding slowly to myself, certain that I was thinking along the right tracks, I was about to turn and follow my companions up the steps when I paused and grimaced. Had the figure out in the distance stopped walking? Were they now staring back up at me as I watched them?

There was no doubt that if I could see him then he could see us climbing the steps.

But did he realise it was me he was staring at?

A shudder ran through me as I imagined the hated fuelled words emerging from the lips of the cannibal as he stared back up at me and then I was shaking my head and turning to find that Andrea and Karl were almost at the top of the stone steps. Cursing, forcing myself to hurry,

I clambered up after them, eventually reaching the top in a state of complete exhaustion and dropping into a crouch, my head down.

"Are you OK?" Andrea asked, her voice concerned and forcing a weary smile I rose.

"Just a little winded...I'll be fine in a minute."

As she nodded back at me, I turned and surveyed our surroundings, discovering that we were stood upon a plateau covered in what appeared to be stone slabs. They stretched away around the sides of the cathedral in both directions and before us another five stone steps led to the arched door of the building. Karl was already at the top of the steps, hands resting upon the surface of the door that hung there, his face turned to the side as if he were trying to listen for any sounds that were coming from within, but I doubted he would hear anything through the thick looking wood.

He turned towards me then as if sensing my eyes upon him and he straightened and gestured to the door behind him. "It sounds quiet inside, but I doubt it is safe. There is every chance that Oliver Queenheart is inside."

"And if he is?" I asked, suddenly curious as to what we were going to do when faced with the man that had brought the seven of us here against our will. "What do we do then?"

Karl laughed bitterly. "Oh, do not worry yourself about that Morgan. I intend to take control of this land for Janet, and I have something up my sleeve which will ensure that Queenheart gives it to me without a fight."

I nodded, frowning in surprise. "You do? What?"

He shook his head. "The less you know the safer you are Morgan...these are dangerous people."

I was about to snap that I wasn't stupid.

That I knew exactly what sort of deranged maniacs we were dealing with when suddenly Andrea was gasping in shock, her eyes wide as she back towards the stone steps where Karl was stood staring back at me. "Oh my God, the cannibal is still coming...we have to hide."

Nodding, I sent her what I hoped was a confident smile and then looked back at Karl. "Is the door locked?"

He held my gaze for a fraction of a moment longer than was necessary and then he was turning and trying the large black metal handle upon the door, his efforts rewarded with a dull, spine-shilling creak as it opened wide before us. Moving to stand alongside Karl, Andrea once more taking hold of my hand nearest her, I stood and stared in a mixture of awe and disbelief at the interior of the building that we could see through the open door. For a moment I let my eyes travel over the rows of wooden pews, the huge marble columns and the bright colours of the stained-glass windows high upon the walls. Then I was grimacing as I saw the figure standing in the raised wooden pulpit to the right of the front of the pews, his body dressed in the robes of a priest and his head as bald as a billiard ball. In shock, I cast quick glances at my two companions, seeing at once from the expressions upon their faces that I wasn't seeing things. I raised an eyebrow, even more stunned as the deep booming voice of the priest in the distance called out to us, the tone friendly and warm. "Come in my children, you are just in time to join us for mass."

Chapter Sixty-Five

"Well?" the voice of the priest boomed out once more when after nearly a minute had passed since his invitation and not one of us had moved. "Don't stand on ceremony, your kind are always welcome in the house of Tsugoth, please, come in and be seated."

"What do we do?" Andrea asked, casting glances between me and Karl. "Do we go inside?"

"It could be a trap," I muttered, grimacing.

"Well, our choices are few," Karl stated shrugging as he met the gaze of each of us in turn. "We either stay here and wait for this cannibal to catch up to us or we enter the church as we have been invited to do."

"But what if Morgan was right?" Andrea asked him, fear in her voice. "What if it is a trap?"

Karl shrugged and turned, entering the open doorway as he spoke. "Well, there is only one way to find out."

Stunned, I stood beside Andrea, still holding to her hand as I watched Karl stride forwards and then stop at the start of the centre aisle between the rows of pews and shaking my head, I entered the cathedral leading Andrea with me. The moment that we were inside the huge building, I released my hold on her and turned, gripping to the huge wooden door as I closed it behind us, calling out to Karl. "Quickly, give me the keys! We need to lock this!"

For a fraction of a second, he stood watching me as I leaned with my back to the wooden door, a strange expression upon his features and then he tossed me the brass ring of keys. "Do you have to lock it? I didn't want them wasted, there are only four left."

I caught them with a snatch of my right hand and then turned, dropping to a crouch as I inserted one of the onyx black keys into the lock, watching as it clicked and then crumbled to black flakes and then dust. Rising once more I threw Karl the keys back. "Now there are three."

He smiled as he caught them and nodded back at me. "Very well."

"Is there some problem I can help you with?"

We all jumped and turned as the voice of the priest sounded much closer than before, and I raised an eyebrow as I found him standing only ten feet away from us down the central aisle, his hands clasped together before him, his form lean and tall. "Is all well?"

I don't know what I had been expecting when I had imagined the tortured figure of Father Archibald Hare roaming his cathedral howling with insanity but the calm, rational man standing there before me and my friends was very much not it. He caught me staring at him then and smiled pleasantly. "Is there something with which you require my assistance, or can I begin the service?"

Unsure what to say, I nodded at him and he smiled again, stepping past me and moving towards the large wooden door that I had just locked, a hand pulling back upon it only to frown as he realised that it wouldn't open.

I flinched as he turned back to face us, the dark look upon his face promising us nothing but trouble. "What is the meaning off this? You have locked the door?"

"Stay calm big guy," I told him, taking a step back, Andrea moving along with me, but Karl held the angry gaze of the priest, unconcerned. "My companion's feels that we had no choice but to lock the door, Father...we are being pursued...we came here seeking sanctuary."

"Sanctuary?" the voice of the priest was barely audible as he frowned back at the black man, his eyes seeming to stare into the past. "You came here for sanctuary?"

"Of course," Karl smiled, nodding as he spoke, one hand reaching out to rest upon the priest's shoulder, "Isn't that what churches provide, help for those in need?"

As if in a daze, the priest met the eyes of Karl and nodded, although he sounded unsure. "Yes."

"Well, we need such help Father, my two friends and I are being pursued by a man who means to harm us. We need your protection and that of the mighty Tsugoth. We have suffered losses."

"Losses?" the priest tilted his head to one side, an eyebrow rising towards the smooth dome of his bald head. "Speak of these losses my child."

Karl nodded, turning his gaze upon me and Andrea as we stood watching in silence and I shrugged, unsure what game the occultist was playing with the clearly disturbed priest but not wanting to get involved lest I ruin the scam that my companion was running. Before me, Karl turned back to the priest and suddenly seemed to slump at the shoulders, his voice growing weary as he spoke. "Father my companions and I are followers of Tsugoth, sent by the Almighty to bring his faith to these unclean lands, to spread His holy gospel amongst the cannibals in the north-east. But on our journey to you we have been attacked and harmed, hunted down by all manner of enemies...we seek your assistance, in our hour of need would you turn your back on the servitors of the God you have come to love?"

Standing with his back to the door of the church, Father Archibald Hare suddenly seemed unable to speak, his lips moving silently for what seemed an eternity until he shook his head. "He sent you...truthfully?"

"Indeed," Karl nodded, holding the others gaze.

"Is this to test my faith?"

"Does it need testing?" Karl asked, the question rhetorical. "Mighty Tsugoth knows of all his followers that you are the most devout...the most loyal. That is why he has sent us to you in his most pure form."

Stood beside Andrea, I watched in fascination as the bald priest raised his gaze from us to stare up at the stained-glass windows that ran along the top of the walls either side of the cathedral. Frowning, my eyes narrowing in curiosity as instead of the usual biblical images one would expect to find I discovered that every one of the panes of coloured glass depicted scenes involving the large white rabbit creature that I had seen upon the stone table mosaic; the deity which we in our white rabbit costumes resembled an incredible amount. Suddenly realising the game that Karl was playing I lowered my gaze once again to find that the priest was now regarding us with bright eyes and a strange smile upon his thin features. "Praise Tsugoth," the voice of the priest when he spoke was full of reverence and despite myself, I felt sick inside for toying with the poor deluded man's faith as he continued, stepping away from the door and striding purposefully back towards the front of the cathedral. "Praise be on high...for his word is law."

Feeling nauseous, the realisation that we were in effect playing catch with a bomb, washing over me, I grimaced and followed Karl and Andrea as they made their way down to the front of the cathedral and stopped before the priest, Karl addressing the euphoric man. "Do you think you can help us Father?"

He nodded; eyes bright with happiness as he smiled back at us. "Of course, it is my duty to serve after all."

With that he was turning away from us once again and heading back towards the base of the pulpit that he had been standing upon when we had opened the door, disappearing behind its bulk. Suddenly there was the sound of scuffling and grunting and taking a step back, leading a scared looking Andrea with me, I cast Karl a grim look. "What's going on?"

"Father?" the American called out, taking a step towards the front of the cathedral, his head angling as he tried to see behind the pulpit. "Is everything OK?"

I cursed as the tall, bald headed priest reappeared, my eyes widening as I saw the hatchet in his left hand and then my stomach was lurching as I saw the fingers of his right hand knotted in the hair off a familiar figure. With a broad grin upon his features, Father Archibald Hare dragged his prisoner towards the front of the cathedral, and I shook my head in disbelief, staring in shock at the unfortunate man's hands tied before him and his purple suit dirty, torn and bloodied. With a dry chuckle, the priest threw the unfortunate man down hard upon the ground and raised his eyes to stare at us, the mania evident for us all to see. "This betrayer sought to leave these lands...before I help you, he must pay"

As I stood looking down at the man in disbelief, McKenzie Hatter raised his face from where he lay sprawled before his former friend, his nose swollen and bruised, and his lips cracked and bloody. For a fraction of a second he stared up at us in confusion and then he was crying out, his voice filled with hope. "Karl...Morgan...you came to save me!"

For a moment, the priest stood staring down at the wretched figure by his feet and then he was raising his head to stare with undisguised hatred and anger at the three of us as we stood before him, his voice little more than a guttural snarl. "Base deceivers!"

"Hey, come on now," Karl raised his hands and took a step back towards where me and Andrea were stood, the confidence gone from his voice. "Deceitful wretch!" the priest rushed forwards, his long legs covering the ground between him and Karl in seconds and then he was swinging the hatchet towards our companion, roaring in rage as he did so. I cried out, the sound echoed by Andrea as we feared the worst only for the blunt side of the weapon to strike Karl across the face instead of the blade edge, sparing his life but lifting from his feet to crash sideways into the long wooden pew to his left. With a growl, the priest turned towards his fallen prey, adjusting his hold on the weapon to make the blade ready to use for its intended purpose and shaking my head I took a step forwards, shouting at the bald man. "Leave him alone!" The tall priest seemed to freeze on the spot at the sound of my voice and then he turned slowly towards me, his thin face grim. "Are you so eager to die first?"

Realising the danger that I had just put myself in but not being willing to stand by and see Karl butchered before me, I was about to curse in dread when with a crash the door behind us smashed open. Heart skipping a beat, Andrea gasping and clinging to my rabbit costume, I spun to find the familiar grim figure of Bert the cannibal standing in the open doorway, the magical lock having been no problem for his brute strength. For a moment he was silent as he stood there staring back at us and then he pointed his rusty spike in our direction. "Ya runnin' days is over...it's time to die rabbits!"

Chapter Sixty-Six

Despite the absence of my memories, I knew that I had heard the phrase between the devil and the deep blue sea many times in my life and I even had the feeling that I had believed myself to have been in such a situation before. But it wasn't until I was standing there beside Andrea in that bizarre cathedral with a raging priest with a hatchet on one side of me and a huge, maniacal cannibal with one eye and a spike for a hand on my other side, that I realised how it felt. Gritting my teeth, I snapped my gaze between them, desperately trying to come up with a way to escape. Frowning I cast a glance beyond the tall thin figure of Father Archibald Hare, dismissing that route as a means of possible escape. Firstly, I had no idea what lay back there and secondly if there was no other route from the cathedral, we would end up trapped and thus easy prey. Taking a deep breath, I cast a look back at Bert, cringing as I found him several steps closer towards us down the central aisle between the rows of pews, his bulky form heaving as he took ragged, anger fuelled breaths. Without a question of a doubt, I knew that I could skirt around him and out of the front of the cathedral, Andrea too.

But that left another dilemma.

Karl was still down and out of sight where he had been knocked amongst the pews on the left side of the huge room. If me and Andrea were to turn and flee from the insane men and the cathedral it would mean leaving Karl behind.

Karl *and* McKenzie Hatter.

Gritting my teeth, I turned my face towards where the silver haired man was now kneeling at the front of the cathedral, my emotions regarding him conflicted. After all, hadn't he turned his back on me and Karl and left us to the less than tender mercies of the Dumbdee twins back outside the Tower of Tsugoth?

He had run and left us to die.

Could I leave him to the same fate?

I had barely considered it when the furious voice of Father Hare roared out in anger, and I spun to face him fully expecting to find the enraged priest rushing me, hatchet raised. Instead, I found him standing staring at the newcomer to his cathedral, his face nearly crimson with anger as he pointed a finger at

Bert. "You would dare violate the home of Tsugoth foul creature!"

"Fuck you!" the cannibal snarled, straightening to his full height, easily as tall as the priest but far broader. Eyes wide as I realised that the two threats to my safety had miraculously turned upon each other, I gripped tight to the hand of Andrea and manoeuvred her back into one of the rows of pews behind us, making sure not to make any noise which might drag their attention back towards us. In no time at all, we were at the end of the row, standing side by side as the two big men stared and snarled at each other, one wielding his spike and the other his hatchet. This time though there was at least twenty feet of wooden pews between us and them providing an obstacle that meant should either of them change their mind and instead try and reach us we would have plenty of time to run in the other direction. My heart lurched as I saw the pained features of Karl suddenly rise above the top of the wooden pew he had fallen behind, the white ears of his rabbit costume broken and bent as he stared at the two men standing in the centre aisle. Beside me, Andrea stiffened and gasped and I winced, praying that Karl would keep still before either Father Archibald Hare or Bert noticed him.

I needn't have worried.

As if on some unspoken signal the two tall men suddenly gave identical roars of anger and charged at each other like ancient berserkers on a battlefield, both their faces twisted in hatred, both raising their weapons. For a fraction of a moment, I paused to watch as they collided heavily, the snarls of hatred changing to curses of pain and then I was charging to my left, dragging Andrea with me and gesturing for the now standing Karl to head towards the front of the cathedral and meet us. The three of us reached it at roughly the same time and I reached out with a hand, grasping at the right shoulder of Karl as I grimaced at the bloody gash on his left temple. "Are you OK?"

He nodded, the pain behind his brown eyes telling a different story but there was no time for hugs and kisses. Flinching as a roar of pain sounded further back down the cathedral towards the door, I turned my head, watching in grim fascination as Father Hare ducked a wild sweep from the rusty spike of the cannibal and chopped his hatchet into the man's shoulder.

"Where's McKenzie Hatter?" the grim voice of Karl snatched my attention and I cursed, snapping my head back to where he was gesturing only to find that the man was gone. "Bastard," I snarled, shaking my head as I recalled how moments ago, I had been telling myself that I couldn't just leave him behind. Yet he had deserted us yet again.

"What the Hell was that?" Andrea suddenly turned her head to the side, staring in the direction of the pulpit that Father Hare had dragged McKenzie from behind earlier. "What was that noise?"

"I don't hear..." I began, straining to listen over the sounds of the two behemoths fighting close by but Karl raised the blade of a hand, signalling for me to be quiet. Grimacing I was about to snap an angry retort when the sound of something breaking came from the direction that Andrea had indicated, followed by the barely audible wail of a man howling in distress and rage. Pausing only long enough to cast each other confused glances, the three of us surged towards the side of the pulpit and the sounds. We reached it in seconds, Karl reaching out a hand to drag back the heavy crimson curtain which was hanging beside the steps that led the way to the pulpit platform above, revealing a series of wooden steps leading down into the depths beneath the cathedral. In seconds I was stepping past the curtain, my footsteps loud as I hurried down the steps beyond, my voice angry as I called out. "McKenzie...where are you?"

For a moment there was no reply, followed by a frightened squeak from somewhere below. "I am here, my friend"

Resisting the urge to ask where here was, I continued down the stairs, the footfalls of Karl and Andrea letting me know that my companions were hot on my heels. Then suddenly the stairs ended, and I found myself standing in a large square room, the area filled to overflowing with piles upon piles of books and heavy leatherbound tomes, piles of bound parchment resting here and there. And amid it all stood McKenzie Hatter. As my companions spread about me at the base of the stairs, I pointed at the small, wiry man in the dirty purple suit. "What the fuck are you doing?"

He flinched at my question, shaking his head as he took a step backwards, his open hands raising before him, a smile creeping onto his features. "Nothing...trust me."

"Trust you?" Karl snarled, taking a step towards him, his voice bubbling with anger. "Trust you...why should we?"

The grey-haired man forced a smile. "Please...I just want to go home...I just want to be free of this place!"

I cringed as another roar of anger echoed down the wooden stairwell to us from the fight above and then I was frowning at McKenzie, realising what he was getting at. "Wait...you are looking for Father Hare's mirror..."

"It has to be here somewhere," the insane man gave a nervous chuckle, nodding at me. "If I can find it...if we can find it then we can take turns leaving here with it."

"Not me," Karl shook his head, a grimace creeping onto his features. "I intend to see this through to the end."

"Me too," I muttered, feeling sick as the words left my mouth, astonished to find that I meant them. "I need to make Oliver Queenheart pay for what he has done here."

"Fine...fine," McKenzie nodded, grinning now as he approached us. "You two stay here and do what you feel you must...but we can still leave"

"We?" I raised an eyebrow, "We?"

"Yes," McKenzie nodded, gesturing towards Andrea. "If you two wish to take on Oliver then that is your choice, but you have to allow me and this young lady to leave!"

I glanced at Andrea then, wincing as I saw the excited look upon her face and the hope in her eyes behind her glasses. It was evident that she wanted to go, and it would be wrong of me to attempt to stop her from doing so. Letting out a sigh, I nodded at her, smiling sadly. "If you want to go then that's your choice."

"Will we find each other in the real world?" she asked, her voice tinged with regret, "Is this goodbye?"

"Is it?" I asked McKenzie, turning around to find him already beginning to root through the various piles of books stacked against a wall. He paused at the sound of my voice and looked back over a shoulder, shaking his head. "What? No, of course not...now help me look before we are joined by one of the maniacs from above, quickly now!"

Throwing him a look of irritation, I nodded and moved to the nearest pile to me, joining Andrea as she began to search for the mirror while Karl shook his head and moved away to stand at the foot of the stairwell. For a moment I fought the urge to demand that he help us search but then I bit my lip and forced myself to concentrate on the task at hand. I had already begun to learn that Karl was a driven man and he sure as Hell had a valid reason for doing so. So instead, I held my tongue and continued rummaging through the books on the pile before me, casting each one aside as soon as I realised that there was no mirror hidden within it, cursing as above us in the cathedral the grunts and curses of the two combatants continued to sound out.

"Oh my God!"

I spun towards the Andrea as she gasped, my eyes widening as I saw her standing there with an old-fashioned silver mirror on a handle. Shaking my head, I moved over to her side. "You found it...you can escape."

"Wait!" McKenzie Hatter was suddenly at my elbow, his expression one of complete horror as he reached out to snatch the mirror from

Andrea, only to curse as I stepped between them and pushed him away from her.

"What the fucking hell are you doing?" I snapped at him angrily. "What's the big hurry?"

"What's this about," Karl was now facing us once again, brow furrowed as he stared at McKenzie. The purple clad man gave a humourless laugh, shaking his head, "I want to go home. That's what is up with me, fool...I want to go home!"

"And you can once Andrea has gone first," I stated, drawing his gaze. "First she goes then it's your turn!"

Before me, his face seemed to crumple with sadness and then he was trying to get past me towards her once again, his hands grasping for the silver mirror that she was holding and again I pushed him back away, this time knocking him back to fall heavily to the ground.

"Wait!" I tensed as a hand gripped at my arm then and I turned, surprised to find Andrea standing there, concern upon her attractive features. "It's OK, let him go first!"

Instantly McKenzie was back on his feet, his face a mask of joy as he placed his hands together and bobbed his head up and down before Andrea. "Bless you my dear, such a wise young woman...after all it will be safer for you if I go first in case the mirror malfunctions!"

With that he stepped forwards, extending a hand towards Andrea as she began to offer him the mirror, me watching helpless at her side.

"Wait," Karl muttered suddenly, stepping forwards and shaking his head. "It's a trick. Don't give him the mirror!"

"A trick?" McKenzie was aghast as he stepped to the side and stared at Karl. "How dare you!"

"What are you talking about?" I asked my companion, taking a step between Andrea and McKenzie Hatter as I spoke. "How is it a trick? I don't understand?"

"He is speaking half-truths, don't listen to anything he says," the man in the purple suit gave a chuckle but the sound was forced and totally devoid of any humour whatsoever.

For a moment I held the gaze of the man and then I was looking back at Karl. "Well?"

"Both the journal of Oliver Queenheart and this fool's own recollection of events have told us that the author, Charles Dodgson, persuaded him to give him his mirror and thus allow him to escape. Both accounts also stated how that had left McKenzie here trapped and unable to return to the real world."

I shook my head, struggling to understand. "So?" Behind me Andrea gave a grunt and I turned to glance at her as she began to speak her face grim as she stared at McKenzie Hatter, anger in her voice. "It means that once someone has spoken their name and returned to the real world the mirror goes with them. He was going to go first and leave me here!"

"Give me the mirror, you fucking whore!" the man in the purple suit was suddenly rushing at her once again, ducking as he did so and slipping beneath my outstretched arms as I tried to stop him from reaching Andrea. With a curse I fell into the pile of books beyond, twisting as I fell in time to see McKenzie collide heavily with Andrea, the pair of them falling to the floor. Shouting in anger, I allowed Karl to help me to my feet and we both stared in complete horror at the man in the purple suit as he rose from where he had fallen atop Andrea, his right hand clutching the silver mirror proudly and the left gripping hold of the screwdriver that I had left behind on the windowsill in the Tower of Tsugoth.

"No!" I cried out, my heart tearing as I saw the blood dripping from the shaft of the tool to the ground below, my eyes then drifting to the still form of the woman upon the ground, the white material around her heart blossoming with blood and her attractive features pale and still. She was dead.

He had killed her to get the mirror and as soon as he uttered his name he would be away from here and free. With a grim chuckle, the little man raised the mirror before his face and cleared his throat. "McKenzie Ha..."

The words died on his lips as his head suddenly seemed to leap from his shoulders, his face registering shock as it spun around and around through the air before hitting the ground with a dull, wet thud and rolling away. Mind reeling, I stood and stared at his face as it peered out at us from beneath a chair, the nose broken and mashed, his neck little more than a bloody stump. Then I was turning my gaze back to watch as his now headless body dropped to its knees and then its chest, the severed neck spouting blood like a fountain. Grimacing I took a step away, Karl going with me, as the tall bald man with the hatchet stood there grinning at us with bloody teeth, his face and body bearing countless serious wounds. Then he too was crashing to the floor leaving just me and Karl alive in the room of death.

Chapter Sixty-Seven

Time lost all meaning to me as I stood there staring down at the bodies of the woman that I had begun to develop feelings for and the two undeniably insane men. Each of them had been a victim in some respect to the machinations of the mysterious and powerful Oliver Queenheart. Despite not having put in a single appearance since we had awoken back in the asylum upon the hilltop, he had been responsible for the deaths of Craig, Tori, Amber, Ian, Andrea, and his followers and former friends, Father Hare, McKenzie Hatter and the Dumbdee twins, not to mention Bert and God knows how many of his cannibal brethren.

There was of course no doubt in my mind that Ian and many of the others deserved the deaths they had suffered, after all if you choose to live by the sword then you get to die by the sword. But the rest of those that had been brought here with me and Karl were relatively innocent except for the small crime of coming to the attention of Queenheart himself.

The man behind the curtain.

Flinching as a hand touched me upon the shoulder, I turned to find a grim-faced Karl there and I smiled weakly. "It's just us now" "All the more reason to find Queenheart and make him pay," he nodded back at me. "Are you ready to go Morgan?"

"Yeah," I sighed heavily, casting another look down at the body of Andrea as she lay on her back several feet away, the chest of her rabbit suit now dark with blood but her attractive features almost serene as she stared up at the ceiling above her with unseeing eyes. "Yeah."

He nodded at me, gesturing for me to go first as he stepped to the side and crouched, rising with the bloody hatchet of Father Hare in his right hand and facing me. Despite myself I felt a tremor of fear pass through my body as I stared back into his brown eyes. "Not you too."

His smile was broad then as he reversed the weapon and offered it to me handle first. "Have some faith in me."

Feeling stupid for doubting him, I nodded, accepting the weapon, holding it by my side as he turned and crouched beside the headless body of McKenzie and I frowned in confusion. "What are you doing?"

"I was just checking to see if this survived the fall," he told me grimly, one hand holding up the silver mirror that had gotten Andrea killed by McKenzie. For a moment I stood staring at the spider webs of cracks upon the reflective surface and then I was shaking my head, physically sickened at the loss of life when the mirror had not even been used before breaking. "Such a waste," Karl muttered as he rose, echoing my thoughts and for several moments the pair of us stood in silence looking down at the body of our companion. Then we were climbing the wooden stairwell together and emerging back out in the cathedral, our eyes widening as we saw the damage that the two combatants had caused during their battle.

On the left side of the cathedral as we faced the distant door, the front half of the wooden pews were all knocked over like dominos, blood pooling on both them and the floor beneath. Amidst that pile of toppled benches lay the hulking great figure of Bert the one-eyed, one-handed cannibal. Grim-faced, me and Karl moved along the centre aisle, stepping over the various puddles of blood that lined its length and then we were pausing and staring at the body to our left, my eyes narrowing as I studied the injuries that had finally claimed his life. His left hand, or rather the spike which had replaced it was gone along with the rest of the arm up to the elbow, no doubt chopped off with the hatchet which I was now holding, and his barrel chest was a battlefield of deep cuts and slashes. However, it was a deep wedge injury in the side of his throat which had been the killing blow, the wound so deep that I could see the glistening white of his spine amid the gore. Staring at the man I remembered how hard he had hit me during our brief fight back in the cannibal town and I shook my head, amazed that Father Hare had managed to kill the giant, even though he had died from his own injuries shortly after. The level of the priest's mania shook me then as I pictured how he must have finally beaten this opponent and then mortally wounded and on his last legs he had come seeking the rest of us, determined to make us pay for what he had seen as affront to the God that he had come to serve.

"Are you ready Morgan?"

I nodded at the softly spoken question from Karl, joining him as we made our way out of the cathedral to stand atop the hill looking out over the land before us as it was bathed in the cold grey light of the twin suns above. A silence descended over us for a moment as we surveyed the landscape and then I was turning to frown at my companion. "So...where do we go now?"

"We find Queenheart," he stated, nodding as he met my gaze. "We find him and end this once and for all."

I cast another look at the land, shaking my head as I looked back at him. "But where do we begin looking? He could be anywhere."

Karl opened his mouth to reply only for the words to die on his lips and his eyes to widen as he stared past me, and I spun about as the sound of a gun cocking reached my ears, followed by a grim chuckle. "There's no need to go looking for me...I'm right here."

I had the briefest of moments to find myself staring back into the face of the middle-aged man that was now standing at the corner of the cathedral, his body clad in a beige Houndstooth suit, one hand pointing a gun in our direction, his face impassive beneath his silver hair. Then with a grimace, I was raised the hatchet and snarled at him only to freeze as I felt an arm grasp at the hood of my costume from behind whilst the head of something metallic pressed hard against my jugular. Lightheaded with shock, I tried to turn, only for the guttural voice of Karl Mackal to stop me in my tracks. "Drop the hatchet Morgan or I swear this screwdriver will go straight through your throat...do it...now!"

Swallowing hard, wincing at the pain the pressure of the tool was causing me as it pressed against my skin, I released my hold on the hatchet, dropping it to the floor. Then I was addressing the man behind me, the man I had foolishly chosen to trust. "What are you doing Karl? Are you in on this with him, you bastard?" The bitter laugh of the black man sounded then and I could picture him shaking his head as he spoke. "Oh no, nothing so devious Morgan. You see I told you the truth. I want this land for myself and my wife!"

"So, what are you doing with a screwdriver against my throat you crazy fucker!" I shouted, my outburst turning to a gasp as he increased the pressure from the tool upon my neck.

"Wait!" the deep voice of Oliver Queenheart had

me snapping my gaze towards him as he called out, clearly addressing my captor. "Wait don't do this!"

Before I could even comprehend the concern, which was etched upon his features, the amused voice of Karl sounded behind me once again, his tone triumphant. "I knew it...I was right. You don't want anyone to kill the last descendant of Charles Dodgson but you...now drop the gun or I will steal that from you Queenheart!"

With a grimace, the grey-haired man in the suit lowered the gun and turned to the side, tossing it down the stone steps that we had climbed up earlier that day. Then he turned back to face us, his expression grim indeed. "Very cleverly worked out Mr Mackal...except for one thing. Your hostage isn't the last descendant of that bastard Dodgson...and Morgan Carew isn't their name."

"What?" both me and Karl spoke together.

Queenheart smiled. "She is *my* last descendant Mr Mackal. Please, meet my daughter Alice."

Chapter Sixty-Eight

"What?" the stunned voice of Karl seemed to come from miles away as I stood there staring back at the grey-haired man before me, my mind racing in turmoil at his baffling words. "You're wrong!" I shook my head, feeling the pressure of the screwdriver increase on my throat as I moved but ignoring the pain. "I am Morgan Carew...I know my own name God damn you!"

Oliver Queenheart smiled back at me, but the light of the emotion didn't reach his eyes. "No, darling, you know your cover."

"Don't call me that," I shouted at him, anger coursing through my body and he shrugged. "As you wish...but you know deep down I am telling the truth don't you...you can feel it deep inside you"

It wasn't a question but rather a statement and I grimaced, hating the certainty in his voice.

For a moment, I stood there, unsure what to say but then I snarled at him again. "No, I remember how I came to be here. Chester..."

"Chester Catt drugged you," Oliver Queenheart finished for me, smiling again. "Another piece of your cover. You invented that story yourself."

"But that's what you would say," the deep voice of Karl sounded from behind me once again, addressing the man before us both. "If you are behind it all then you would naturally know how and why she got here."

"Indeed, I would," Oliver Queenheart nodded, clasping his hands before him. "So, let us just assume that you are right and that she is the descendent of that bastard Dodgson, I have disposed of my firearm...now release her as you promised you would."

The soft chuckle from the black man sent a shudder up my spine. "Now hold on...I never made that agreement. I just told you to throw the gun away or I would kill her myself. I never said I would let her go!"

"Bastard," I hissed, and he pushed the small tool even harder against the side of my throat.

"Nothing personal. I'm doing this for my family!"

Grimacing, Oliver Queenheart stared hatred past me for a moment then turned his eyes to mine. "Are they dead...McKenzie...Archibald?"

I grimaced as I saw a shadow of regret pass over his face before vanishing again. "Yeah. Everyone is dead. McKenzie Hatter, Father Hare, the

Dumbdee twins and everyone you sent here with us you sick bastard!"

"Everyone I sent here?" he gave me a surprised look then, the expression making a dark, cold space open somewhere way down deep inside of me. "I take it you mean everyone that we sent her Alice…you helped me choose them after all…just like you have been doing for the past three years."

"Liar!" I roared at him, the word catching in my throat and coming out soft and weak. "My name is not Alice."

"Oh, but it is," he nodded, the sadness in his eyes making my stomach lurch. "Named after my first wife, though if your mother had known she would have been more than a little put out."

"Shut up Queenheart!" Karl Mackal snapped at him then, anger in his voice, the volume making me wince as he continued. "Do you really expect me to believe that you willingly send your own daughter…out on these hunts!"

The grey-haired man looked aghast at the suggestion and he shook his head, a grim smile creeping onto his features. "Willingly? No…never…the choice to partake in these hunts

has always been Alice's. Ever since she has been aware of them, she has enjoyed them greatly."
As Karl gave a grunt of disbelief behind me, I shook my head, holding to the gaze of Oliver Queenheart as he continued to address the American. "Of course, I tried to talk her out of it, but she would not listen. I had lost my wife and did not want to lose my daughter as well."
He paused for a moment, shrugging as his gaze flicked to me and then back to my captor. "And so, it went on with each hunt, she would be hypnotised to not have her memory available to her at first. It was part of her fun you see...thinking that she was one of them. That way they would trust her and when her memory returned, she would be hiding amongst them. She does have a wickedly violent temper."
"No," I shook my head, my voice little more than a whisper and he turned his gaze upon me.
"Think Alice, now is the time to remember."
Gritting my teeth, I shook my head, trying to do just that, desperately trying to come up with some memory that proved I wasn't who he was claiming I actually was. Surely if I was his daughter one of his followers would have remembered who I was wouldn't they?

As the thought occurred to me, I grimaced, remembering the way McKenzie had questioned me when I had first encountered him, acting as if he had known who I was for a moment before asking if *I* even knew who I was. I shuddered as his words returned to me then, telling me that he wasn't sure about trusting me as I shared the same blood as someone that had betrayed him. I had thought he had been referring to Dodgson. Had he meant Oliver Queenheart?

Gasping, I closed my eyes, screwing my face up as another memory returned to me, this time of Craig as he had used his last breath to tell me with surprise that he suddenly knew who I was before he had died. Craig had been one of the journalists along with Tori that had been investigating the life of Oliver Queenheart.

Had he too recognised me?

I shook my head. "If this is true and I have done this before why can't I remember this time?"

"I don't know" he shook his head, his eyes narrowing in thought. "Perhaps it is because the woman responsible for your mother's death was on this hunt. Perhaps some part of your sub-consciousness is holding on until all the hunted are dead...you always were persistent Alice, you never liked leaving any behind."

I won't leave anyone behind; words that I had said throughout my time in New London.

I had thought them to be some indication that I had a strong moral fibre and yet now it seemed they were part of something more sinister.

The grunt of shock that left me then sent a grim smile back onto the face of the man claiming to be my father. "It is all coming back to you know isn't it my dear?"

And it was.

As I stood there with the screwdriver pressed against the side of my throat by the black man in the rabbit costume that was stood behind me, whilst meeting the curious gaze of the man in the Houndstooth suit before me my memory suddenly stirred and began to swirl like snow. And just like that it all fell in to place.

Me and father sitting with a list of people and various photographs upon a huge table, picking and choosing who we would place into the hunt as we ate and drank. Me and father standing in a room at his mansion in the real world, his face concerned as he told me to prepare myself mentally for the next hunt.

Me standing before my bed in my room at the same mansion, grinning as my raven-haired lesbian lover beckoned to me from beneath the sheets, eager to send me off on what she thought was a business trip more than satisfied. Me and father hugging farewell; him smiling as he told me that he would see me on the other side, once the woman that had killed my mother and the last descendant of Charles Dodgson were both dead.

Me putting on the white rabbit costume and entering the cell in which I had awoken with no memory, laying down upon the ground as father stood above me and began to use hypnotherapy to cloud my thoughts.

I was Alice.

I was Alice Queenheart.

That was how I had seemed to know my way around the land so well, that was why I could hold my own ground in a fist fight.

I was a survivor; shaped by New London to avenge my mother's death and my father's tarnished honour. In that moment disgust washed over me as I considered how I had kissed and hugged the woman responsible for my mother's untimely death, my sexual preference for my own gender having allowed me to get far closer to the woman than me and father had ever intended. A cold smile crept onto my face as I remembered that the woman, Andrea, was dead and gone and opening my eyes I looked in those of the man who I knew beyond doubt was my father. "I remember." For a moment he stayed frozen in place and then a huge smile split his features as he nodded. "Then you know what to do my dear." In a blur of motion, I snapped my head back, laughing as I felt the nose of Karl Mackal break under the blow from the back of my head, then I was gripping at his right wrist even as he thrust futilely at my neck with the screwdriver.

He cursed, the tool flying from nerveless fingers as I rolled his arm, snapping his wrist with embarrassing ease before spinning to face him, my leading elbow catching him hard in the throat. With a strangled cry he fell back to the ground, his eyes wide as he stared up at me, shaking his head. "Please Morgan...Alice, no...!" For what seemed an eternity I stood staring down at the terrified black man, my mind running quickly over everything that I had been through with him since we had met and then I was bending and retrieving the hatchet that he had made me drop only minutes before.

He gasped out loud as I dropped, knees first onto his chest, the hatchet raised above my head and I couldn't help but chuckle. "It's nothing personal…it's for my family"

About the Author

Born in Portsmouth, England in 1973, Kelvin V.A Allison has somehow found his way to the hill strewn paradise that is County Durham, where he lives a life of calm and insanity in equal measure, in the village home that he shares with his fiancée and their three children. An author of over thirty novels, including the ten book World of Sorrow series, he mainly writes horror but has dreams of being a fantasy author.

By Kelvin V.A Allison

PHINEAS LUCK SERIES
Highgate
Desmotarion

THE BLIGHTED
Kraken
Ascension

WORLD OF SORROW SERIES
The Demon Dilemma
Wonderland
Angelous
Rebirth
Cursed
Hell Diver
The Returned
Downfall
Endgame
Prophecy

HOPE CHRONICLES
Hope & Glory
False Hope

STAND ALONE NOVELS
Skin Shifters
Thorns
Renascentia
Pariah
The Trouble with Rabbits Fluid
Bad Seed
Blood Harvest
Ubasute
Witch Rock; Ubasute 2
Bloody Geese
Pandemonium
Juggernaut

THE DAMORAN SAGA
All the King's Animals

Made in United States
North Haven, CT
03 March 2022

16731012R00252